Secret Servant

Also by Kate Westbrook

The Moneypenny Diaries: *Guardian Angel*

The Moneypenny Diaries

Secret Servant

Kate Westbrook

JOHN MURRAY

© IFPL 2006

First published in Great Britain in 2006 by John Murray (Publishers)
A division of Hodder Headline

A CIP catalogue record for this title is available from the British
Library

Hardback ISBN-13 978-0-7195-6767-4
Hardback ISBN-10 0-7195-6767-X
Trade paperback ISBN-13 978-0-7195-6768-1
Trade paperback ISBN-10 0-7195-6768-8

Typeset in Sabon MT by Servis Filmsetting Ltd, Manchester

Printed and bound by Clays Ltd, St Ives plc

Hodder Headline policy is to use papers that are natural, renewable
and recyclable products and made from wood grown in sustainable
forests. The logging and manufacturing processes are expected to
conform to the environmental regulations of the country of origin.

John Murray (Publishers)
338 Euston Road
London NW1 3BH

To Amber Lily
Fletcher, and with thanks to the
Fleming family and all at IFP

Introduction

I was leaving for the library one morning, the manu-script of my aunt Jane Moneypenny's 1964 diaries almost ready for the publisher, when a letter arrived. It was typed on official Cambridge University Department of History writing paper, and was short and brutal:

Dear Dr Westbrook

We have recently received several official communications from government sources, to the effect that you are guilty of contravening the Official Secrets Act with the proposed publi-cation of The Moneypenny Diaries, *on which you are named as editor. Further, that you intend to release additional volumes. After some considerable intervention from this Department, they have decided not to prosecute. However, since you did not inform us of your intention to publish – which, under section C2, subsection 4, you are bound by the terms of your contract to do – we have no option but to with-draw your junior lectureship forthwith. You have therefore been struck from the staff register of this department.*

Yours sincerely

By the time I got to the familiar signature at the end, I was shaking. I felt both humiliated and furious.

I wanted to hide away in a burrow for a decade, but also to catch the next train up to Cambridge to bang on my former boss's door and tell him exactly what I thought of his cowardly kowtowing to the secret forces of authority, his downright bloody rudeness. Instead, I took a deep breath and made a vow to myself that I would not be beaten. My aunt's diaries would be published. I would brave any threats to see that they were.

It was a fateful moment when Jane Moneypenny's diaries were delivered to my rooms in Cambridge on 10 October 2000, wrapped in scarlet tissue paper and locked in a large metal chest. It kick-started a chain of events that have overturned my life, slamming shut familiar doors while opening up new worlds.

One of my first feelings, on opening that Pandora's box and reading the confessional letter that accompanied the diaries, was of betrayal. I thought I knew my aunt as well as I knew anyone. It turns out I hardly knew her at all. Throughout all those birthdays and Christmases, those long summer holidays when I would travel by train and boat to her small island hideaway in the Outer Hebrides, the time we spent together travelling through East Africa, I had no clue. Throughout weeks and months and years of talking, when I confided everything to her and thought she did to me, she never told me that she worked for British intelligence.

I wish I had known. I wish she had lifted the veil of secrecy for a moment. She might have sat me down and said, 'This is who I am really; this is what I want to tell you.' Her diaries tell the story of her hidden life, but I would have loved to have heard it all from her.

She started writing a diary when she was a child, growing up semi-wild in Kenya in the early 1940s. Her father, Hugh Moneypenny, had been called back to England to join the war effort. One of his last acts before disappearing, apparently killed in action, was to send Jane the first soft red leather journal and urge her to commit her thoughts and observations to paper. For the next fifty years – until shortly before her death on 10 October 1990 – she obeyed him.

It was not a strict diary; she did not write every day, nor record much of the routine stuff of life. She chose what she found interesting, and used the pages as a confidante – much as most women would use a friend or sister. She concealed the growing pile of identical journals in a safe built into the bathroom wall, covered by a cabinet, retrieving them only when she was alone, behind a bolted and chained door.

I must have glanced in that mirror a thousand times, never once guessing the cache it concealed.

She came into the secret world by chance, but once there she was hooked, drawn in by the excitement and sense of being at the centre of events that most people can only read about. She loved the feeling of close community between her colleagues, particularly her fellow secretaries, whose centre of gravity was the Powder Vine, the first-floor ladies' cloakroom. It was in the Powder Vine that office romances were discussed, and rumour and scandal dissected; where the safe return of a missing agent was celebrated and grief permitted to flow when someone didn't come back. But it wasn't just of that she wrote.

Even secretaries and administrative staff at the Secret Intelligence Service – the Office, or the Firm, as those on the inside refer to it, or MI6 as it is also known – are required to sign the Official Secrets Act the day they join. They are then sent on a training course, to give them a grounding in the basic skills of an intelligence operative: shadowing, evading surveillance, cryptology and secret signals. Jane Moneypenny excelled at them all. And recorded her experiences in her diary.

She described the tension and barely suppressed frenzy of the eighth-floor Communications room where she was working as a junior cipher clerk in 1956, when the Suez situation turned into a Crisis. She found herself spending fourteen straight days at the shoulder of the then deputy chief of the Service, Admiral Sir Miles Messervy.

Two weeks later she was summoned to his office. He informed her that he had been appointed the next chief of the service, and offered her the job of his personal secretary. As the guardian at his gate, Miss Moneypenny was privy to most of the secret machinations of state: she saw all the papers that passed his desk; she was present at meetings with ministers and spymasters from England and afar; she typed his letters, decoded the 'Top Secret – Eyes Only' incoming signals, and encoded those that M sent to his agents posted around the world.

Although I did not want to believe that my aunt would lie to me, her diaries were so potentially explosive that I needed to be absolutely sure they were genuine. I hired a document expert in the East End, and took him one volume to examine. It was clear, even to me, that some entries were hurried, some written at a more leisurely pace. I was fascinated as the old gentleman in white cotton gloves was able to decipher fear or anger, contentment or distraction. When she was tired, her loops were exaggerated; if she was uncertain, they disappeared. Without studying the content, he showed me a large chunk of entries which, he said, had been copied into the journal at the same time. I glanced at the section he was talking about; all referred to a trip abroad when she had presumably left her journal at home.

'As far as I can determine, by the ink and natural wear of the paper, this journal was written some time in the mid-1960s,' he pronounced. 'It was written by one person, almost certainly female, not under duress and over a period of time.' It was enough to satisfy me that the journals were authentic. But other obstacles soon presented themselves.

During the last year, I have been forced to make major changes in my life; I have lost my job, and have had to move out of my house, abandon my students, and, for the present at least, wave goodbye to the prescribed and secure life of academia. All as a result of the diaries. It is not my aunt's fault: she never asked me to follow this path. But, as an historian and her only living relative, once I read what she had written I felt compelled to dig deeper.

Jane Moneypenny would have understood that. She too had committed herself to discovering the truth: about what had happened to her father – my grand-father.

In October 1940 her mother, Irene, received the telegram that every wartime relative dreads: Commander Hugh Moneypenny had been reported missing in action. He was later presumed dead, and a death certificate was issued. Despite an active campaign of letter bombardment and banging on ministry doors by his widow, the details of his disappearance were never released. Jane and her sister, Helena, had a secret dream that he had not died and would someday walk back into their lives with a smile on his face and great adventures to relate. As the years passed, however, their hope faded. In time they stopped talking about it. But Jane had not forgotten.

When she came to London and started working for SIS in 1953, she made a private pledge: to do everything in her power to find out what had happened to him. She searched through files, and dredged the fading memories of old colleagues and acquaintances. It was not until 1962 that she came upon the first hints that he had not died in action.

My aunt could find no written records of her father's last mission, but, as she confided to her diary, her hope was reignited by some evidence that suggested that he had been taken captive by the Germans and locked away under an assumed name. His death – like so many aspects of her life – had not been what it first appeared to be.

The same is true of Harold Adrian Russell 'Kim' Philby, the man dubbed 'the greatest traitor of his generation'. This volume of my aunt's diaries describes the time when she became entangled with this master deceiver.

By the time of his flight to Moscow in January 1963, Philby had been married three times and had five children. During the war, he had worked for the Special Operations Executive, from where he joined MI6, rapidly climbing the ranks to become head of the Soviet Section, and tipped as a future chief. Throughout all this, for twenty-seven years he had been reporting to the KGB. For him, every day had been a deception; every action or utterance was preceded by a check, a furtive glance from side to side. It took its toll: he drank increasingly heavily; he had sweating, screaming nightmares. But, until the day he was finally unmasked as a Soviet agent, he never let slip his true allegiance.

Forty-two years later, I can see the parallels between my aunt's life and Philby's. As I study her diaries and spend more time with the inhabitants of their secret world, so I find myself increasingly estranged from my own circle, the people I thought were my friends. By choosing to reveal my aunt's life – at least an edited version of it – I have been drawn into her world, and taken on new secrets of my own.

Kate Westbrook
Kenya, 2006

1963

January–July

Six years ago I read my aunt's diaries for the first time. I initially found them almost impenetrable, filled with acronyms for places and people I did not know. But gradually, as I have read them again and again, her world has come alive for me. Her friends and colleagues have risen off the page to enter my life.

During that first reading I kept a piece of paper beside me at all times, and whenever she mentioned a new person I made a note of who they were, along with some of their key characteristics, which I would add to when I learned more. It seems strange now that I ever thought of them as strangers:

- **M.** Pipe-smoking ex-admiral and Chief of SIS. Brilliant strategist, respected by all. Loved and hated by JM (Jane Moneypenny) in equal measure. Bald patch on back of head. Favourite tipple: cheap Algerian wine.
- **Bill Tanner.** M's Chief of Staff (CoS). In practice, number two at SIS and responsible for keeping the 'War Book', a daily account of the workings of the Office, so that, in the event of both of their deaths, the whole story would be available to their successors. Devoted to JM, whose office adjoined his. Best friend of James Bond.

- **007**. James Bond, legendary seducer and agent, with a licence to kill. Head of the oo section. Drives a custom-converted Bentley; fond of expensive wines and fine food (half an avocado for pudding). Habitually smokes seventy bespoke Morlands cigarettes per day. Reported missing in action in December 1962, after blowing up the fortress hideaway of his old adversary Ernst Stavro Blofeld. Ongoing flirtation with JM.
- **CS**. Dr John 'Bookie' Booker, Chief of Soviet Section – the largest and most important foreign section of SIS. Tall and thin, with one arm and a patch on his left eye. Adored by his secretary, Pamela. Gambler???
- **CME**. Chief of the Middle East department – Alexander 'Dingle' Delavigne: old-school SIS, polished, aristocratic, charming. Speaks six languages. Dresses immaculately, plays piano – show tunes – smokes Turkish cheroots. Married to Margaret. Secretary: Janet d'Auvergne, queen of the Powder Vine and close friend of JM.
- **'Bobby' Prenderghast**. Chief of Southern Africa Section until 1962, when it emerged that he had been recruited as a Soviet agent after falling into a KGB-laid 'honey trap' while on holiday in the Greek islands ten years earlier, and had been supplying the Soviets with information ever since.
- **Dorothy Fields**. Broad-beamed chief research officer and mole-hunter. One of only three women intelligence officers. Drives a Citroën 2CV; wears hats at all times.

The complete list covered two pages. The vast majority of names belonged to colleagues of my aunt's. It seemed that she saw few people outside the Office apart from her immediate family: her sister, **Helena Moneypenny**, and **Lionel Westbrook** (my mother and father), and her great aunt **Frieda Greenfield**. Jane Moneypenny's parents had both died when she was young; her father, **Commander Hugh Moneypenny**, a renowned sportsman, had worked as a naval attaché in the colonial government in Nairobi before the war. Her mother, **Dr Irene Moneypenny**, was involved in developing rural health initiatives in Kenya when she was killed in the Mau Mau uprising on 26 March 1953.

One notable exception was Richard Hamilton, whom she referred to in her diaries as **R**, and of whom she wrote with increasing regularity – and fondness – from the time of their first meeting, in Barcelona in 1961. By the middle of 1962, however, their relationship had faltered in an atmosphere of distrust. Neither, it transpired, had been entirely honest about what it was they did for a living. But it wasn't until December 1962 that he made the extraordinary revelation that he was not, as he'd maintained, an architect, but in fact an agent of the British domestic Security Service, MI5. She learned of this in dramatic circumstances: **Boris**, a pale-eyed KGB officer, had broken into my aunt's flat and, after a struggle, tied her to her bed and threatened to kill her if she did not reveal office secrets. R arrived unannounced and leaped on Boris, who shot R in the chest, before he, in turn, was shot by my aunt.

These were just some of the individuals on a list which grew ever longer as I read the forty volumes my aunt had written over a period spanning half a century. It became covered with more notes, scribbles and scrawls about their backgrounds and behaviour, until I realised that it was no longer just a cast of characters, but a list of suspects.

Friday, 18th January

This afternoon, M called me in and, without warning, swivelled his chair to face the clock and dictated James's obituary, which he ordered me to send directly to *The Times*: 'A senior officer of the Ministry of Defence, Commander James Bond, CMG, RNVR, is missing, believed killed, while on an official mission to Japan,' he dictated. 'It grieves me to have to report that hopes of his survival must now be abandoned. It therefore falls to my lot, as the Head of the Department he served so well, to give some account of this officer and of his outstanding services to his country . . .'

He showed no emotion as he recounted, fluently, the sparse details of the life of the man we both knew so well. As I turned to leave, my hands were shaking and for a ghastly second I lost control. 'Sir,' I blurted out, 'you can't do this. You're burying him alive. We have to search more. If you'll give me leave, I'll go myself. He can't have just been blown into dust.'

I can't believe I said it. As my mouth snapped shut, I felt the colour drain from my face. It was all I could do to stop crumpling to the floor. 'I'm sorry, sir,' I said. 'I forgot myself. Please forgive me.' Without looking at him, I turned and rushed towards the door. My hand was on the handle, when he called, 'Jane.' He had never before used my first name. 'I know you were fond of 007, but I'm afraid there is no hope. Tanaka's* been over there twice and 006 spent a week out there, talked to everyone and found no

---

* Head of the Japanese secret service, a trained, kamikaze woman-iser and bon viveur.

sign of him. We have that woman's – Kissy Suzuki, I believe her name is – first-hand testimony of watching the castle explode. There is absolutely no point in your going. I expressly forbid it. Believe me, he would have given his life willingly if he took Blofeld with him. We will miss him, but he left the world a safer place. Now, we're going to have to start thinking about a memorial service, and I would like you to be in charge of drafting a suitable response to the letters of sympathy.'

The brief window of humanity left and his voice regained its usual authority: 'Miss Moneypenny, please circulate a memo to the effect that 006 has assumed charge of the 00 section, with immediate effect.' I suppose I should be grateful that I escaped without further admonishment.

Sunday, 20th January

I am going out of my mind with worry about R. When I dropped by the hospital on Friday, he was sitting up and joking that the nurses' bedside manners left quite a lot to be desired. Though whether he desired them or not, I never found out. Early on Saturday morning, I got a call from the matron asking me to come in urgently. He'd started fibrillating in the night. His heart stopped briefly, but they managed to revive him. He's still unconscious and there's a small chance his brain was damaged. I cannot allow that possibility.

The doctors said they had no idea why it happened. He'd been making excellent progress; this was totally unexpected. I stayed at the hospital all weekend, holding his hand and listening for each breath, worried that the next might not follow the last. I prayed, for the first time in years, and begged forgiveness. R would not be hovering on the knife-edge of death if it wasn't for me. He would not have come through my door a month ago and Boris would not have shot him. It's all my fault and I don't know how I can make it better. He must recover.

Monday, 21st January

R has regained consciousness, thank God. I went to see him after work and he was sitting, propped up against the pillows. He was a little groggy and could barely talk. He smiled when he saw me and squeezed my hand. I sat with him until they asked me to go, and as I bent down to kiss him goodbye, he whispered into my ear, 'I dreamt of Boris. Please be careful.' I stood up and in his eyes I thought I saw a shadow of fear. I hope it is just the after-effects of the drugs.

Thursday, 24th January

I arrived early this morning to find the red light on outside M's door. When he buzzed me in, I found Bill [Tanner, M's Chief of Staff] and Dingle [Chief of Middle East (CME)] hidden in a cloud of pipe smoke and the Old Man in a state of high dudgeon. 'Any new signals from Beirut, Miss Moneypenny?' When I replied in the affirmative, he sent me out to decode them 'all sails open', which I took to mean 'soonest'.

I found a growing pile, all from our Beirut station head. I got out the Triple X and set immediately to work deciphering them. It was only when I had finished and read over the plain text that I began to grasp what was happening. Agent 279 failed to turn up to a dinner party at the house of one of the Foreign Office chaps last night. He appears to have disappeared into thin air.

It was immediately clear why everyone was in such a state: 279 is the numerical designation of Kim Philby, former Head of Sov. Section here and chief liaison officer in Washington until '51, when he was forced to resign under a cloud of suspicion surrounding his friendship with Guy Burgess. I know X* spent years trying to confirm his guilt, but nothing stuck – except Philby's implacable denial that he had ever worked for the Russians. He's an old friend of Dingle's and has been stringing for us in Beirut for the last three years or so – though on a short leash and under, I suspect, some degree of surveillance. I have deciphered a number of his reports and M has always insisted on seeing a copy of each of them; I don't think he has ever quite trusted Philby's innocence. Could he be the Third Man we've all been so afraid of?

Dingle went to see him out there before Christmas and again a couple of weeks ago. On his return, he spent the whole day in with M, delivering his report in person. When he came out, there was a perceptible frown in place of his usual mask of patrician sang-froid and his shoulders were slumped beneath the immaculately tailored

---

* Chief interrogator of the SIS and inventor of various techniques of reportedly painless information extraction that are used by intelligence organisations around the world to this day.

suit. Since then, the Old Man's been in a black mood. He's had Philby's file on his desk constantly and there have been a series of huddles with Dingle and various other section heads. I hadn't before seen the connection, but now Philby's disappeared it's flashing loud and clear. From the signals that keep arriving, describing his wife's surprise and consternation, the lack of any clue as to where he might have gone and the steps being taken to gag the press out there and over here from reporting it, I would guess that the questions being asked are: did he go of his own accord or was he snatched, and is he heading to where we fear he might be?

It was nine o'clock when M buzzed through from his office, ordering me to go home. He sounded weary, but would brook no objections. I hope he doesn't overdo it. This situation, if it plays out how one fears it might and we fail to contain it, could prove to be his downfall. He tried to resign over Prenderghast, but this is potentially far more explosive. M can be a miserable old so-and-so sometimes, but we need him. He carries the nation's safety in his arms. I know I sleep more easily because of him.

Friday, 25th January

M stayed at the office last night. I ran into Bill getting coffee at Franco's this morning. He looked spruce as usual, but the tired crumple at the corners of his eyes gave him away. He sat down at the tiny table at the back to drink it, beckoning me to join him. When I asked what time he had made it home, he looked at his watch and said, 'About an hour ago. Time enough for a quick shower and change of shirt and back here for breakfast with the Old Man.' I asked how he was. 'He's a tough old gull, used to weathering the night on deck in a storm, but this is hitting him hard, especially coming on top of James. It's what he always feared. He came on board here just as Philby was off to Beirut – never worked with him before, of course. We didn't start using Philby at once, but there were certain friends of his here who maintained he'd been dealt an unfair hand and lobbied for us to put him back on the books. Then, when Dingle went out there in '60, he activated Philby. Against his instincts, M gave the green light. Suspect he saw it as a way to smoke him out, once and for all.

'Now, of course, he's kicking himself – and Dingle, for that matter. It's not so much what Philby has given away in the last couple of years, as the appalling cost of what he may have told them over the last thirty – and what he still has to tell.'

Bill ran his hands through his hair and rubbed his eyes and I thought again how much older he looks than his years. For a slight man with narrow shoulders, he carries above his weight of responsibility. The Firm is everything to him – he has no wife, no children and no space in his life for anything except work.

'Of course, there's a chance he might have just gone walkabout like his old man* used to, or fallen into a wadi in a drunken stupor, but my best guess is that he's going to wash up in Moscow with Burgess and Maclean before too long. A pretty triumvirate.' He gave a bitter laugh.

---

* Harry St. John Bridger Philby (1885–1960), also known as Sheikh Abdullah, a renowned Arabist, explorer, writer and eccentric.

'The last bloody thing we need – the press would have a field-day. First Bobby Prenderghast and now Kim Philby. No wonder the Old Man's in a state.'

The Office had a feeling of static electricity about it today, as if anything you might touch would pack a mighty shock. There was perhaps more movement than usual, more Registry girls scurrying along the corridors and up and down stairs, carrying signals and files from one section to another, and even they seemed to sense the undercurrent of unease that has percolated the building. Most people stayed late this evening – in M's parlance, there can be no rats on this ship. We just have to batten down the hatches and hope the news doesn't leak out. I couldn't help but think about the events of last year – what Bill called the 'sieve' effect. Too much leaked out and some of it after Prenderghast had been caught. I know Dorothy and Bill think there's another mole in here somewhere – but who and where?

By ten, when he sent me home again, M was still closeted in his office with Bill, Bookie,* Dingle and Dorothy. I hope he takes some time off over the weekend. Even the captain needs to sleep.

I had planned to stop by the hospital to see R on my way home, but by the time I left, visiting hours were long since

---

* John Booker, PhD, Chief of Soviet Section – in his day, Oxford's youngest maths graduate, at the age of sixteen years and six days. Famous among his peers for being able to think to eleven decimal places, and calculate the odds of any eventuality in the blink of an eye – hence his nickname. During the war, he was siphoned directly into the decryption huts at Bletchley Park, where he worked alongside Alan Turing on breaking the Enigma codes. He joined SIS in 1945. Fluent in five Slavic languages.

over. They let me speak to him, however, and I was relieved to hear him sounding cheerful again. He's still croaking a little, but definitely in full possession of his faculties, chafing at the concerns of the doctors that keep him there. He claimed to have got the crossword down to under ten minutes and said he felt like going to Quaglino's for dinner.

I laughed. I'm torn, in many ways. Before R made his dramatic re-entry into my life, I had thought our relationship was over. When he revealed that he was one of us, my first thought was of relief, my second, of betrayal. While he's been in hospital, especially these last few days, I've put all consideration of our relationship to the back of my mind; all I want is for him to recover. Until I know he has, I can't concentrate on the other.

Saturday, 9th February

I went to see R at the hospital to find that he had been moved to an end room. There was a man sitting outside his door with a perceptible bulge under his jacket, who demanded I show identification and searched me before allowing me in to see him. When I asked R what it was all about, he tried to shrug it off. 'Probably nothing. GCHQ thought they picked up my name in a signal from Moscow. The powers that be decided to give me a bit of protection, just in case.'

I wasn't fooled by his show of unconcern. I tried to ask more, but he insisted that he knew nothing. When I left, however, he looked serious for a moment and urged me to take care. 'I'll look left and right before crossing the road, I promise,' I assured him.

Monday, 11th February

The nightmare has not ended. I went to see Bill as soon as I got in and asked him whether he knew why R had body-guards on his door. He ushered me into his office and sat me down. 'I was contacted by my opposite number at the end of last week,' he said. 'Seems they have an idea that your friend's relapse wasn't entirely natural.'

'He was attacked in some way?'

'We don't know, but we certainly can't rule it out, par-ticularly in light of some traffic that was recently inter-cepted, in which his name was clearly spelled out. The KGB are going to be after him. That contretemps with Boris at the end of last year will not be forgotten quickly.'

'Is he in serious danger?' I asked.

'To be honest, we don't know. He's been given round-the-clock guards just in case and extra security in place on the entrances and exits. He should be all right in hospital. We don't yet know what will happen when he's well enough to leave.'

Neither of us raised the obvious next question; am I at risk, too? I was the one who shot Boris, after all.

Friday, 22nd February

Boris stalks my nights. He's there when I wake in the dark, small hours, a moving image of past horrors unspooling in front of my open eyes. I can see his pale, hairless hands strapping mine to the bed-head, smell the scent of fresh sweat and musky aftershave, feel the sting of his slaps on my cheeks. Each night, again the click of the light-switch, running for the door, his hand grabbing my ankle, pulling me down, R bursting in, two shots, the heat of a just-fired gun in my hand. Blood on the carpet. I wish I could expunge the memory from my subconscious. It's been nine weeks now since it all happened and Boris is safely locked up behind bars. It's time to stick pins in a Russian doll and move on.

I miss James. He would have laughed and told me to put my chin up and stop skittering at ghosts. Without him, the Office seems drained of colour. Yes, he spent most of last year in an uncharacteristically depressed state, but I never doubted that he was going to snap out of it, saunter through the door one day with the twinkle back in his eyes, perch on my desk and suggest an early afternoon at the Ritz. It's not that I would have said yes – or that he would have thought for a minute that I would – but I wish he was around to ask me.

I think we all miss him, his levity and ability to draw the best from any given situation. M gets increasingly terse, the lines on Bill's face are burrowing deeper into his premature frown and Dingle just cracks more jokes in what appears to be a desperate charade to hide the blame he has undoubtedly laid upon himself. Philby has not yet resurfaced. His wife reported to Beirut station receiving letters and telegrams postmarked from around the region, but that signifies little. Anyone could have posted them for him. Standard evasion practice.

This evening, M surprised me. He called me in to see him, then said, 'Miss Moneypenny, I know this has not been an easy time. I don't want you to think I don't notice or appreciate the extra hours you've been putting in. I wanted to tell you that I hereby grant your request for a week's leave, effective immediately. It will not be counted against your holiday allowance.'

'But, sir, I haven't requested . . .' I protested.

'No buts. You deserve it. There is only one condition: you are not to get into trouble. Anywhere within a thousand-mile radius of Japan is strictly off limits.'

'Of course, sir. Thank you, sir.'

Bill was waiting when I got out of the office. He looked grave. 'It's a little more complicated,' he said. 'Hamilton has insisted on checking himself out of hospital. The doctors say he's well enough to go, but his people are not sure that he's in the clear, from a security point of view. However, he's refusing to have a bodyguard. He says he wants to go away for a while and that the only person he's prepared to go with is you. I had his section chief on the phone for twenty minutes this morning asking me to persuade the Old Man to let you go. He wasn't keen on the idea. To be honest, nor was I. They were very persuasive, but it was only after your man Hamilton telephoned and insisted on talking to M himself that you were given the green light. Apparently he satisfied the Old Man that he would take very good care of you.

In the face of that determination, who was I to refuse? So tomorrow evening, R, Rafiki* and I are catching the sleeper train to Scotland. Our final destination is a secret. My stomach is knotted with nerves which, I suspect, have more to do with spending time with R than with any real or imagined danger we may be in.

---

* JM's gunmetal grey standard poodle, with an outsized character and the instincts of an actor. At the utterance of the word 'dead', he would collapse to the ground with his head on one side and his four legs in the air.

Sunday, 3rd March

The strangeness of being alone together evaporated once we'd got on to the train and R had satisfied himself that we weren't being followed. We were a little jittery for the first few days, jumping at any creak or bang, but we soon let go of our fears.

He had rented a beautiful little crofter's cottage on a bay on the north-east coast of North Uist, a remote island in the Outer Hebrides. Uneven whitewashed walls, thatched roof and the combination of a low ceiling and a huge, peat-burning fire made it as cosy as a caterpillar's cocoon. From our cottage, we could see for miles around and Rafi would have alerted us to a stranger's presence. Through the whole week, we hardly saw a soul.

The island is a heavenly, heavenly place. I feel like a different person – cleansed inside and out by the bitter winds that whipped sand into our faces and threatened to blow us off the sides of hills by day and lulled me into an untroubled sleep at night. I love the unfettered power of the elements at their most extreme. There was a tiny islet at the mouth of the bay – which at low tide could be reached on foot across the sands – but apart from that, nothing but the ocean between us and America. A liberating thought. It is only when I go somewhere like Uist, where life seems to be battened down, concentrated on surviving the winter, that I realise how divorced we are from nature in the big cities. It's not immediately obvious, but I had a strong sense of Africa there. R laughed when I told him this, as we were fighting our way against the wind along a wide beach of the purest white sand. 'Funnily enough, I had a hunch you'd think that.

It's obviously these pesky mosquitoes everywhere – and as for the sunstroke . . .'

For the first few days, we avoided the big issues. He made no demands on me and I offered nothing in return. We just laughed and talked and revelled in the beauty of our surroundings. It was on the third evening, after a delicious dinner of fresh mussels, scavenged from the beach, that he gave me a glass of wine and beckoned me to the fire.

'Jane, I'm truly sorry,' he began. 'Please forgive me, and please believe that I never wanted to deceive you. As time went on, I was too afraid to tell you that I knew what it was you did. My work has destroyed every relationship I've had and I couldn't bear for it to consume this one too.'

'Did you know from the start?' I asked.

He shook his head. 'No. I promise. I was on holiday. At first, I was just relieved by your reluctance to discuss your work, as it gave me an excuse to bury mine. Then, as my feelings for you grew, I found myself wanting to know more. Every time I tried to ask, you evaded the question, until one day it dawned on me that perhaps you too had something to hide? I tried to telephone you at the Foreign Office and when they said they'd never heard of you, the penny dropped.'

'Why didn't you just ask me?'

He gave a sad smile. 'Force of habit, I suppose. Eventually, I had a drink with a chap I know from your outfit and he confirmed it. By then, however, things had begun to implode and it was too late to start afresh. I wish I'd tried.'

'Instead, you ran away.'

He poured me some more wine. 'Yes, I suppose so. Then I came back and . . .'

'. . . took my bullet.' I laughed and felt myself leaning forward to embrace him, and suddenly everything was all right.

We stayed in front of the fire through the night, talking, unpicking and restitching our relationship. So maybe he isn't the architect I thought I'd fallen in love with, but does that mean he's a spy I couldn't love? Once I'd got over that hurdle and stopped thinking purely in terms of truth and lies, I felt myself soaring again. After all, I hadn't been entirely straight with him either.

Over the next days, our conversation continued unabated and unfettered. We slept separately, but it felt as if we were coming ever closer together. It was an extraordinary relief, for me, to be able to talk freely outside the Office, without having to filter out careless remarks. The only subject we shirked was the future. Time enough for that. All R said was that he wasn't prepared to live in fear of Boris or any other faceless bogeyman.

One night, after a fierce game of Scrabble, we sat up late listening to the wind howl around the chimney and talked about Pa. Since R had told me that a man using his code name, Hugh Sterling, was on the catalogue of prisoners at Colditz at the end of the war, the thought of it has haunted me – images from books and films, of POWs starved and half-crazy. R offered his help in any way he can in my search for the truth about Pa. I will start looking for Colditz survivors. The half-knowing has become worse than not knowing.

Friday, 29th March

Still no sign of Philby. Bill came by my office this morning and sat me down again, before telling me that Boris had escaped custody and is thought to be on his way back to Moscow. I closed my eyes and felt myself begin to shake. Just as I've managed to lock him out of my nightmares, he reappears in my life, at large and presumably even less fond of me than I am of him. What does that mean for R? More bodyguards? A return to hiding? Suddenly, Moscow doesn't feel so many miles away.

'How did he get out?'

Bill replied that he was having trouble getting the exact details, but he suspects that the Russians made a deal with Five to ensure a blind eye was turned to their plans to spirit him out of the country. 'They must have wanted him very badly — and were prepared to make the arrangement a sweet one. What did they get in return — that's what I want to know? We're bloody furious about it. It's not that Boris has given us anything, but while we had him, he was a potential embarrassment to the Sovs. Now he's gone, the egg's on our faces,' Bill said.

'Was it anything to do with R? Does he know?' I asked.

Bill shook his had. 'If it was, they're not telling. Penny, I don't want you to fret. As long as you stay out of his backyard, you should have no cause for unease. There's no way he could ever get back into the country.' I could sense that he was concerned, though, and so was I. I hope R will be safe.

Then, this afternoon, an extraordinary report passed my desk. It came in letter form, plain text, from an irregular agent based in Vladivostok. The source, who I understand is a woman on the auxiliary service staff at the KGB headquarters there, claims that the KGB have a man in their custody who they are treating with extreme secrecy and caution. The source saw a zapiska – a file – that had been sent over from Moscow headquarters, marked SOVERSHENNO SEKRETNO, 'Top Secret'. The name on the front was 'James Bond, British Secret Agent'.

M was still at Blades, so I took the report straight to Bill. He looked at it and frowned, then picked up the phone. He came into my office a few minutes later. 'Don't get your hopes up,' he said. 'Bookie's checking it out, but he doesn't set much store by this source. Says it's stretching the odds too far. He's convinced that the two events are unrelated. Just because the Russians have 007's file knocking about, doesn't mean that they've got him. We'll do all we can to find out, of course. Please make sure M gets the report.'

Saturday, 11th May

I can't believe that more than two months have passed since we came back from Uist, and since I last wrote in these pages. It's madness – I feel guilty when I write and also when I don't. The Scylla and Charybdis of the secret diarist. It's almost a relief that R has been called away, though I do miss him. I always look forward to our weekends together, the laughter and companionship and underlying frisson of what might be. I feel wonderfully at ease with him, more so than with any man before. I know he wants our relationship to progress, but he's being very patient with me, giving me every reason to trust him, which I'm beginning to do.

The run-up to the Prenderghast trial has put us all under pressure, especially M. We don't know whether Prenderghast will testify and if he does, to whose benefit it will be. Throughout his interrogation, he has flatly refuted any idea that he had an accomplice within the Office. He belongs in jail, I know, but I can't help but feel some sympathy for his plight. When They are determined to catch you and have found an appropriate hook, it is hard to resist.

Dingle arrived back from another trip to Beirut on Thursday. He's now convinced that Philby is in Redland, probably Moscow, Janet told me this evening. He spent much of his time out there with Mrs Philby, who still won't admit to herself her husband's true colours. She appears to be genuinely confused as to his present whereabouts and the reason for his disappearance. She clings to the idea that he was taken against his will.

Dingle brought back a copy of a letter from Philby that had been hand-delivered to their apartment. Against her husband's strictest instructions, Mrs P had kept it and, worse still, shown it to our side. I made a copy of it for M. It was three pages long and type-written and had originally included $2,000 in bills, with which Philby directed his wife to buy a return aeroplane ticket for herself to London and one-way tickets for the children. (Children? How could a man like this have children?) These tickets, however, were for show only. At the same time he instructed her to destroy them and choose a flight to Prague. When the date was set, she should write it in white chalk on the white wall in the alley beside their apartment, or, if she was having problems, mark the left-hand side of the wall with an X. A 'friend' would be visiting her to help with the arrangements, he added. He would produce the book token she had given Philby for his birthday as confirmation of his identity.

The letter only served to convince Mrs P more firmly that her husband had been kidnapped. The book token she had given him was still in the top drawer of his desk; it must be his way of warning her about a trap. Furthermore, his youngest son had no valid passport and so could not leave the country. Unsure what to do, she told all to Dingle, her husband's old friend. He responded with an offer to help, but only if they all flew to London. 'This is the only realistic avenue available to her,' he reported. 'I feel confident that she will be on British soil by the end of the month.' So, when Philby's 'friend' turned up on Eleanor's doorstep with a book token and an offer of help, she was suspicious and turned him away, reporting the incident to the British Embassy.

I can't help but feel sorry for her. I know only too well how it feels to discover that the man you love is not who you had believed him to be, but it must be so much worse for her. Philby is her husband, they lived together, but all the while, he was working for the enemy. Now she's living in a distant country, away from her family, with no income, his children to look after and no idea what the future holds. On top of it all, she's about to be pulled this way and that by opposing intelligence forces, to whom she is a mere pawn in the great game.

Monday, 13th May

Two days ago, in Moscow, Oleg Penkovsky* was convicted of treason and executed. They should have fêted him. Were it not for the information he passed to the West about the relative weakness of the Soviet nuclear arsenal, the Cuban Missile Crisis might have had a more explosive conclusion.

Wednesday, 5th June

Profumo resigned today, at last. What a fool. I always thought he had a weak chin. He finally admitted having lied to Parliament about his affair with Christine Keeler.[†] The Powder Vine has talked of little else for weeks. Like most of the country, I've found the details riveting – pillow-talk with call-girls and pool parties at Cliveden. It's the stuff of spy fiction, though hardly what the Services need at a time like this. That Keeler can have been

---

* Code-named Source Ironbark. During the eighteen-month period that he was in play, he passed over innumerable priceless intelligence documents to his Western handlers.

[†] John Dennis Profumo(1915–2006), Conservative Secretary of State for War, told the House of Commons in March 1963 that there was 'no impropriety whatever' in his relationship with Keeler. However, it emerged that the married Old Harrovian had enjoyed a brief but passionate relationship with her, having been introduced to her by the 'society osteopath' Stephen Ward. Ward was prosecuted for living off immoral earnings, but committed suicide on the last day of his trial. Keeler was tried and imprisoned on related charges. Profumo resigned, and devoted much of the rest of his life to charity work in London's East End.

sleeping both with the Minister of War and a Soviet attaché – almost certainly KGB – seems extraordinary. How had the Watchers missed it? It's some comfort for us that it's Five this time who have been caught with their pants down. The other fortunate consequence of this monumental scandal is that it has pushed Prenderghast way down the news agenda.

Perhaps as a result of this, on the eve of his turn in the witness-box, he confessed all to X. I overheard X reporting to Bill this morning. 'It was almost as if he couldn't bear to be thought of as a minor spy any more. He just blurted it out. He said, "Nobody tortured me! Nobody blackmailed me! I myself approached the Soviets and offered my services to them of my own accord!" We just listened in amazed silence. In those three sentences, he sealed his fate and tripled his sentence.'

No word from R for a week now. I feel his absence more than I care to admit.

Saturday, 15th June

Eleanor Philby is in London and under siege from the press. She arrived two weeks ago. I knew from the Powder Vine the minute she touched down – Janet had arranged her flight from Beirut and Dingle spoke to her the following day. Apart from a sore toe, which we arranged for a doctor to see, she was well and in hiding from the media. That lasted about ten days and once they caught scent of her, they were all over her like a pack of hounds.

Friday/Saturday morning, 21st/22nd June

Mary's* leaving party was meant to be a drink after work at Bully's, but perhaps inevitably, degenerated into a bun fight. The Prenderghast judge had called an extended recess at the Old Bailey. Unusually, all the oos were in town. It was the longest day of the year. What more reason did we need to celebrate? For one evening, at least, it was like the old days, when the Office was a place of light and laughter. Events culminated with Mary being dunked in the lake at St James's Park by three large men, with her successor, Jo Comely, dressed only in bra and pants, cheering her on from the side. James would have loved that. Luckily it was too late for passers- by, who would probably have called the police. Then we would have been in trouble. Not the sort of behaviour expected of Her Majesty's Secret Servants.

Mary looked radiant. She told me in the Vine as we were getting ready to go that she was relieved to be leaving the pressure-cooker of the oo section. 'After James went (still nobody can refer to him as dead) I couldn't bear any of them going on a mission,' she said. 'I found I was alternating between clucking over them and pushing them away so that they didn't have the power to hurt me. It was affecting my work. Do you think I should warn Jo?' I shook my head; she'll find out soon enough by herself.

On Sunday, while I'm – belatedly – spring-cleaning the flat, Mary will be flying to Kingston, Jamaica, to become

---

* Mary Goodnight, attractive blonde secretary to the oo section. Enjoyed a passionate but ultimately unsustainable liaison with oo6.

Commander Ross's new number two. On Monday, Joanna will be installed at her desk, dressed to suit her name. Perhaps I'll go out to Jamaica to visit Mary one day? I know James would have loved to. I still miss him, every day. We all do.

Monday, 1st July

Philby has officially been revealed as 'The Third Man'. After our dam-stopping operations with the British press, American *Newsweek* finally broke the story, forcing Ted Heath [then Lord Privy Seal] to make a statement to Parliament today. Heath admitted that it was now known that 'former Foreign Office official' Philby had warned Maclean, through Burgess, that the intelligence services were on their trail, and advised him to flee. No one expected Burgess to go with him. This was twelve years ago. 'Since Mr Philby resigned from the Foreign Service in July 1951, he has not had any access to any kind of official information,' Heath said. 'For the past seven years he has been living outside British legal jurisdiction.' I hope that doesn't come back to haunt him.

Heath confessed that it was now apparent that 'Mr Philby was a double agent working for the Soviet authorities during his time with the Foreign Office. This information, coupled with the latest message received by Mrs Philby, suggests that when he left Beirut he may have gone to one of the countries of the Soviet Bloc.' It's out there now, as M had feared. Our intelligence stock must be at an all-time low. The Americans must despise us, the Russians mock us.

Surprisingly, M looks relieved. He had an almost devil-may-care attitude when he swept out of the office for lunch at Blades. I hope that doesn't mean he has decided to go.

This evening's papers had a quote from Burgess in Moscow, to the effect that it was 'ridiculous' that Philby was the Third Man. I suppose he would say that.

Friday, 12th July

The day of James's memorial service began, ironically, with another strange sighting, this time in Leningrad. A doctor who has been working at the Institute of Experimental Medicine on Nevsky Prospekt, and who has secretly approached our consulate expressing a desire to defect, reported that the KGB had a top secret patient in there. The doctor himself had not seen him, but had overheard his colleagues who had, talking about the 'Angliski spion'. The patient was being accorded the privileges of a VIP and received regular visitors from KGB top brass.

The report was sent overnight in the diplomatic bag from our Moscow station, along with a note from our section head out there, suggesting that the patient could be Philby or Burgess – who is known to be desperately ill with lung disease. Scrawled in royal-blue ink at the bottom, as if an afterthought, he had added, '007???' It's another long shot, but it still gave me a tingle of hope, especially in advance of the afternoon's events. I don't think I'll ever believe he's dead – not until we have definite proof anyway. What is it about the men in my life? They have a tendency to disappear without trace.

James's memorial service, at St Martin-in-the-Fields, was a dignified and moving occasion. Apart from May, his elderly Scottish housekeeper, and an obtrusive cluster of glamorous women with expensive hats and large diamonds weighing down their wedding-ring fingers, most people were from our world. The Minister was there, as was C, James's first boss. M delivered a moving address, talking of Commander Bond's bravery and patriotism. 'He didn't always obey orders, but he certainly got results, as some of you know only too well,' he said, with the briefest of glances at the expensive hats. That raised a titter. 'The Commander's actions will pass into Foreign Office legend,' he concluded. 'He will always be missed by his colleagues and many friends, but never forgotten.' I felt unbidden tears roll down my cheeks, and beside me, Lil* let out a stifled whimper and blew her nose.

Then Felix Leiter† limped up to the pedestal. It was the first time I had seen him since he was half eaten alive by sharks in Florida at The Robber's aquarium. He looked better than I expected. Apart from the missing limbs, there was only the slightest visible scar evidence above his right eye, and this was mostly hidden by a lock of blond hair, far longer than the regulation American cut. He drew a piece of paper out of his pocket with his right hand, then anchored it on the stand in front with the steel hook projecting from his left sleeve. 'I would

---

* Loelia Ponsonby, secretary to the oo section until she retired to marry the heir to a dukedom.

† Sometime CIA agent and employee of Pinkerton's Private Detective Agency. First encountered by Bond in the casino at Royale-les-Eaux, where they became firm friends and subsequently partners on numerous missions.

have given my life for James,' he began, in an attractive drawl. 'Come to think of it, I nearly did. On several occasions.' Over the next ten minutes, he had most of the congregation if not actively rolling in the aisles, then laughing openly. At times, I feared he was swimming rather too close to Official Secrets, but as an American, I doubt that worried him unduly and I can't believe that the assembled congregation had many illusions as to what it was James did for the MOD. Suspecting, I imagine, that the speeches might not have been going to be marked by discretion, Bill had taken precautions to ensure that the gathering was unsullied by press. He had put Paymaster Captain Troop* in charge of enforcing this – one time when his over-developed sense of duty served us well.

There was tea afterwards in the crypt, with egg-and-cucumber sandwiches lovingly prepared by Joanna and a team of Registry girls. We stood around, swapping anecdotes about James – some spicy, all affectionate – until Bill struck his teaspoon on his cup to silence us. 'This is all very well and proper,' he said. 'However, I'm not sure it's exactly up our friend's street, so to speak. Everyone is therefore not so cordially invited to the American Bar at the Savoy at six. There's a case of champagne behind the bar, a side of smoked salmon, and for those who want

* Head of Admin and James Bond's bête noire, after he served under him on a committee investigating the impact of the Burgess and Maclean defection. Described by Bond as a bigot, 'the office tyrant and bugbear . . . cordially disliked by all . . . the one man who has real impact on the office comforts and amenities and whose authority extends into the privacy and personal habits of the men and women of the organisation'.

something stronger, Joe* will be on hand with the Martini shaker.' There was clapping and some cheering.

As I turned to go back to the Office to tidy up before the evening's revelry, a hand touched my arm. I turned to see an extraordinarily beautiful tall woman, with ash-blonde hair, golden skin and wide-set blue eyes. 'Are you Jane Moneypenny? I thought so. James spoke about you with such fondness.' When I looked a little puzzled, she smiled. 'I'm sorry, I'm Honey Levin – Honey Rider that was. I met James in Jamaica, on Crab Key. He changed my life.' She briefly touched her perfect nose. I told her that James had always enjoyed receiving her Christmas cards. She beamed with delight and I warmed to her. 'Would it be all right if I came along to the wake?' she asked. 'I fly back to Philadelphia tomorrow. I know I don't exactly fit in, but I don't feel I've said goodbye to James properly yet.'

I urged her to join us and the last I saw of her, well past midnight, she was sitting on a stool by the mirrored bar, crooning ballads to an admiring audience comprised of some of the most senior members of British intelligence. How James would have laughed.

Tuesday, 30th July

From our Moscow station: it was reported in today's *Isvestia* that Kim Philby had been granted political asylum in Moscow and full Soviet citizenship. Further fuel to the Opposition, who are intent on exploiting the Government's

---

* Joe Gilmore, the legendary long-serving head barman at the Savoy and author of *Joe Gilmore and his Cocktails*.

embarrassment. The debate has been hot and fierce since Heath's announcement and looks set to continue for many weeks.

It is a horrible blow to the Office, to M, and to the country.

Wednesday, 31st July

I had just delivered the morning signals to M, when he asked me to sit down in the high-backed chair opposite him. Although it was a beautiful day outside, he had drawn the curtains and switched on the green-shaded desk-lamp, which lit his face with a ghostly glow. He had a file open in front of him. For the first minute he just flicked through the pages without once looking up at me. I waited quietly.

'Miss Moneypenny, I know this is highly irregular, but I have a small mission for you,' he said at last. 'It's a sensitive project.' He reached for his tobacco and slowly filled his pipe and tamped it down before lighting it.

'It concerns Mrs Philby. As you know, she is currently in London. Her husband is in Moscow, where she is apparently keen to join him. That would not be ideal, from our point of view. However, that's not your concern. Mrs Philby is being pestered by the media and deserted by many of her friends. According to CME, who sees her on a fairly regular basis, she feels isolated and lonely. I would like you to', he cleared his throat, 'befriend her. Nothing more. She will know from the outset that you work for us. I do not want to put one of our women agents on to this – Miss Fields is too busy, for one thing, and Miss

Pelham-Hill is not, perhaps, the kind of woman to engage another's trust. You will do the job very well. All I want is to make her happy. You know the kind of thing,' he looked slightly perplexed – 'tea, shopping, a woman's ear . . .'

He took his pipe out of his mouth and started fiddling with it. 'I am bound to say, at this point, that you are in no way compelled to do this. It is outside your job description and you would be within your rights to refuse.'

I stopped him. 'Sir, if it helps, I'd be happy to do it. I would find it interesting to meet Mrs Philby and will try to do anything in my power to make her happy in London.'

M gave one of his rare smiles and pushed the file across his desk. 'You will find all the background in here. You'd better have a word with CME first. He knows her well. Anything else, ask Chief of Staff.'

I returned to my desk, excited at the prospect of an assignment of my own.

August

As an undergraduate, I had always taken a perverse pride in the knowledge that I shared an alma mater with 'the Cambridge Spies'. Their names added a frisson to the long list of Trinity College alumni that I would trot out for the benefit of any passing visitor: Newton, Wittgenstein, Marvell, Thackeray, Nabokov, Byron . . . Philby, Burgess and Blunt. Certainly they seemed to me to have done no lasting damage to the largest, richest and arguably most venerable of Cambridge's colleges. It was only relatively recently, not long before my peremptory dismissal from the university, that I realised that a degree of sensitivity remained about these more infamous former students. I was sitting at High Table next to a senior colleague, who had joined the college in 1952 – the year following Burgess and Maclean's flight to Moscow. 'Wouldn't want any more scandal of that type,' he muttered over the port decanter. 'Best keep the college well away from any taint of espionage – for the wrong side, you understand.' He jiggled an unkempt eyebrow at me, before shuffling off to the Senior Common Room. I was surprised: I'd assumed that the upper reaches of academia were exempt from that sort of stuffy patriotism.

It is now generally accepted that there were five members of the inner circle: Philby, Burgess, Donald Maclean (a Trinity Hall alumnus), Anthony Blunt and John Cairncross. All were members of the Apostles, a dining and debating club where the clever young men of the day would argue passionately about the causes closest to their hearts. Many of the Apostles were members of the Cambridge University Socialist Society (CUSS) and later the Communist Party. In the 1930s, it made intellectual sense: the economies of the West were sunk in depression, with the starving forming long lines at inadequately supplied soup kitchens, and as fascism swept across Spain and Germany its antithesis appeared increasingly attractive to independent thinkers.

Philby was never going to be a conformer. His father, Harry St John Philby, was an ardent Arabist, who converted to Islam and served as adviser to the King of Saudi Arabia – who, as a token of gratitude, gave him a Baluchi slave girl to be his second wife. Kim – born in India, fluent in Urdu, and nicknamed after Kipling's hero – excelled at Westminster School, but found the lure of politics more exciting than his academic studies at Cambridge. He canvassed for the Labour Party in the 1931 general election, and became treasurer of the CUSS. Handsome, slightly built, with a stutter that became more pronounced when he was nervous or angry, by all accounts he was a charming man. After graduation, he bought a motorcycle and drove to Vienna, where he threw in his lot with the Communist underground and met and married his first wife, Litzi Friedman, a Communist activist in need of a British passport.

Back in London, in May 1934 Philby was visited by a friend from Vienna, who asked whether he would like to meet a man of 'decisive importance'. Two days later he had his first rendezvous with 'Otto' in Regent's Park. 'Our conversation lasted less than an hour, but within a few minutes it was clear that, although Otto said nothing in so many words, I was being approached with a view to recruitment into one of the Soviet Special Services,' Philby later recalled. 'Long before he finished, I had decided to accept.'

It was the beginning of twenty-nine years of secret servitude. It was Otto who asked Philby to compile a list of his Cambridge friends and acquaintances, with biographical details about each of them – particularly their political sympathies. Donald Maclean was near the top of the list. Burgess was there, and probably Blunt and Cairncross too, although Philby never admitted to having had a direct role in their recruitment. It was Otto's successor as handler, 'Theo', who suggested some years later that Philby should find a way to join the British Secret Intelligence Service, MI6.

That Philby – and his cohorts – should have managed to work at the heart of the British intelligence services for upwards of a decade does not reflect well on the internal security of those organisations. In other areas, however, the SIS and the Security Service (MI5) were mostly admired and feared by their counterparts and adversaries around the world. Both had an outstandingly 'successful' war, helped in no small measure by Philby and his Cambridge comrades, even though they were sharing classified information, particularly about the German Enigma codes, with our allies in Moscow in what seemed to them be a justifiable deception.

It was after the war, when the West's allegiances shifted and resettled, with the Soviet Union placing itself firmly on the other side of an ideological – and increasingly physical – divide, that their work became more hazardous, and damaging for Britain. But by then, the spies had no possibility of an elegant exit. As Philby knew, to break with Soviet intelligence would lead either to a British cell or to a Russian bullet. So he maintained his faith and continued to serve his Soviet master with whatever he could supply – until the point, at the end of 1962, when he was confronted with the knowledge that the KGB defector Anatoly Golitsyn had irrevocably betrayed his secret.

When the Chief of the Middle Eastern section, Alexander 'Dingle' Delavigne, was sent to interview Philby in Beirut in December 1962, he reported back to London that Philby had shown no surprise. He had clearly been forewarned by someone in the inner sanctum of SIS.

Thursday, 1st August

I got in early this morning and opened Eleanor Philby's file. On the first page, there was a photograph of an attractive woman with a warm smile. She was sitting in a deckchair, on a balcony perhaps, wearing an over-sized man's shirt and smoking a cigarette. I liked her face; she was older than me, but looked as if she could be a friend. I started reading the dry details of her life. She was born in

Seattle in 1913, the only child of Irish-American parents. She graduated from the University of Washington and, aged twenty, moved to California to study art. When war broke out, she moved to New York and in 1943, in search of adventure, to Istanbul. After peace came, she continued her wanderings around Europe. In 1948, then thirty-five, she married a *New York Times* journalist, Sam Pope Brewer. They had a daughter, Ann, and a series of far-flung postings which culminated, in 1956, with his appointment as the paper's chief Middle Eastern correspondent, based in Beirut. Even in dry black and white, it sounded like an exciting life, but the real adventure was still to come.

According to the file, it was later that year – while her husband was out of town on an assignment – that she first met Kim Philby, who was working as a correspondent for the *Observer* and the *Economist*, in the bar of the St George's Hotel. Their relationship developed and on January 24th, 1959, soon after the death of Philby's previous wife and only months after her divorce papers came through, they married, at Holborn Register Office in London. According to unnamed sources, it appeared to be a happy marriage, though both Philbys exhibited an increasingly voracious appetite for spirits. Frequently over the year before he disappeared, after a session in a bar or even on a picnic, Kim had to be poured into a taxi and sent home, with Eleanor not noticeably more in control of her faculties. On New Year's Eve, three weeks before he disappeared, he slipped in the bathroom and cracked his head open. The doctor at the American Hospital said that had he one more ounce of alcohol in his blood, he would have died. Throughout all this, he always managed to file his articles on time – and never gave any hint of his double life.

With hindsight, his drinking problem was explicable. He must have known the net was closing in on him. She, presumably, drank to keep him company. I looked again at the photograph and felt a growing sympathy for her. I phoned Janet and asked if I could see Dingle.

He was full of wit and courtesy, as usual, as he ushered me into a comfortable leather armchair in the corner of his room and came to sit opposite, crossing his polished half-brogues elegantly at the ankle. 'Margaret and I are very fond of Eleanor,' he told me. 'She's a good, brave gal and she adores Kim. She hadn't the foggiest what he was up to, of course. He took us all in, I'm afraid.' His eyes, behind round-rimmed spectacles, did not waver, though when I happened to look down, I saw that the whites of his knuckles were showing where his hands were tightly grasped together. 'I'm furious with Kim for what he did, but as much as anything for how he abandoned Eleanor. He couldn't have done so in a manner more calculated to distress her. You'll find her in a pretty sorry state now: she alternates between high excitement at the idea of joining him in Moscow and fear when she contemplates what she'll have to forgo for him – her daughter, her family, possibly her freedom. If she goes to Russia, I don't know whether she'll ever be allowed back. It's sad, because she's not a political creature. She married Kim because she loved him, for better and for worse, and she still does. He's a damnably charming fellow. He's always had this great effect on women: they love him dearly, though he's not always treated them fairly. Not at all.' He shook his head.

'Eleanor will like you, Jane, and God knows she needs a friend.'

Monday, 5th August

Prenderghast was sentenced today. Forty-two years for three counts of contravening the Official Secrets Act. Everyone I spoke to was stunned at the severity of the sentence, even though the Chief Justice had referred to 'hundreds of agents' having been blown by P, at least forty of whom had been killed as a result of his treachery.

Talking to Bill later, he said it was a political sentence, designed to placate the Americans. Between them, the PM, the Attorney-General and the Lord Chief Justice had apparently cooked up a term that was meant to demonstrate how seriously we take betrayal, and the degree of our 'commitment to eradicate the cancer of treachery within the intelligence services'. I know M has had repeated meetings with his opposite number, who was in London for the verdict, stressing that the necessary security adjustments had been made to ensure that this couldn't reoccur. He surely did not mention the fear here that Prenderghast had an accomplice within the Office.

On the news, there was footage of a small man with a jacket over his head being bundled into a police van and driven off to Wormwood Scrubs. Forty-two years: when his sentence is served, he'll be eighty-six – too old for further treachery.

Wednesday, 14th August

A day like no other. It started this morning with a telephone call from the Chief Security Officer. He sounded unusually agitated and asked for an immediate appointment with M. I told him that M was over with the Minister. A few minutes later, he bounded up the stairs, a cigarette between his fingers, and rapped sharply on Bill's door. 'Tanner,' I heard him say. 'I need to talk to you urgently.' He walked into the room and, without shutting the door, proceeded to recount the details of a telephone conversation he had just overheard.

'Twenty minutes ago, a man telephoned the Ministry switchboard and identified himself as James Bond, agent 007. He was transferred, as per protocol, to Liaison. Walker was on duty – extremely bright chap. When he asked who was calling, the man once again said, "This is Commander James Bond speaking. Number 007," and repeated his request to speak to M.'

'Another crank?' Bill asked.

'I'm not so sure. Just wait. Liaison patched the call through to me and I listened as he kept him talking long enough for Special Branch to trace the number. Walker asked him again who it was he wanted to speak to. "Admiral Miles Messervy," he said, in a low voice. He is head of a department in your Ministry. The number of his room used to be twelve on the eighth floor. He used to have a secretary called Miss Moneypenny. Good-looking girl. Brunette. Well let's see, it's Wednesday. Shall I tell you what'll be the main dish on the menu in the staff canteen? It should be steak-and-kidney pudding."'

Bill looked up at that. 'Good God! Do you think it might be him?'

'I didn't like that bit about the steak-and-kidney either. I've passed him on to the Soft Man* at X Section. X is on leave, sadly, though it's probably best anyway that it's not someone 007 knows . . . if indeed it is 007. He's on his way now to Kensington Cloisters.'†

'Thank you,' Bill replied. 'I'll notify M as soon as he gets in. We should be on our guard about this.'

Once he had gone, Bill appeared at my door. 'Heard all that, Penny?' he asked. 'A good-looking brunette, eh?' I could tell, despite the attempt at levity, that he was tense. I didn't quite know what to feel. My heart was beating fast and I had an inexplicable urge to cry, which I just managed to control by repeating over and over, 'It is probably another hoax, probably another hoax.' I couldn't begin to think about what would happen if it wasn't. James back from the dead?

M returned from the Ministry and Bill told him the news. I wasn't there to see his reaction, but can imagine that he exhibited no emotion, if indeed he felt any. He is impenetrable.

Over the next hour, reports kept coming in, which I took immediately into M.

Special Branch had traced the phone call to the Ritz and picked up the target at the Arlington Street entrance.

---

* The proverbial 'good cop' in the two-man re-entry interrogation team.
† The West-London headquarters of X Section, the department concerned with the cross-examination of foreign spies and of suspected double agents within the Secret Intelligence Service.

His room had been taken under the name of Frank Westmacott, company director.

A photograph taken was sent over here immediately by dispatch rider. Q Branch developed it and brought it up. I got a brief glimpse as M opened the file. It certainly looked like James, but then I know what can be done with skilled plastic surgery.

Fifteen minutes later, we received details of his coat – a Burberry mackintosh bought yesterday.

Then information on his arrival in the country from Immigration: he had flown in yesterday from West Berlin.

Then his fingerprints.

Next, the Chief Security Officer called up, asking to see M immediately. I showed him in and as I was closing the door, I just caught him saying, 'The Soft Man thinks it must be 007 . . .' James back? It was too good to be true. I suppressed the urge to run along the corridors, shouting the news. Bill was summoned into M's office to join them and when he came out he rushed straight through my room with a deep frown on his face.

Twenty minutes later, he marched back through M's door, barely stopping to knock on the door. He was still in there when I was notified by the concierge that Commander Bond was on his way up. With a stomach-tightening cocktail of nerves and excitement, I went to the lift to meet him. The doors opened and my heart gave a jump. It was James all right – no doubt about it: the same grey-blue eyes, the wayward comma of hair straying over his right eyebrow. I was on the point of rushing forward to embrace him, when he stepped out and said, 'Hello, Miss Moneypenny. Good to see you again,' in a cold, emotionless voice. There was only a pretence of a smile, no joke, and when had he ever called me Miss Moneypenny? That instant, I knew there was something seriously wrong.

In a state of turmoil, I started walking towards my office, with James following a few steps behind. I opened the door and went over to my desk and automatically pressed the intercom to notify M of his arrival. Then I sat down. My mind was churning furiously, trying to think of a way to keep him away from M.

He stood in front of my desk, looking at me with that same empty smile, as I fought desperately for something to say. After what seemed like hours, Bill came through M's door. James looked up and said, 'Hello, Bill,' but he didn't hold out his hand. Bill is – was – his best friend. How could he greet him so coldly? I had to do something. I looked at Bill, trying to convey my doubts, hoping that he wouldn't let this strange husk of 007 go through M's door. Nothing good could come of it. 'Hello, old chap. Long time no see,' he replied, in a forced attempt at jollity. I shook my head at him, but he gave me a fierce glare. 'M would like to see 007 straight away.'

I said the first thing that came into my head. I can't remember exactly what it was – something to the effect that M had an important meeting – but Bill was not to be swayed.

'M says you must get him out of it,' he said curtly. Then he turned to the James figure and told him to go in. 'Come and have a gossip after M's finished with you.'

As James walked through the door, I started shaking uncontrollably. 'Oh, Bill,' I said. 'There's something wrong with him.'

He gave me a quick squeeze and told me to calm down and then swiftly disappeared into his office, shutting the door behind him. A bare ten minutes later, he burst back through, along with Head of Security, and straight into M's office. I didn't see what happened, but they must have leapt on James, as by the time I got to the door they were heaving him to his feet. He appeared to be in a dead faint.

I looked past them to where, to my astonishment, there was a glass screen in front of M's desk. Brown liquid was dripping slowly down the middle of the glass. I couldn't drag my eyes away; it was as if I were paralysed. Still rooted to the spot, I was aware of some movement, as M walked around the side of the glass. Suddenly everything was happening at once. Someone was shouting, 'Cyanide. We must all get out of here. Bloody quick.' A foot kicked out and I saw a pistol skipping across the carpet. Then M was being ordered to leave the room. Head of Security and Bill followed, dragging James with them into Bill's room.

I was still frozen to my spot. M turned to me and told me sharply to close the door and get the duty medical officer right away. 'Not a word of this to anyone. Understood?' I managed to gather my wits and follow orders. Even now, recalling the events, I feel a tightness in my chest. I hadn't known about M's protective shield. What if? It is too horrendous even to speculate. I can only thank every deity that M survived.

M followed Bill into his office and closed the door behind him. They were joined minutes later by the doc and soon after that by two orderlies carrying a stretcher. I caught a brief glimpse of James as they took him out, supine and still unconscious, his face a shade of pale putty. M came out to collect his bowler hat. 'I'll be at Blades for the next hour,' he said as he left. I wonder at his composure.

Bill was soon back. He came up to me and gave me a hug. 'Feeling all right, Penny?' he asked. 'Must have been a tremendous shock for you. Can I get you some tea?' I shook my head. Typical of Bill to be solicitous of others at a time like this. What must he have gone through? I collected myself. 'I'm perfectly fine, thank you. Just a normal assassination attempt by a dead man on my boss. Now, how can I help? You need a cup of tea.'

He smiled. 'You're right, I do. Thank you. Now, if you're really up to it, there's a list of things to do.'

He sat down and got out his notebook as I made tea for us both. As I got back, a troop of men dressed head to toe in white, with masks covering their faces, went through to M's room, dragging heavy-duty equipment. Bill raised his eyebrows. 'The cleaners are in early today then?' Suddenly we were laughing. Shock, I suppose, mixed with relief.

'Right. I've got a list of commands from the Old Man. We had better share them out. Can you contact Sir James Molony, please? Explain that there's been an emergency with 007 and that he's been taken by ambulance to The Park. See if he can call in there before talking to M this afternoon. Then, if you could order the Scaramanga file up from Records for M's return, please. We also need to collect James's things from the Ritz and pay his bill.'

I told him I would take care of that myself. It would be a welcome excuse to get out of the office. Bill thanked me. 'That will be a great help. M wants me to get a statement out to the Press Association, announcing James's return from the dead.'*

'What's going to happen to him? 007, I mean?' I found it hard to say his name. 'Will he be court-martialled?'

'Apparently not,' he replied, drily. 'The Old Man wants to try to get him straightened out and back in the saddle again.'

'I suppose that's a good thing?'

'We shall see, Penny. We shall see. Thank you again.'

The walk across the parks gave me a chance to calm down. The Office had always felt like a sanctuary. I knew what had befallen one of M's predecessors, of course,† but the idea that the threat might come from within is horrifying. Despite his apparent heartlessness, I respect M more than any man. He is our country's protective shield. Had anything happened to him . . . Then 007 – even when I conjure up images of his limp body being carried out of the room, I can't believe it. That he, who has done so much for our country, could turn around and try to stab it in the back is beyond contemplation. He must have been brain-washed by the Russians. Surely, though, he has

---

* The statement read, 'The Ministry of Defence is delighted to announce that Commander James Bond, CBE, who was posted as missing, believed killed, while on a mission to Japan last November, has returned to this country after a hazardous journey across the Soviet Union which is expected to yield much valuable information. Commander Bond's health has inevitably suffered from his experiences and he is convalescing under medical supervision.'

† The third 'C' was shot with a poisoned dart through the open back window of his official car at the traffic lights on Hyde Park Corner. The assassin was never caught. From then on, it was official policy to rely on air conditioning to cool the car in summer.

undergone training to combat that? Even so . . . What a strange, twisted world we live in, where death is common currency and, on occasion, our friends are indistinguishable from our enemies.

I finally persuaded the manager to let me into James's – Frank Westmacott's – room, by claiming to be his sister. I found it eerily free of personal belongings. There was an unopened bottle of vodka on the table (unopened? James?) and a clutch of empty shopping-bags at the back of the wardrobe. I sorted through them: Turnbull and Asser for the shirt and black knitted-silk tie, Huntsman of Savile Row for the navy single-breasted suit, Church's for the black soft-leather slip-on shoes. It was as if he was 007 dressed by numbers. There was no sign of the clothes he had arrived in – nothing except for a pair of ordinary cotton pyjamas folded under the pillow. James in anything ordinary would be stretching credulity enough, but pyjamas?* Impossible. As was the standard cut-throat razor in the bathroom.† Whoever moulded this James Bond was good enough to get him through the Office door for a one-shot mission, but no better.

I couldn't wait to come home this evening. I ran myself a deep, hot bath and sat in it until my fingers shrivelled. I still felt shivery when I got out. I phoned Helena and talked to her for almost an hour, about inconsequential stuff mainly. I would have liked to have seen R, but he's still away, goodness knows where, and it seems an age

---

* Bond habitually slept in a navy silk pyjama coat – loose almost to his knees, with wide, short sleeves and a belt around his waist instead of buttons.
† His razor of choice was a heavy-toothed steel number, bought from Hoffritz on Madison Avenue in New York.

since I last heard from him. I hope he's safe. So I'm sitting here now, wrapped up in my gown, drinking hot chocolate and trying to exorcise the day's events from my memory by writing them down.

Tuesday, 20th August

I can't stop thinking about what happened. Whenever I walk into M's office, my eyes are drawn to a small patch of carpet a little paler than the rest, where the drops of poison were scrubbed clean with powerful chemicals. Whenever I think about James, images of those dead eyes haunt my mind. They were not the eyes of my friend, the bravest man I know. What has been done to him?

My thoughts turned to R: I don't know where he is, but I hope it's nowhere behind the Iron Curtain. I couldn't bear it if he was hurt again.

I finally met Eleanor Philby today. Dingle thought it would ease matters if I was introduced to her by his wife, Margaret, at their Belgravia flat. So I rang on the doorbell shortly before four. I was looking forward to meeting her, but not without some trepidation. What if she didn't like me? After the events of last week, especially, I was keen for everything to proceed smoothly.

Margaret, a mirror version of her husband, tall, elegant and well bred, answered the door and led the way upstairs into the drawing-room. As I walked in, a slim, dark-haired woman stood up from the sofa. She was wearing a simple white short-sleeved cotton dress, belted at the waist, and flat shoes. She was almost as tall as me, not beautiful, but with an attractive, friendly face. Only her eyes betrayed her unease: they were wary, like a deer in long grass. 'Jane Moneypenny, I presume?' she said in a soft American drawl. I laughed. 'Mrs Livingstone?' She smiled, and from that instant I knew it was going to be all right.

Margaret excused herself to go and collect her children from school, and we started to talk. Eleanor was reserved at first, confining herself to the most benign chat, but I could sense that she wanted to open up and reach out to someone. It was lucky for me – and for M – that I turned up at the right time.

She asked if I wanted some tea and when I replied yes, suggested the Lyons' Corner House. 'I get out so rarely, you see,' she explained as she got up to look for her bag. 'I started out staying with Kim's sister, Patricia, in Kensington, but the press soon found me there. I was offered £10,000 by one paper for my story – can you believe it! I was mobbed every time I set foot out of the door, so I stayed in. Then I moved to some friends in St John's Wood, but they aren't keen on the attention. Can't blame them. I don't care for it myself. I've been trying to keep a low profile. I see Alexander and Margaret every week, but otherwise I'm just waiting.'

We walked to Knightsbridge. I noticed that Eleanor kept glancing behind her, but apart from that she was easy company. She chose a table at the back corner of the restaurant and we ordered tea and scones. We talked for an hour, though I said little. Understandably, her feelings and thoughts were in a jumble, and lacking anyone to sort through them with, she was almost bursting with frustration. She mentioned her husband only infrequently – and then with care. It was as if she measured every word she said about him, for fear of exposing too much. Most of her focus was on her daughter – back in America with her father – and Kim's children, currently scattered among relatives in England. What should she do about them? They were like her own children.

We talked a little about London. She told me about her first visit here with Kim, when they had married. Walking around the city together, he seemed to have friends in every corner. 'Many of them won't talk to me now,' she said, sadly. 'I'm a pariah. I hate to think of how they regard Kim.' Then, pulling herself together, she looked at her watch and, seeing it was shortly after six, suggested we pop across to the Hyde Park Hotel for a drink.

I excused myself with regret. We've made a plan to go to the cinema together next Saturday. I like her very much indeed. It will be no hardship being her friend. I only wish I could do something to ease the inner agonies that she's undoubtedly experiencing.

Friday, 23rd August

Bill passed by my desk this morning, whistling. I asked why he was looking so chipper. He replied that he had just got back from seeing James at The Park. 'He's getting on well. Should be back to his old self fairly soon.'

'Do we know what happened?' I asked.

'Not yet, but we should do soon, if he keeps on recovering at this rate. Have dinner with me tonight?'

When I said I'd love to, he suggested Scott's. I was expecting something more along the lines of Bully's; for Scott's, one needs a new frock.

At lunchtime, I dragged Janet out shopping. She was desperate to hear about James. News of his dramatic return had inevitably penetrated the Powder Vine. She asked endless questions – how he'd looked, what he'd said to M, where he'd been all this time. I tried to be as non-committal as possible, but it wasn't easy. Janet has a way of wheedling the truth from anyone. I hope I didn't say too much.

It has been ages since I bought something special. I'm longing to get a 'trouser suit', but I'm not sure I have the self-confidence to walk into a restaurant wearing trousers. I admire the women who do. Only last week, I read about a woman who was turned away from the Savoy Grill because of her trousers – Yves Saint Laurent, of course. Without a word, she wheeled round and disappeared into the Ladies. She returned to the restaurant wearing only her jacket and nylons. When the maître d' tried to protest, she argued – successfully – that her jacket was no shorter than the average mini dress. I read a similar story from New York. I'm not sure, however, that M would enjoy the publicity if I tried to emulate them. Instead, I found a very smart navy and white short linen dress by Jane & Jane. Janet said it made me look ten years younger. The sad truth is that I am about ten years younger than I normally look. This evening, I entered the Powder Vine as safe old Miss Moneypenny and emerged as swinging young Jane, complete with false eyelashes. When Bill came into my office, he literally stopped in his tracks and told me I looked beautiful. He has perfect manners.

Scott's was lovely. What a treat. We ordered smoked salmon and champagne. I asked Bill what we were celebrating. 'James's return to good health,' he replied, firmly. I raised my glass.

'You know that some of the others are not going to be this forgiving?' I said.

He shook his head. 'I fear you're right. We've got to persuade them, Penny. You have to help me. Think about it: do they honestly believe that James would try to pull a stunt like that if he was in his right mind? I talked to Molony at The Park today. He said that James had suffered a huge bang on the head, probably when he was blowing Blofeld's castle up to high heaven. He was almost certainly unconscious for a while and suffered total amnesia. The first thing he can remember is lying in a cave having his brow mopped by a beautiful girl, with the sound of the sea crashing against the cliffs below. That was Kissy Suzuki, the awabi diver who had affected such grief at James's death when 006 went to see her.

'For several months after that, he believed he was a Japanese fisherman. Now, this is where Molony is surprised. He's done exhaustive tests and found the remains of APV in his system. It's a memory-blocking drug, used by the Japanese in the war. There's a chance it was administered to James by the Russians when he got there, but Molony says, from an analysis of his hair follicles, it appears that if James had been ingesting it for at least six months – probably longer. If he's right, that means someone was giving it to him in Japan. Missy Kissy has some serious questions to answer. James can't remember much about it, of course, but says he drank a lot of what she called 'herbal tea' – sounds disgusting. We're doing a search on her background now. Apparently, she spent some time in Hollywood a few years ago. Dikko Henderson's going back to the island to see what he can dig up.

'As far as James is concerned, we can assume he's been to hell and back and it'll take time before he's right again. Molony's putting him through some fairly intense treatment and his memory is returning, but we can't push it. We don't know yet what the Russians did to him – on past form, it's likely they used some sort of mind-altering serum, on top of psychological manipulation. James has talked a bit about an institute in Leningrad, and to M he mentioned a Russian colonel who had "helped him to understand what British intelligence was really up to". Molony says it's a miracle that he's with us now. James is a strong man – brave and determined – but even he has limits. I don't doubt that, when he recovers his full wits, he'll hate himself for what he did. We have to ensure that he's not censured by everyone.'

It was a long and impassioned speech from a man used to measuring his words. I lifted up my glass and gently clinked it against his. 'We will,' I told him. 'How's the Old Man taking it all?'

'You know him. Hard to say. He's approaching it in an entirely pragmatic fashion. Doesn't mean he's not determined to wreak revenge on the KGB. He's convinced that Philby had a role in preparing James for his mission. Can't see any other way the KGB could have learnt the information they needed to infiltrate James back into the building. They must have known about Kensington Cloisters – but that's so top secret that only a small handful of us have the details.'

I nodded. Even I had no idea of the procedures for vetting suspected double agents. 'Philby left the Firm twelve years ago. Surely personnel have changed since then?'

'You're right, but procedure hasn't, to any great extent. I looked through Philby's files. He was CS [Chief of Soviet Section] after the war, when the protocols were put in place; he would have been instructed in them during the Volkov case.* Philby was in charge of it. He flew out to Istanbul, but by the time the mechanisms for Volkov's defection were in place, the Russian had disappeared. With hindsight, Philby must have blown him to his Soviet controllers. He was so clever that no one guessed at the time.

'Kim Philby was a supreme intelligence agent. I met him on a number of occasions. He came across as some-what shy, with his stutter and deferential matter. With hindsight, it was the perfect foil. Underneath, he must have been ruthless, but people liked him and confided in him. He made it his business to find out everything he could about this organisation. At one point, he was tipped for the top chair. He had an instinctive feel for the busi-ness. With his deep background knowledge, he would have been able to tell the Russians exactly what they needed to know to prime James – and exactly how to go about finding it.'

'His defection really is a big deal.'

----

* Konstantin Volkov was a senior Soviet intelligence officer in Istanbul. He contacted the British Embassy in 1945, wishing to defect and promising to name three Soviet agents working in Britain – two for the Foreign Office and one for SIS. Fortunately for Philby, the papers landed on his desk. He contacted his Russian handlers imme-diately, while stalling the British end of the operation. By the time authorisation had come through to contact Volkov, the would-be defector was already on his way back to Moscow, and a bullet in his head.

'Bigger than you can imagine. It's certainly not just a piece of propaganda. At one point he knew everything – agent rings, methodology, personnel – and he has an extraordinary memory. If he was indeed working for them from the beginning, the damage he's caused is inestimable – and he's compounding it in Moscow as we speak. He makes Prenderghast look like a small-time hustler. It will take us years and years to unravel. Then there's the future. What else might he and his KGB chums be up to? Did he turn any others? Until we have him back here, his knowledge and skill are a constant threat.'

'Surely there's no chance of him returning?'

'Strictly between you and me, M's got clearance from the top to give him full immunity from prosecution and a comfortable retirement – something he certainly won't get in Moscow, where the Russians will suck him dry of information, then, when he's got nothing further to offer, grow tired of him and cast him aside. Here, he'll be able to do the *Times* crossword, watch cricket, see old friends . . . everything he can't do in Moscow.'

'He'd get immunity? After all he's done?'

'Yep. It would be embarrassing for a short while, but I'm sure, with some well-placed whispers in friendly ears, we would be able to persuade the great British public how galling it must be for Moscow to swallow Philby's return.'

'So this is where Eleanor fits in – she's a lure?'

'Not to put too fine a point on it, yes. It's up to you to ensure that she feels happy and wanted in the West.'

September

Acres of newsprint were devoted to the trial and sentencing of Robert Prenderghast, including long biographies by people who claimed to have known him, and analyses of his career as a traitor by so-called 'intelligence experts'. I've trawled them all, but found no hint that he had an accomplice. Yet, from what my aunt had related, he must have had a contact on the inside. Information had leaked out of the Office that couldn't have originated from him. But, however hard I searched through the archives, I could find no mention of this mystery mole.

My thoughts turned to my aunt's friend and colleague Bill Tanner. Over the last few years, I have been down several times to visit him in his genteelly worn old rectory in Wiltshire, and it's always been a pleasure. He has an energy that belies his advancing years, and mischief still burns behind his clear blue eyes. From when I first revealed to him the existence of my aunt's diaries, and he greeted the news with obvious amusement, I've had a wonderful feeling of being at home with him. I've sat at his scrubbed oak kitchen table, drinking red wine and listening to faintly scandalous stories of life at the Office in the good old days, and felt like I belonged. From the beginning, he treated me as a member of the family that I later discovered he never had.

Like my aunt, Tanner had not married. 'Never had the time,' he told me on one of my early visits. He had interrupted his Oxford career when the army appealed for officer recruits with a knowledge of engineering. By 1944, when a landmine exploded just yards away from him in Normandy, rupturing the nervous system on his left side, he was a full colonel in the Royal Engineers at the age of only twenty-five. When peace broke out, he joined SIS and, on M's accession to the top chair, was appointed his Chief of Staff, a position he held for twenty-one years.

'Thought the world of your aunt,' he told me. 'Held the whole thing together. The Old Man would have been lost without her. Couldn't find his pipe without her help, let alone his way around a Triple X decoder. Brilliant mind, but hopeless practically. Fell apart when he was pushed aside. Thought he'd be perfectly happy with his paints and his orchids and his naval-battle jigsaws. He wasn't. According to your aunt, who visited him every other weekend, he was increasingly paranoid. He claimed to see Reds under every bed, and was convinced he was being poisoned. Drove poor old Hammond and his wife, who were only trying to look after him, into a home, and was so foully rude to his visitors that they soon gave up coming. Except Penny, of course. She rode all the waves and was with him the day before he died.'

'Did you ever find Prenderghast's ally in the Office?' I asked. Tanner cleared his throat and got up from the faded velvet armchair in front of the fire, where he'd been idly fondling his labrador's ears. He picked up a small replica of a cannon that was sitting on the mantelpiece, put it down again, and turned to face me. 'Don't believe he had one,' he said finally. 'Know there was talk of it at the time, and the Old Man was convinced we had another blind tunneller, but I never really thought so. It was the climate of the times. Moles were popping out from every cubbyhole – we thought there had to be another one because we couldn't believe there wasn't. Funny sort of logic, I know. But we dug hard and never found a trace. Led me to conclude that he was a figment of our oversensitive imaginations.'

I shook my head. From what I had read in my aunt's diaries, I knew that he was, at best, dissembling. 'So what about the leaks?'

He shrugged his shoulders and walked over to the window, where the sun was setting in a blazing riot of burnt umber over the Downs beyond. 'There's always seepage of some sort – idle gossip, signal intercepts, that sort of thing. For God's sake, your aunt wrote a diary the entire time she was working for the Firm. Who knows who got hold of that? No, there was no other leak. The Office was secure, and to the best of my knowledge has not been penetrated at that level again.'

After being persuaded to stay for cottage pie, I drove back late across country to Cambridge. I wasn't persuaded that even Tanner believed what he was saying. From my aunt's diaries, it was clear that she was convinced that there was a mole, and she wasn't the only one. I went back to my rooms and reread the 1962 and 1963 diaries. There it was, in December 1962, in her own writing: 'I told Bill, who raised his eyebrows. "We've been afraid of that," he said. "Both Dorothy and X say it doesn't add up; Prenderghast must have had a comrade on the inside. But he's not admitting to anything." ' In the volumes that followed, it became clearer still. Tanner was clearly holding something back from me. I would need to try another angle.

At a dinner party in Cambridge shortly afterwards, I was placed next to an ageing modern-languages don from Corpus, who introduced himself as 'Snuffy' Wilden. When the conversation turned to espionage – as somehow, these days, it seems to quite naturally – he told me with some relish that he had 'always been on the lookout for bright chaps and chappesses who might be interested in that line of business'. Fascinated, I asked how it worked. 'Well, I was involved with the Firm myself after the war,' he told me, 'and, when I retired to teach up here, they asked whether I'd be prepared to do a spot of scouting. I accepted, of course; one gets an appetite for secrecy, you see, and once one's been in that world it's hard to let go. So I ask around, look for the usual signs – an aptitude for languages, an engaging character, some intimation of a desire for foreign adventure – sound them out gently, and then point them in the direction of the Firm. It's all fairly open these days, of course – little of the old hush-hush stuff – but not unuseful for all that.'

I asked him if he had a contact there I could talk to about certain events in the 1960s. I explained that I'd made several written requests, all of which had been politely rebuffed. He gave a typical donnish snuffle, then got out a gold pen and wrote down a name and a number on the back of his napkin, which he told me to burn once I had committed them to memory. I wasn't sure whether he was joking. 'Don't expect great things though, m'dear,' he warned as I thanked him. 'They might be out of the closet, so to speak, but they still guard their secrets closely.'

The next day I telephoned Ferdy Macintyre, who the old don had described as 'a senior chap there'. A woman answered and very politely took my name and number. She said she would pass on the message, though she advised me to put it in writing. Two days passed, and when I heard nothing I sat down to write a letter to Macintyre on Trinity College headed paper. I explained my position; I said that I was researching the Prenderghast affair and that I would appreciate assistance in verifying my sources and filling in some of the gaps.

The following Monday I received an email from his secretary, requesting a list of questions. These I duly submitted, slipping in a brief query about whether the identity of Prenderghast's accomplice within the Office had ever been determined. The reply arrived a week later and while, somewhat to my surprise, the rest of my questions had been carefully answered, no reference was made to Prenderghast's sidekick. My original query had been omitted from the list. I sent my thanks, resubmitting the unanswered question. This time I received no reply.

A few days later I ran into a colleague of mine from the history department – a distinguished professor of twentieth-century history, and a senior member of the college now headed by a former chief of MI6. 'A word in your ear, Kate, if I may,' he said, steering me into a small tea shop on King's Parade, frequented exclusively by tourists. 'I understand you're doing some research into the Office,' he said. Surprised, I nodded. It was some months before the publication of *The Moneypenny Diaries*, and, on my publisher's urging, the project was being kept under wraps until its release date. 'Look, not to beat about the proverbial, but you'd better be careful that you don't make any unsubstantiated allegations concerning matters about which you have no proof. The Office takes seriously any breach of the Official Secrets Act, and would far prefer to take a look at any allusions that you might think of making in advance of publication, so as to avoid any messy legal wrangling. Do you get my drift?'

I didn't exactly, but I was beginning to find his confidential tone – not to mention his halitosis – claustrophobic, so I stood up and shook his hand. 'Don't worry. I don't intend to step on anyone's toes if I can possibly help it,' I said. 'And, as a historian, I wouldn't dream of publishing untruths. Thank you for the tea.' Without a backwards glance, I left the café and strode off along the road to Trinity, his words circling around in my head. I had received a warning from the Office. That much was clear. But why? And what were they afraid I might discover?

Sunday, 1st September

A strange afternoon with Eleanor. She came to me straight from lunch at the Dorchester with Dingle. When I opened the door, her face was slightly flushed and she announced that there was a change of plan: 'Alexander says we must see *The Birds*.' I was somewhat surprised. We had arranged to go to *Tom Jones*, which I thought would be a bit of bawdy light relief for her, portraying England in its sunniest light, as a place of fun and green meadows and high jinks. I asked her if she was sure. She said yes – could I believe it, she was an American and she'd never seen a Hitchcock movie before? If Alexander recommended it, then it must be worth seeing. I let it pass and we walked to the Curzon. It's my favourite cinema and soon to be closed down for renovations. Still, I was wary about *The Birds*.

We settled down in the middle of the cinema and, from the opening announcements, I was filled with a sense of foreboding. One knows what Hitchcock horror can be like, of course, but I couldn't help but view it through Eleanor's eyes. Tippi Hedren arrives in a pretty seaside town outside San Francisco, bringing with her a pair of lovebirds for Rod Taylor. As she and Taylor go through the motions of flirtation, the town's gulls start to behave increasingly erratically. I watched with mounting disquiet as the birds started to attack Tippi and the local people, crashing through shop windows, hunting down children. By the end of the film, Tippi was in a cage with birds swooping from all directions to attack, and the town had been devastated. What at first seemed so normal, so safe, a game for her, turns into hell on earth.

It was a truly disturbing film. I worried about what it would do to Eleanor's fragile mental state. Why had Dingle been so determined that she see it? Eleanor sat throughout without moving a muscle. When we emerged from the dark, she was pale and silent and shivering. I took her by the arm and led her to the bar at Claridge's. It was only after two double brandies that the colour seeped back into her face. 'What a horrible story,' she said. 'I love birds. We had several in pretty little cages in Beirut. In his last letter, Kim wrote that he had bought me a gold canary and a pair of blue and green budgerigars for the flat in Moscow. I wish we hadn't seen this.' Then she smiled. 'It's only a film, though. Come on, let's have another drink.'

We sat in deep armchairs and talked and gradually the colour returned to her face, but she was still obviously agitated. 'Guy Burgess died on Friday,' she said. 'I read about it in today's paper. What a sad life. Kim was fond of him. He talked about him occasionally. He told me how Guy had insulted the wife of a high-ranking CIA official at one of his dinner parties in Washington, shortly before he fled to Moscow. I asked him whether he had known that Guy was working for the Russians.'

'What did he say?'

Eleanor laughed drily. 'He said that Guy was such a flamboyant creature that no one in their right senses would recruit him as a spy. Typical Kim – avoiding the question without appearing to. He's a very clever man. He's got the best mind of anyone I've met. He's also a romantic. When I was with him, he always made me feel like the most special person in the world. Now I wonder, was it true?' Her voice dropped and she looked down. 'In those quietest moments in the middle of the night, when everyone is asleep and dawn is still a few hours off, I wonder whether it was all a sham: whether the Russians told him to marry an American to deflect suspicion from his true passion?'

I wanted to lean forward and hug her. Her pain and confusion were achingly evident. I didn't know what to say; I had no more insight into Philby's motives than I did into M's love life. Before I could say anything, she appeared to collect herself. 'No, I know that's rubbish. He loves me and I'm still not sure he went to Moscow of his own accord, whatever Alexander says. They kidnapped him. He couldn't have lied to me for so long. He couldn't have.' She looked at her watch. 'It's eight o'clock. How about another brandy?'

As I walked home after escorting her back to her lodgings, some hours later, I wondered again why Dingle had been so insistent she saw that film. I assume he meant to unsettle her, to show how seeming normality can be turned upside down? Or did he mean to show her the dangers of an unfamiliar world?* I suppose he knew that Kim had bought her the birds.

Even after so many years at the Office, I don't fully understand the mind of a professional intelligence officer. It seems to operate in extra dimensions, considering whys and wherefores, bluffs and counter-bluffs that most of us would not think to conceive. Is R like that too, I wonder? Sometimes I realise that, however much time we spend together, I still have so much to learn about him. Perhaps that is part of his attraction: he's a book that I could never finish?

---

* Film historians now see *The Birds* as an allegory about the spread of Communism into the West. The birds represent the Warsaw Pact nations swooping in to threaten – and ultimately overpower – humanity and the institutions of Western democracy, which is incapable of defending itself.

The longer he's away, the more I yearn for his gentle humour and quick-fire mind. Wherever I go outside the Office, I find myself imagining what it would be like if he was with me. When he's back, I want to take him up to Cambridge to meet Helena and Lionel. I'm sure they will like each other. I hope so. My sister and my – I don't know what to call R: what is he to me?

Tuesday, 3rd September

Yesterday morning, M asked me how I was getting on with Mrs Philby. I told him we had established good relations.

'She likes you?'

'I think so,' I replied.

'Trusts you?'

'I hope so.'

'How does she feel about her husband?'

I told him that I believed she loved him very much.

'He's a bounder you know.' M said. 'Treated his previous wife very unkindly. She was the mother of his five children; went round the bend. I suspect she guessed what he was up to. He used to taunt her with his mistress's virtues. She loved him very much, too,' M said drily. 'D'you think the current Mrs Philby plans to join him out there?'

'I believe she hopes to,' I replied.

'I had better have a word with her. Set it up, please. Better not in here. Have a word with CME.'

After some discussion, we decided it would be easiest for Eleanor if the meeting took place at Dingle's flat and that I shouldn't be present. 'Don't want you to be tarred with his brush if he gets a bit firm,' was how Dingle put it. So he and Margaret invited her to lunch today. When they were finished, he telephoned M, who went directly to join them. He returned to the Office a little over an hour later and made no comment as to how it had gone.

This evening, soon after I arrived home, my phone rang. It was Eleanor. She sounded distinctly shaky. I told her to get in a taxi and come straight round to the flat.

It was raining and she looked miserable when I opened the door to let her in. She had a silk scarf around her head but no coat, and her thin cotton dress stuck to her skin. I think she'd been drinking. Her hands were shaking a little. I gave her a towel and made her a cup of strong tea.

'I met your Chief this afternoon,' she said. 'He's an impressive character, doesn't pull his punches.'

I said nothing and she continued.

'It was after lunch today. He arrived at Margaret and Alexander's apartment and we were left alone in their drawing-room with coffee and a bottle of brandy. He took neither. We started talking about Kim. I told him that I couldn't have been more surprised when he disappeared, and that I believed he'd been taken against his will. I told him that I still can't believe Kim was a Russian agent. He said firmly that I had to. He claimed that he had known for the last seven years that Kim had been working for the Russians without pay. He asked if I could identify Kim's friend, who had come to the flat offering his help in easing my journey to Kim. He showed me a book full of photographs – and there he was, a stocky young man with thinning blond hair. I couldn't help but point out his picture. I hope I haven't done anything wrong.'

She started kneading her handkerchief. I looked down. It was large, white and man-sized, with the initials H.A.R.P. [Harold Adrian Russell Philby – Kim's full name] embroidered rather shakily in the corner in navy thread.

'I started to cry. In front of your Chief. He just sat there. I don't think he knew quite what to do. You see, I'm beginning to accept that what he said is true. What do I do now? Apart from Annie, Kim is all I have. He's everything to me. All I dream about is going out to join him, giving him a happy home. It must be difficult for him too, mustn't it?' She looked up at me, almost beseechingly, tears once again in her eyes. I didn't know what to say. I went to sit next to her on the sofa and put my arms around her as she wept and wept.

Sunday, 8th September

Bill came by my office on Friday afternoon. He had a smile on his face. 'Just spoken to Molony. James's making good progress. Nearly back to his old self. Why don't you pop down to see him? He'd love a visitor. I think he's bored out of his wits. The worst thing is that M gave orders that he was to be cared for by male nurses only.' Bill chuckled. 'Not exactly 007's cup of tea.'

The thought of James being tucked up in bed by effete men in white uniforms made me laugh. 'All right,' I told Bill. 'I'll try to go down there tomorrow.'

It was a beautiful morning. I took Rafiki for a walk in the park, popped in to R's flat to water his plants – he must be back soon, surely – then came home to change. I had great problems deciding what to wear, which annoyed me. Indecision is a waste of energy and I wasn't sure that James deserved it. On the one hand, I strongly believe that one should always wear bright, cheery colours to hospitals, but a part of me still wanted James to suffer for what he had done. I compromised with a white shirt and turquoise skirt. Work clothes.

I hadn't been to The Park before and wasn't sure what to expect. I suppose I had a vague idea that it would be a large grey institution, with barred windows and burly orderlies walking around with bunches of clanking keys hanging from their belts.

Fortunately, it defied the caricature and instead lived up to its name. I turned off the A2 at Ashford and, after a few more miles, found myself at an imposing pair of wrought- iron gates. There was a discreet sign on the manicured grass to one side: 'THE PARK. PRIVATE.' As I pulled in, I noticed the blinds twitch in the gatehouse window. I pressed on the intercom and announced my name. After a few minutes, the gates began to swing open.

The drive was lined with chestnut-trees; there were sheep grazing in the fields to one side, horses on the other. I rounded the corner to see, in front of me, a very large, very grand mansion – the sort of place one could imagine playing host to an international summit. Parked on the immaculate gravel – raked, I assume – I saw a row of long, dark, shiny cars. I tucked the Mini in as inconspicuously as possible between a Bentley and an Alvis. As I got out, the drivers of both gave me a look of ill-disguised disdain. 'In my opinion, size is severely overrated,' I told them. They looked momentarily shocked before settling their peaked hats back over their eyes and resuming their midday snooze.

There was a uniformed commissionaire at the front door. I said I was there to see Commander Bond. He gave me a form to sign and asked to see my identification, which he handed to an official sitting at a large desk to one side of the grand marble hall. He read it carefully, looked me up and down, then sidled off. It hadn't really occurred to me before, but I suppose they have to take all possible measures to ensure James's security. Presumably, his failed attempt on M's life has made him a prime target for the KGB, and whatever now passes for its counter-intelligence directorate, SMERSH.

After another long wait, a young man dressed in a suit and white coat approached and introduced himself as Dr Gordon. 'Miss Moneypenny. Good to meet you. The Commander has been looking forward to your visit. Please follow me.' As we walked up the stone staircase and along a deeply carpeted corridor, he told me that he had worked with Sir James for five years. 'You will find the Commander much improved,' he told me. 'His memory is perhaps 80 per cent recovered and we confidently expect the rest to return within the next week. You must under-stand, however, that he's undergone some fairly intense treatment. It has been physically as well as mentally demanding. We've given him twice the normal dose of ECT – seventeen bashes so far, almost one a day. That on top of hours of one-on-one psycho-analysis. The patient has responded exceptionally well, but he is tired and – how shall I put it – somewhat frustrated. He realises the mag-nitude of what he has done and is eager to make amends in any way he can.'

We had reached a heavy wooden door, guarded by a uniformed officer. Dr Gordon showed his identification and I signed my name, before we were buzzed in. On the other side, there was a metal gate. Another guard produced a key and turned the lock to let us in. Dr Gordon shrugged. 'One can't be too careful. We have a lot of high-profile people coming through here, for whom the need for privacy is paramount. This is our high-security wing. At the moment, the Commander is the only inmate.' I looked up. 'Patient, I mean,' he corrected himself quickly.

He knocked on a door – again guarded from the outside – then turned the handle and ushered me through, remaining outside and closing the door behind me. I entered a large, comfortable room, furnished like a drawing-room in a grand hotel, with upholstered arm-chairs and a fireplace. The sun was flooding through tall sash windows. A figure got up from a chair and walked towards me. His face was in shadow and at first I couldn't make out his features, but when he said, with a familiar smile in his voice, 'Penny, as desirable as ever. Thank you for coming,' I knew it was truly James.

'How could I not? It isn't every day a girl gets to meet a ghost,' I replied, as I walked across the room and into his open arms.

'Missed you, Penny,' he said as he hugged me tight. 'It's been a long journey home.'

I looked up, and saw in those grey-blue eyes a rare hint of warmth. 'Don't ever try that poison trick on us again. It was hell to clear up,' I said sternly.

He laughed. 'Thank heavens, still the same old Penny. Don't worry, it's strictly patriotism for me from now on.

"Land of Hope and Glory" and all that stuff. As soon as I can break out of this prison.'

He led me to the window and looked out over beautifully landscaped gardens. 'Who'd have thought that one could feel incarcerated in luxury like this? Of course I understand why they're doing it – and, apart from severe torture,' he smiled, 'they've taken good care of me. As my memory returns, though, I can't help but feel that I'm imprisoned in my thoughts. I can't wait to get out, apologise to M and get back on the job.'

'Is that an offer?'

He laughed again. 'With you, any day – you know that. Right now, however, I need to try to do whatever I can to prove my loyalty towards M and the Firm.'

We walked over to the comfortable chairs and sat down. James seemed to want to talk, and I was more than content to listen. 'I can't believe what's happened to me,' he said. 'It was only a few days ago that I recalled my original mission to Japan. Now it's flooding back. Tanaka disguising me as a Jap, showing me Blofeld's castle. The swim over from the island and up the craggy wall into the Garden of Death.' He broke off at that point, his eyes far away, as if he was conjuring up a picture of Blofeld's compound of biological horrors.* He shivered slightly. 'I hid out all day, and that night I managed to break into the castle. Once there, however, I made a mistake. That

---

* In the guise of a wealthy Swiss naturalist named Dr Guntram Shatterhand, Blofeld had bought a fortress on Japan's south island of Kyushu, and created a Garden of Death, with beds of rare and lethal plants, and ponds stocked with piranhas, which acted as a magnet to Japanese 'suicide tourists', in search of a dramatic and painful end.

bastard Blofeld had booby-trapped the corridors. I fell through a trapdoor and that was that. She recognised me, of course, the hideous Bunt.* Even with my eyebrows shaved upwards and yellow-stained skin, there was enough of a resemblance to Sir Hilary.† I said nothing. They knocked me about a bit, then tied me to a stone chair in this ghastly place they called the Question Room. All I could hear was the loud ticking of a clock. Blofeld told me that I was sitting above a fumerole, a volcanic geyser that erupted every fifteen minutes, sending boiling mud shooting into the air. If I didn't move before the next eruption, my lower body would be flame-grilled to cinders.' He turned towards me.

'So I capitulated. I admitted my identity. They took me back to the library – Blofeld and Bunt, mad as hatters both of them. He went for me with a samurai sword. We had a bit of a scuffle and he ended up worse for wear.' James smiled, acknowledging the understatement. 'I managed to float away hanging on to a helium balloon. I know, it sounds like the product of a fevered imagination, but it's true. At last I remember it. I remember the look on that murderer's face as I strangled his last breath out of him.' The grim triumph on James's face would have been unattractive had it not been coupled to the memory of what he had suffered when Blofeld had killed his wife, Tracy, only hours after their wedding.

---

* Irma Bunt, Blofeld's consort and partner in crime – 'a stumpy woman with the body and stride of a wardress'.
† The alter ego adopted by Bond when he first encountered Blofeld and Bunt, in Blofeld's Swiss-mountaintop lair.

'The next thing I remember was waking up in a cave on Kuro with a girl with the face of an angel wiping my forehead. You know, Penny, I honestly believed I was a Japanese fisherman. I was happy. When spring came, we went diving together for abalone from Kissy's small boat. She took care of my every need. It was a simple, contented life, but there was always some little seed of doubt hovering in the back of my mind. Something told me that there had been more to my life. I knew deep down that I wasn't one of them, whatever Kissy said.'

He must have caught sight of my raised eyebrows, as he interrupted his narrative to insist that Kissy had had his best interests at heart. 'I know Bill and Molony have this half-cocked suspicion that she was doping me and holding me captive, but I don't believe it for a second. What would she have to gain?'

'I'm sure there are many women who would have tied you up for the extended pleasure of your company,' I told him. 'In fact, I met quite a few of them at your memorial service. That turns out to have been a waste of the tax-payers' hard-earned money.'

James chose to ignore me and continued: 'When I saw the word Vladivostok printed on a piece of torn-up newspaper in the loo, it was like a flash of blinding light. I knew it was something to do with my past life. From that minute on, all I could think about was going there and finding out, somehow, who I was.

'That was how I ended up on a wharf in the eastern Soviet Union, dressed as a Japanese fisherman, in search of my true self.' He closed his eyes. When he opened them, I was still looking at him. 'Sorry, Penny. Rather tired. These treatments take it out of one somewhat. I haven't

even offered you a cup of tea – I've even got all the para-
phernalia for making it. Think I'd better take a nap.
Thanks for coming. Dinner when I get out of here?
Please?'

I told him that I wouldn't miss it for the world, hugged
him and knocked on the door to be let out. James was
indeed back.

Saturday, 14th September

Spent the day with Eleanor. It was unusually hot. We took
our bathers and a picnic and went up to Hampstead
Heath. We swam in the ladies' pool, then laid our towels
out on the grass and let our bodies soak up the soft heat.
Apart from a few gently scudding clouds, the sky was a
deep blue – 'the colour of Kim's eyes', according to
Eleanor. She talked about him a lot. She described their
first meeting and how she had been immediately struck
by his wonderful manners. 'I was living in some style
with my husband in central Beirut,' she said. 'We had a
large apartment, staff, a driver, membership of a country
club – everything that went with the job of chief Middle
Eastern correspondent of the *New York Times*. Kim, on the
other hand, had very little money. He had lodgings out of
town and only used to come into the centre a couple of
times a week, to fetch his mail, or file his stories. He
seemed perfectly content. He accepted Beirut for what it
was, without trying to turn it into an European pleasure-
land. He always had a great affinity for the Lebanese, a
sensitivity towards them – in that respect he was his
father's son. I found all this terribly attractive, of course.

'My husband was away a great deal. Kim and I started to see more and more of each other. We would go for lunch in Arab coffee-houses on the waterfront, where foreigners rarely ventured. It wasn't long before we'd fallen in love. He would send me messages – love-notes, really – almost every day. When he was away, I missed him inordinately. I suppose Sam cottoned on soon enough, but I don't think he really cared. The *Times* was his number one, two and three priority. Kim was different to anyone I'd ever met. He adored Annie – he'd spend hours and hours helping her with her French homework. He loved cooking and listening to music. Sometimes he'd read me German poetry – his stutter disappeared and he was able to make even that most unmelodic of tongues sing to me. Yes, he drank – we both did – but then so did most people those days. We were perhaps just a little more uninhibited about it. You know, Jane, growing up in America, there was no one like Kim. I couldn't help myself.'

Then she turned to me with a smile: 'What about you? Is there a great love in your life?'

'I don't know,' I replied. 'It's a little complicated.'

'Don't let minor issues stand in your way,' she said. 'Don't let anything stand in your way. Hell, I'm not going to let a mere technicality like the fact my husband's been spying for the Russians and has disappeared behind the Iron Curtain stand in my way.'

'You've decided to go?' I asked, even though I felt awkward about probing.

'I think so, but it's more than a little complicated. I had a letter from Kim last week. Re-routed from his sister's house. He said he was well and begged me to go out and join him as soon as I could. He said I would be free to leave any time I wanted.'

82

'Will you go?' I couldn't help but ask.

She looked away. 'I don't know. Alexander says I'd never be allowed back. There's Annie to think about. I honestly don't know.'

Friday, 20th September

R is back. Glory be. He telephoned from the airport to ask if I would consider spending the weekend with him. I accepted without thinking. My bag is packed. He's going to pick me up at seven. I don't know where we're going. It will be a surprise.

Sunday, 22nd September

An extraordinary weekend – exquisite both in its pleasure and agony. Why do we have to be part of this strange, strange world?

R picked me up on Friday night in a beautiful silver Citroën DS, borrowed from a friend. It was another balmy night, the sky so clear that it seemed as if we could see a thousand galaxies. We drove west for hours, stopping on the way for a picnic that he'd brought with him, beautifully packed in a wicker basket with proper linen napkins and a hurricane lamp. It was wonderful to see him again, after all these months. He looked thinner, and I thought I could detect an extra worry crease on his forehead, but he made no mention of where he'd been and I didn't ask. It's odd, despite these no-go conversational areas, we never run out of things to talk about. I don't think I've ever felt so at ease with anyone. I don't know whether spending this time with Eleanor has made me more accepting of R's comparatively minor deception. I expect so. In any case, our reunion was rather less inhibited than previous meetings.

He had booked a small inn, under the name of Mr and Mrs Jones. As we walked up the stairs behind our host, I pinched him. 'Jones?' I whispered.

'Well, I believe there's already a couple of Smiths here,' he whispered back. 'Wouldn't want to be too obvious.' I felt a shiver of anticipation. Outside our room, R asked for the key and said we could manage on our own from here on. Then he pushed the door open, bent his knees, put his arm under my thighs and swept me into his arms, before striding into the room and throwing me on to a huge double bed. It was a wonderful night.

We slept late on Saturday morning. When eventually we woke, I opened the French windows leading out to a small stone exterior staircase. From there, I could see rolling hills and smell the sea. We dressed quickly, ate a huge breakfast and set off towards the salty scent. It was only then that R answered my repeated questions as to where we were. 'Dorset,' he told me. 'A few miles east of Bridport. I used to come down here as a boy. My grandfather lived over that hill. My mother brought us to stay with him during the war, when my father went off to fight. We used to collect clams on the shore. I've always loved the sea.'

We walked in companionable silence until, breasting a hill, we saw the coast in front of us. Waves were slopping on to the shingle beach, where families clustered at the water-line, hobbling across the stones, in and out of the lazy surf. I told R about our childhood holidays at Watamu, up the coast from Mombasa. 'It was miles and miles of white sand, palm-trees bowing into the clear turquoise water. On our last holiday before the war, we went goggling with Pa. He speared lobsters, which we cooked on a brushwood fire on the beach and ate for lunch, washed down with coconut water.'

'A little more exotic than sausages in Dorset,' R replied, with a laugh. 'Despite the war, life was certainly more simple in those days, wasn't it?'

I wasn't exactly sure what he was referring to – which part of our complicated lives – but I nodded anyway. It was a glorious, perfect day and I didn't want to have to think. We walked until we were hungry, and then we turned inland and found a small pub in the nearest village, where we ate fresh clams in celebration of R's boyhood and drank cider out of pewter tankards.

That night, R had booked a restaurant for dinner. After much deliberation, I decided to risk my white linen trousers and striped off-the-shoulder jersey. 'Will I be allowed in?' I asked R. He laughed. 'You look wonderful – like a delicious sailor-boy. They wouldn't dream of turning you away. This isn't the Savoy.'

As we were driving there, I noticed him looking repeatedly in his rear-view mirror. 'Is there anything wrong?' I asked. He put his hand on my knee. 'Of course not. Just habit.' I caught a glimpse of his face when the moon peeped out from behind the trees, and he was frowning. When I switched on the interior light to reapply my lipstick, he reached sharply across to turn it off. Looking in my wing- mirror, I noticed a car appeared to be following us a hundred yards or so back.

R said nothing more. He just drove with precision and concentration. When he pulled into a small car-park on the wharf, however, I noticed his shoulders relax as the car behind us kept going. He jumped out and came round to open my door before I could do it myself, and we walked arm in arm into the restaurant.

He was right about the trousers: it was a darling place and we were greeted warmly by the owner, an old man with ruddy, wind-beaten cheeks, who recognised R on sight and couldn't have cared less if his companion had been wearing a monkey-suit. He showed us to the best table – in the corner, overlooking the water – and proceeded to ply us with dish after steaming dish of delicious seafood. It was a feast unlike any other and, in both quantity and atmosphere, quite put Scott's to shame. R regaled me with tales of his eccentric, seafaring grandfather – who I envisaged as a grizzled old fisherman, until R admitted later that he had been a Rear Admiral of the British fleet – and his childhood adventures in Dorset. It was straight out of *Swallows and Amazons*, which I must have read thirty times when I was a child, sitting in the acacia tree at Maguga, with my legs dangling over the lake.

It was a wonderful dinner and, although we didn't discuss the future, I felt the growing possibility that we would spend more time together. We left the restaurant well fed and happy.

It had started to rain softly and the moon was reflected in the glistening streets. On the way home, I leant my head on R's shoulder and closed my eyes. Suddenly, I felt him tense. I sat up. He was looking in his rear-view mirror again. He told me to hang on tight – 'Probably nothing to worry about, but we can't be too careful.' He swung the car to the right, down a narrow lane. I turned around; the car behind had followed us. R accelerated until we were hurtling into the deep night along roads barely wide enough for a single car, and crumpled with bends. I clung on to the dashboard, truly scared. I looked behind again. 'He's still there,' I gasped.

We turned sharply to the left and right again, down an even narrower road. The rain was getting harder, the visibility softer, the road ahead of us fading and emerging through the swing of the wipers. The car was gaining on us, its bright lights blaring through our rear window. R reached up to turn the mirror away, then he muttered 'Hold on' again, before slamming his foot down hard. I could hardly bear to look; low branches bore down from either side, corners seemed to materialise out of the darkness right in front of our noses, there one minute, whipped around the next. We sped through puddles, glanced our wheels against the steep bank on the roadside. I was rigid with tension, trying to anticipate each turn so I wouldn't be flung against R and disrupt his concentration, my eyes fixed on the dark ahead of us.

Then we were at a junction with a larger road, brightly lit. Without dropping his speed, R spun to our left. I looked behind again. There was nothing but a pair of red tail-lights disappearing rapidly in the opposite direction. R drove back to the hotel in silence, his hand squeezing mine. Nobody followed. It was only when we'd let ourselves in, and he had poured us both large brandies that he carried up to our room, that he spoke. 'Are you all right?' he asked, and when I nodded, he sat down. 'We had better talk,' he said. I agreed, glancing at the door which led directly outside.

'No need to worry now. That little performance was designed to shake us,' he said, getting up in any case to check the door was locked. 'It was also a message. We need to take extra care. Tanner's told you that Boris is back on the loose?' I looked up, surprised. I didn't know that R and Bill had been in contact. He guessed what I was thinking. 'We've spoken on a couple of occasions, about business. Well, mostly as it concerns you and our friend Boris. Your outfit and mine have, together, been keeping tabs on him. It's not been easy, as he's kept a low profile since returning to Moscow, mostly burrowed away in the depths of the Lubyanka.*

'Last week, we received transcripts of more conversations recorded by GCHQ between the Soviet Embassy and Moscow KGB. This, in itself, was not unusual. We monitor their signals and they know we do. They send their private stuff by scrambler and whatever new means they have come up with – but leave a certain amount for us to "intercept", so that we don't search too hard for the rest. We know this and, since it is, at least partly, designed for our consumption, most of the traffic is fairly worthless. However, it is routinely translated and analysed. Last week's exchange included details of your and my identities and locations. The recipient was designated "Colonel Boris".'

I frowned.

---

* The feared former KGB headquarters in central Moscow was originally built in 1898 to house the offices of the All-Russia Insurance Company, and was renowned for its beautiful parquet floors. During Stalin's Great Purge, the offices become so overcrowded with secret police that another two buildings were constructed on adjacent blocks.

'Yes, I think we can safely take that as a warning. It looks as if Boris wants to scare us. He was humiliated by what happened here last year: getting shot and then failing to kill me was a disgrace. Having to be rescued from British detention puts him very much in his organisation's debt. In normal circumstances, he would've been sent to a punishment camp, at best. I don't know how he's managed to escape that, but I would hazard a guess that he's been given a last chance to rehabilitate his career, and that this chance somehow involves you and me.'

I felt the beginnings of a chill climbing up my back. 'What must we do?' I asked.

'That's what I was talking to Tanner about. We believe that on a day-to-day level you have little to fear. As long as you follow your usual routine and don't impinge on his business, you should be left alone.'

'What about you?'

'I'm afraid I can't leave him be. Boris is obviously a weak link. He was operating here as an illegal;* but he took matters into his own hands. Now he's gone back on some sort of probation, I imagine. To be honest, this isn't the first time I've been harried like that. Remember the hospital? We now think that was an attempt, if not to kill me, then to put the frighteners on. I'm followed most of the time I'm in this country, and frankly I'm not prepared to take it any more. We won't be able to relax fully until he's somehow been put out of operation.'

'But do you have to . . .'

---

* KGB term for an undercover agent, a Soviet national who assumed a foreign identity by adopting the papers of a real person who had died – or of a fictional one created by the KGB.

He cut in before I had a chance to finish my question. 'Yes, Jane. It has to be me. I can't let it go. Just think,' he looked into my eyes – 'once it's over, it will be truly over. No more looking over our shoulders. We'll be able to see each other more freely.'

'Do you mean . . .'

He stopped me again. 'I'm afraid that, together, we're too much of a target. My identity was compromised last year. You're not perceived to be any kind of threat, which is why you shouldn't be unduly perturbed, but if you're seen with me, that puts you at increased risk. I'm afraid I'm going to have to go away again for a while. I hope it won't be for long.'

He reached forward to take me in his arms. I didn't ask where he was going, but I suspect he'll be heading towards the morning sun, rather than away from it.

I have a dreadful premonition that this is going to end horribly.

Monday, 23rd September

I collared Bill at Franco's this morning. We sat at our usual little table at the back. 'I suppose you've talked to Hamilton?' he said. 'I thought it would be better if it came from him. We'll be keeping an eye on your place, but I think – and M agrees – that you're not in imminent danger. You proved you weren't a soft target last year and, since you're not a threat, they shouldn't come after you. The possible side-effects of being seen to threaten a member of the administrative staff . . .'

I cut in: 'You mean a woman?'

'Yes, that too . . . are hugely embarrassing. Even Redland will not stoop to that.'

'This Boris: is he a serious danger?' I asked.

'We've got Moscow station working on his true identity. He's obviously got powerful protection within the KGB.'

His words failed to comfort me. I feel suddenly terribly vulnerable.

I wish R wasn't going.

Tuesday, 24th September

Eleanor telephoned me last night and sounded in such a state that I offered to leave work early to be with her. We arranged to meet at The Fountain in Fortnum's at five. I couldn't help but glance around me as I went, but I saw no obvious sign of a tail. She arrived clutching large Harrods bags. Her cheeks were flushed and her eyes glittering. When she kissed me hello, I caught the unmistakable whiff of brandy. She sat down and immediately lit a cigarette. 'I've been shopping,' she said. 'Winter's coming and I need a new coat. I had no use for one in Beirut, though, when the storms came, it could pour with rain for days. Look!' She pulled a handsome camel-hair coat out of her bag, put it on and twirled around. The restaurant was full of ladies taking tea and they all turned to look. 'I also got this hat, some boots, some gloves and sweaters . . .' They all came tumbling out. I thought – though I couldn't be sure – that along with her fur-lined gloves, I saw a larger men's pair.

For the next hour, she talked and smoked. She was clearly in an excited state. If she didn't have a cigarette in her hand, she fiddled with the sugar, or stirred her tea. Only once did she stop twitching. She looked at me and then said, 'I'm going, Jane. Don't tell them, I beg you. I just needed to tell someone. I'm going to join Kim in Moscow. I know Alexander has warned me against it, but I must be with him. I don't want it to be in Moscow any more than you do, but he needs me. I will do what Alexander asks, however: if your outfit is serious about the immunity offer, then I'll do everything in my power to persuade him to come back to London.'

I reacted instinctively. I gave her a huge hug and wished her luck. I told her that if she needed serious help, she could write to me care of Helena and include the sentence 'I hope your sister is well.' It was the first thing I could think of, in the circumstances. She repeated the phrase and nodded. 'Please promise that you won't tell your Chief until tomorrow morning. Please, Jane.' I saw the desperation in her eyes, and gave her my word. When it was time to leave, she hugged me hard and thanked me over and over.

'We'll see each other again real soon. Promise?' she asked. I nodded. 'I hope so,' I told her. 'Go safely.' When we parted, both of us had tears in our eyes.

Thursday, 26th September

Eleanor has gone. I lay awake most of the night, torn apart by conflicting loyalties, questioning whether I should break my promise and alert the Office about her impending departure. Then I thought of her happy shining face and I couldn't. I even considered not admitting to M that she'd warned me – out of fear of his displeasure. In the end, however, I went in at my usual time and told him as soon as he got in. To my surprise and relief, he seemed fairly sanguine about it. Instead of the slap on the wrist that I'd expected, he praised me for proposing a channel of communication. 'We'll make an agent out of you someday, Miss Moneypenny. I haven't forgotten our conversation last year. I'll get Chief of Staff to look into some training courses. Let's give your Mrs Philby until lunchtime and then please alert CME to check on whether she's gone. I expect that we'll hear from her before the year is out.'

I walked out of his office in a slight daze. It was as if M had expected her to go – the grand master always a few steps ahead of the game. I am truly pleased for Eleanor, if a little apprehensive. If she hadn't joined Kim, she would have lived with regret for the rest of her life. Right now, he is her centre, her reason to be. I hope Moscow isn't too much of a shock for her. I hope he doesn't let her down.

October

My aunt may have confided most things to her diary, but she was circumspect when it came to describing her personal relationships. There are references to men dotted through the volumes, and she undoubtedly had relationships with some of them. But she was never one to parade her intimacies. She kept her work, her private life and her family life strictly compartmentalised. In my memory, she never brought a boyfriend to stay with us in Cambridge. I asked her once why she had never married. She just shrugged and, with a smile, said that there had never been a right person at the right time. As far as I know, Bill Tanner was the only work friend she ever introduced to my mother.

My mother liked Tanner, and I overheard her once speculating to my father about the nature of his relationship with my aunt. But, if she pressed her sister for details, we never heard the response.

The romantic content of Miss Moneypenny's entanglement with James Bond has been more widely debated. Certainly they were close friends, and undoubtedly there was an element of mutual attraction. The first time she saw him, in the lift shortly after joining SIS in 1953, she described him as 'coldly, darkly handsome, with a hint of reserve that makes one want to discover more'. But, from reading her diaries closely, I believe their relationship was more complex.

Aunt Jane was seemingly the one woman who did not melt in a pool of desire at Bond's feet. Their flirtation, at first anyway, was conducted within the safe confines of the Office. He would stop by her desk on his way into and out of M's office, always armed with a witticism or a seductive barb, which she would bat back with equal verbal dexterity. It was when he was in hospital, fighting for his life following his poisoning in a Paris hotel room by the Russian KGB queen Rosa Klebb, after escaping from Istanbul on the Orient Express, that their relationship changed gear. Jane was at his bedside every evening, initially sitting quietly, holding his hand, and then, when he began to regain consciousness, reading to him for hours on end. Although he favoured adventure yarns, she couldn't help but choose books that he would never have picked. She read him *Middlemarch*, and to his surprise he enjoyed it. There was something soothing and comforting in its essential Englishness.

When he recovered sufficiently to move back home, they continued to see each other outside the Office for a while: quiet dinners at Bond's King's Road home or at her flat in Ennismore Gardens, maybe a film or a walk in the park on the weekends. There was little in the way of flirtation then – even he was still too weak for that – and once he was back to fighting fitness he was sent on his next assignment, to Jamaica and Honeychile Rider. When he returned, he was his old self again: the extra closeness conferred by his weakness had faded.

Jane accepted this. Bond was not the kind of man she wanted to share her life with – as she once wrote, 'He is about as cerebral as a football.' His pleasures were more sensual: he liked fine wine, food, fast cars and beautiful women, the thrills of speed and danger. And yet, as she confided to her diary, she couldn't help but feel flattered by his regard. He was by no means exclusive in his attentions – his secretaries were always in love with him, and he did little to dissuade them – but it still felt as if he and my aunt had a special bond. She knew he felt he could trust her and talk to her; he did so at length after his wife, Tracy, died on their wedding day. Jane was the only person that he confided in then. Perhaps, she thought, it was because they were both orphans. Or did he see her as some kind of mother figure? She was a decade younger than him, yet he brought out her nurturing instincts, as well as setting her senses tingling. Or was it her proximity to M, the man she knew he revered and respected above all others?

Bond exasperated her too. She loathed his view of women as the 'weaker race'; he saw them as adornments, partners only in the bedroom. But, at the same time that excited her. She couldn't help but feel a thrill in his presence. The men she tended to go out with respected her originality and independence in a way that Bond would never dream of doing.

She found 'R' instantly appealing in a completely different way. They had met in Barcelona in October 1961. She had gone for a week's holiday on her own, armed with guidebooks, novels and a comfortable pair of shoes. She was looking around the building site of

Gaudi's Sagrada Familia when the rain started. She ran under a parapet, which chose that moment to flood, sending water gushing on to her head. A man rushed up with an umbrella and ran with her to a nearby café, where he insisted on buying her a cup of hot chocolate. Tall and wiry, with thick dark hair and blue eyes framed by spectacles, he turned out to be English. He introduced himself as Richard Hamilton, and told her he was an architect.

Their conversation, as often happens with countrymen drawn together in a strange place, moved rapidly from the general to the personal. He invited her to dinner, and she accepted. That evening, in a small fish restaurant in the medieval quarter, he told her that he had been married once, but that his wife had run off with his best friend soon afterwards. Now thirty-five, he had spent five years mostly alone, working hard, frequently abroad. After dinner, they went to a bar for late-night whiskies, and when he walked her back to her hotel he kissed her goodnight. 'It felt like the most natural thing in the world,' she related to her diary. 'I knew then that this was going to be no passing flirtation.' They spent the next five days together, acting like a young couple in love, picnicking in the park, taking long midnight walks along the beach, eating late in small restaurants in the artists' quarter.

When he left, the day before her, she found herself missing him, but enjoying the solitude. It had been years since she had spent that much time intensely with another person. 'I don't want to think about how this relationship will unfold,' she wrote. 'I wish, for once, it could be straightforward; I wish I could tell him everything.' But she didn't, and for a while it didn't seem to matter. R appeared to be as independent and unquestioning as she was, as bound up in and consumed by his work.

They started seeing each other on a regular basis – maybe one night in the week, and most weekends. They went cycling together. He stayed at her flat near the Albert Hall, and she stayed at his in Marylebone. They spent a long winter weekend together in Norfolk, walking the beaches, reading in front of log fires. She felt, so she wrote, 'remarkably happy and at ease with him'.

But then, in early 1962, he started talking about the future and asking questions about her work. Despite her deep affection for him and her secret internal debates about whether she could give up her work for him, she froze. The walls started building themselves around her, and she could do nothing to stop them. Her secret work for the Office drove a wedge between them until it had cleaved them apart. He took a job abroad. She missed him.

By returning when he did, in December 1962, when she was being held captive in her own bedroom by Boris, he probably saved her life. In revealing that he worked for the Security Service and knew what it was that she did, he opened another door of possibility on to the relationship. I cannot believe it is a coincidence that, when she left the service, she went to live on North Uist, the small Hebridean island he had introduced her to. Certainly, after their visit there together and their weekend in Dorset, she appeared to be once more considering a future with him.

Sunday, 6th October

Dinner with James last night. He was released from The Park a week ago. Bill went out there to pick him up. M has decreed that he is not, at present anyway, permitted to return to the Office – said it would be bad for morale. What happened with M was meant to be hushed up, but inevitably it leaked out somehow. The Powder Vine had it the very next day, though they were shaky on details and not best pleased when I refused to illuminate them.

Instead, James has been put on an intensive programme of physical rehabilitation. He spent this week down at the Fort, being assessed by the instructors. Nobody knew to what extent he had forgotten basic tradecraft, but according to Bill, who spoke to the boss on Friday afternoon, the skills are still there, though he's out of practice and still physically weak. The good news is that he hasn't suffered any permanent brain damage from the drugs.

It looks as if the angel-faced Missy Kissy Suzuki is in trouble. The evidence suggests that she used some sort of memory-depletion drug on him and, contrary to first suspicions, it wasn't supplied by the Japanese. Our American office has been digging and yesterday sent us an interesting snippet: when Kissy was in Hollywood seven years ago, acting in a film about a Japanese pearl diver, she came into close contact with an acrobat who has subsequently been exposed as a Russian agent. Did he recruit her? Was it pure chance that 007 landed on her island? Or was there a longer game, involving an alliance between Tanaka of the Japanese Secret Service and the KGB? The analysts are going to have a fine time unpicking this one.

Whatever the machinations, James was clearly caught up in a horrible situation, from which he was lucky to escape. He went through hell on earth at Blofeld's lair and afterwards (despite the succour offered by Kissy) and is obviously now racked with guilt over what he did – or attempted to do – on his return. I'm just delighted that he's alive and on his way to full recovery.

I arrived at his flat at eight. May answered the door, even managing to raise a smile as she greeted me. 'The Commander's in the sitting-room. Please follow me.' It felt curiously formal, and when I walked in and James rose to greet me, I was pleased that I had chosen my silk Sybil Connolly. I get few enough chances to bring it out from the deeper recesses of my wardrobe. He was wearing a dark navy serge suit, a heavy white silk shirt and his habitual black knitted-silk tie, navy socks and soft black leather moccasins. He looked every bit his former self. He had a slight tan and his blue-grey eyes were alive again with a hint of mischief. People have often described him as having a 'cruel face', with 'cold eyes', but if you get to know him it's not hard to locate the emotion behind the surface froideur.

'Champagne, Penny? I've got a '53 Krug Grande Cuvée – there's not much to beat that. And something to go with it? May, bring the caviar, please.' I walked over to fetch my glass. 'You are too spoiling, James,' I said. 'To what do I owe this special treatment?'

'It's all you deserve – and a proper prelude to seduction.' I laughed. 'I wanted to thank you, Penny, for standing by me through all this . . .'

'Well, if you can't forgive your friends for trying to murder your boss, then what can you do?'

'Seriously, you listened to me and gave me a chance, and you're here now. I'm not sure many from the Office would be.'

He sounded uncharacteristically lacking in confidence. I went to join him at the window, where he stood gazing out over the pretty, tree-lined square.

'You'd be surprised. We're all just relieved to have you back – especially the girls in the typing-pool. They can't wait to see you and have been emptying the stores of pretty frocks in anticipation of the day you walk back through the Office doors. James, you're a hero. What you did, in getting rid of Blofeld, was incredible. We all owe you a debt of gratitude.'

'What happened with M . . .'

'Nothing happened. The Old Man's still in his chair and fighting fit, and so will you be, soon.'

We walked over to sit down on an elegant walnut Biedermeier day-bed, upholstered in navy raw silk. James lit a cigarette, and when I frowned at him, he laughed and gave me a squeeze.

'Don't nanny me, Penny. The doc said to cut down to twenty a day and I'm only failing by five. Anyway, you're far too pretty to hector, and too young too.'

'And you're too old to flirt,' I replied. 'With a young woman like me, anyway.'

He laughed again and we chatted easily until May called us into the dining-room to eat. She had produced a feast: smoked salmon washed down with Puligny-Montrachet, followed by beef tournedos in a cream, brandy and green-peppercorn sauce, with fine French beans and pommes dauphinoise. It was quite the most delicious dinner and, when I told her so, she blushed a deep red. 'Aye took a cooking course while the Commander was away,' she said. 'Aye always knew he was coming back.'

'She was determined on that,' I told James when she left the room. 'Wouldn't let anyone into the flat, refused to talk to the solicitors about your will, generally was stubborn and obstructive in a very Scottish way.'

He smiled fondly at the door. 'Dearest May. If she was just thirty years younger . . .'

We ate, we talked. So much had happened in the year since he left for Japan. I filled him in on R's return into my life. I was describing the events of last December, in what I hoped was a suitably light-hearted manner, when he suddenly froze. 'Boris?' he said. 'What did he look like?'

I described him as best I could – his pale eyes, faded red hair and smooth, hairless skin; his broken nose and accented but correct English.

'It couldn't be . . . it's too much of a coincidence. No, definitely not,' he appeared to satisfy himself.

'Not what?'

'I was picked up by the police in Vladivostok. I suppose I must have looked a sight – a Caucasian dressed in the clothes of a Japanese fisherman. No wonder they were suspicious. They asked me who I was and, when my answers failed to satisfy them, they tried to extract the information by more forceful means. I must have got a bump on my head at some point, because I suddenly remembered that I wasn't a fisherman – though I still hadn't a clue as to my real identity. They took me to the local KGB headquarters, a gruesome grey building close to the harbour. The officers there were more refined in their interrogation techniques – but no more pleasant, I must say.

'They took my fingerprints and Belinographed them to Moscow – and it was only after they received the results that they started to treat me more gently. By this time, I think they were convinced that I wasn't just feigning amnesia. I see now – thanks to Molony and the quacks at The Park – that they must have realised the value of what they had, for they started to treat me very well indeed.'

May came in to remove our plates and asked whether we were ready for pudding. James told her to hang fire for a while. He poured us both another glass of the excellent Château Grand-Puy-Lacoste red, and continued. 'In the middle of the night they flew me to Moscow, where I was put up in this small flat in a hideous building on the outskirts of the city. It was comfortable, by Russian standards, but the food was execrable. I barely ate a fresh vegetable for weeks – if you don't count potatoes or beetroot. I was under full-time guard and only allowed outside for an hour a day, and then with a four-gorilla escort to make sure that I didn't try to escape. No chance of that. Their surveillance techniques are legendary; everyone is being watched by someone. The only civilian I exchanged a word with during that entire period was Anna, the hatchet-faced housekeeper who came each day to cook for me. She had clearly never learnt even the basic skills of feminine enhancement.'

He called for May to bring in the pudding. 'You're going to love this, Penny. A proper old-fashioned treacle pudding. Forget about your waistline and dig in. May, my darling, you're a saint.'

The Scotswoman left with a huge look of pride on her face. 'She used her own savings to keep this place going y'know. Where was I? Yes, in Moscow – a drab place, by the way: no holiday destination. I'd steer clear if I were you.'

'I'm planning to,' I told him, but I couldn't help thinking about Eleanor. She had a Californian's love of fresh fruit.

'I was interrogated for weeks on end. They took it in turns, but I honestly couldn't remember a thing. Sometimes they prompted me with stuff that they knew, which helped to dredge up a few nuggets of memory. Nothing of importance. I couldn't even remember you, Penny. They had to show me your picture. It was several weeks later that I first met Colonel Boris – or that was what he called himself: all KGB officers operate under assumed names. He was different – extremely charming, for a start, and cultured too. His suits were unmistakably Savile Row, and his shoes hand-made. He told me that he had lived in London, Paris and Berlin. He took me to dinner at a Georgian restaurant – we had a private room – where the food was excellent and the drink copious. He told me that I was being moved the following day.'

'What did he look like, your Colonel Boris?' I asked.

'He also had pale eyes, and spoke good English, but his hair was white-blond and he wore a moustache. You see, it can't have been the same person. Half the men in Russia are called Boris, and that's the ones using their real names.' Despite his assurances, I couldn't prevent a shiver of apprehension. It is not hard to grow a moustache, and blond hair can always be dyed red.

James was continuing, 'I was taken to Leningrad on the overnight train. It was rather wonderful actually. They played the national anthem at midnight and everyone stood to attention. There was tea in samovars at the end of each carriage and women walked up and down selling cigarettes and caviar. I had a compartment to myself – an untold luxury. Boris was in the compartment to my left and the gorillas to my right. They took turns to guard my door – but I had no urge to escape. Where would I have gone? They were my only link with a past I no longer knew. They're impressive, Penny – organised, fiercely disciplined and determined to better us in whatever way they can. They fight dirty, too.

'A car met us at the station and I was taken to The Institute. It's their equivalent of The Park, just more Russian and rather less plush. A beautiful building, nonetheless – one of the few to escape the German bombardment during the last war. They also bashed my brain, but without the Pentothal. Just strapped me down, cupped cathodes on each temple' – he put an index finger on each side to demonstrate – 'then, whack. It was not a pleasant experience. Afterwards, to put me in a co-operative mood, I suppose, I would be given a drink and a massage by a beautiful girl – surprisingly, they do have them over there. To tell you the truth,' he gave a dry laugh, aware of the irony of the phrase, 'I would have done anything they said. I was their captive both physically and mentally. I had visitors four, five times a day – brain surgeons, top KGB brass. They talked to me about the political situation, how they were working for peace and we were holding the world back.' He laughed again, but there was no trace of mirth on his face.

'Boris would come each afternoon. It was his job to fill me in on the Firm. He had photographs of everyone: you, M, Bill, Dorothy, Goodnight – how is she, by the way?'

I told him she was fine; now wasn't the moment to reveal her departure. I urged him to go on.

'They even had a picture of old Fletcher in the lift. They had detailed plans of the Office, where each section is based, the Registry, the range in the basement – the Powder Vine too. I wonder how they got that one? They seemed to know everything, even the daily special at the canteen. Boris told me all about it. From time to time, he would disappear for a couple of days to Moscow, and on his return he would have something else for me. When I asked him how he knew all he did, he just smiled and said "Vee hef our saucers" – or something like that.'

'You believed everything?'

'I wasn't in a position to do otherwise. They made it all sound so damn reasonable. I honestly believed', and here he poured himself a brandy and lit another cigarette, 'that they had a point. You don't understand – and I am only now beginning to myself – they blew my brain to pieces and then put it back together again how they wanted it. I was theirs. Bloody bastards. They convinced me that I had devoted my life to working for a warmongering, blood-thirsty operation, and the damned thing about it was that I couldn't remember a thing to contradict what they said. They told me that I had to strike at the heart of the organisation. Boris said it would be an honour, that I would be striking an almighty blow for peace – or "piss" as he called it.'

The tension broken, we both started laughing.

106

'So I was primed, directed and fired. I still can't believe it. It was as if I was some kind of walking zombie. Mr Big* would have approved – but, then again, he was one of their men; he probably taught them how to do it. Oh, Penny, now that I'm back to my senses, I need to make amends. I must show M that he can trust me again. I want to destroy them, humiliate them as they did me. I hate them.' He looked at me, and his eyes, drained of their warmth, glinted coldly in the candlelight.

'Enough of that. I've talked too much. Thank you for listening. I needed to get it off my chest. Come on, old girl, let's go next door and dance. I haven't danced in a year.'

Even now, as I recall what he said, I appreciate the effort that it took him – not the most emotional of men – to recount his trials. Sitting there, across the polished mahogany, I was shocked and horrified by what he had undergone, chilled by the stark picture he painted of the inhuman world we inhabit. More than anything, I wanted to take him in my arms and tell him that everything would be all right.

Monday, 7th October

James and I are under surveillance – by our own side. Bill asked this morning if I had enjoyed my dinner on Saturday night – just blurted it out, then blushed in an

---

* Larger than life, Harlem-dwelling black hoodlum and SMERSH power-broker, who had convinced his followers that he was the living corpse of Baron Samedi, the Prince of Darkness.

uncharacteristic manner, as if he knew he shouldn't have asked. I hadn't told him I was going and I know James hadn't either. 'We need to keep an eye on you two,' he said defensively. 'Make sure you're safe and all that.'

I just looked at him, puzzled as to what I thought. I suppose I should have been reassured, but I wasn't.

'Bill, do we know if it's the same Boris?'

He knew what I was talking about. 'It's a possibility, certainly. We had the same question. Moscow's looking into it.' I must have shuddered noticeably, as he took my hand and patted it. 'Please don't worry about it. It's a long shot. Just in case, though, we had better get both of you on to the Identicast.' He sidled out of my office, still embarrassed.

This evening, he came back in, smiling and waving a piece of paper. 'I wanted you to be the first to see this, Penny. It's just come in from Washington. Today, Kennedy signed a treaty with the Russians to limit nuclear tests. You should be proud of yourself. This is a direct result of Cuba. Without you and James, we might never have got to this point.'

It was lovely of him to say so, but I don't believe we influenced the course of history, even in the most minor of ways. The President must take the credit – he's an extraordinary man and it was an honour to have met him. Sometimes I look at my Orange Star and pinch myself. I truly believe he's going to change the world for the better. Maybe, with his leadership, we will no longer have cause to live in fear of the mushroom cloud?

Friday, 11th October

This quarter's Q Branch report was circulated today,* as fascinating as ever, crammed with obscure technical information and written in the stilted style of someone for whom English is not a first language. I've always maintained that boffins are a different race. Appropriately, considering the prevailing obsessions around this place, it focuses on the KGB. I read it with interest. The KGB is our main enemy, to a large extent our *raison d'être*. Every day, the greater part of the Firm is dedicated, in some way, to plotting how to infiltrate them, steal a march, better them in some way – while 1,500 or so miles away, in Moscow, they are trying to do the same to us. In a sense, we are mirror images: our aims and objectives, even the way we go about trying to achieve them, are similar but opposite. We have democracy; they have Communism. Each of us believes vehemently in our own system. Rarely do we doubt it, on our side, anyway. Yet, looking at this report, there is so much that we share.

I hadn't thought about it in quite that way before. I've always assumed that all that is Red is bad, but spending time with Eleanor, and hearing her talk about Kim, has injected some shades of grey into that assumption. How could a man who, by all accounts, is cultured, intelligent, sensitive and a good cook – how could he have devoted his life to a regime that is brutal and repressive? What was it about Redland that led him to sacrifice – and betray – his family, his friends and the country that educated and nurtured him? I am too young, I suppose, to understand

---

* See end of chapter.

the fear of Fascism. Communism has been our enemy for as long as I can remember, but perhaps if I had felt Hitler creeping up behind me, I too would have made for the opposing corner?

Reading about the level of the KGB's surveillance and their techniques, I couldn't help but think of Eleanor. She had told me about the instructions Kim had given her for leaving the country, the signals that she had to chalk on the wall of the alley near her apartment. At the time, it sounded like Boy Scout stuff to me, not the way to plan one's future, but reading this report, it appears that it was standard KGB procedure. Is she followed by some invisible person every time she steps foot outside their flat? I assume so. That being the case, does she know, and does she perform her own version of 'dry-cleaning'* to lose her tail? Surely Philby must be aware of his constant shadows, but how much does he share with her about the realities of their new life? Despite myself, I hope for Eleanor's sake that being back with him has lived up to her expectations. I can only imagine what it must be like, the questions she must be asking, the doubts she must suppress every time she looks into the face of the man she once trusted implicitly. I hope she finds some way of letting me know how she's getting on.

I think of her when I step outside my front door, knowing that our people are out there, somewhere, watching me – and perhaps theirs too? Was it me they were following in Dorset, or R? The thought of them is with me constantly; I feel their breath on my spine.

---

* The name given by the Americans to the intricate and protracted procedure performed to shake off any unwanted surveillance.

Sunday, 13th October

I woke to the first frost, early this year. I walked around the corner to buy the newspaper and read it over hot chocolate in the brasserie. Jean Cocteau and Edith Piaf both died the day before yesterday: the poet and the little sparrow.

R has gone. Our relationship sometimes seems like one long chain of farewells. Is it a chain made of paper or of metal? We met yesterday for lunch, then after a spot of window-shopping (was R performing his own subtle version of surveillance evasion, I wonder?) caught a bus to Richmond Park. He had brought a kite and we ran around for hours before it became permanently entwined in a tree, much to our amusement. On the way home, we stopped at a small restaurant in Barnes that we'd never heard of, nor ever seen before. The food was excellent. We ate coq au vin and drank a bottle of red wine. Although these times happen far too rarely, there will be a hole in my life when he's gone.

Over an excellent pear tart, he took my hands in his and said that he was determined to sort out the situation. 'Please take care,' I entreated him.

He smiled. 'Of course. Don't worry about me. Promise me you'll be careful too, and when I get back, we'll . . .'

He leant forward to kiss me. We'll what, I wonder? I still don't know what I want. I would love to be with him more, but the Firm means a great deal to me. For ten years now, it has been my family, my friend and my life.

When R left early this morning, to get his bag and go to the airport, I didn't ask when he would be back.

Sunday, 20th October

Weekends are lonely places without R. I wanted to go up to Cambridge to see Helena, but she called on Friday to say that Lionel has the lethal combination of flu and a book deadline and has quarantined the house. She sounded exasperated. We talked again about going to Kenya together. She won't be able to go until L's book is finished, but that should be within the next month or two. Maybe then he'll agree on a wedding date? This damn book's been an excuse for perpetual delay.

R hasn't forgotten me. The day after he left, a parcel was delivered early in the morning. It was tightly wrapped and taped. The lad who brought it insisted I showed him my passport before he would hand it over. 'Orders, miss,' he said, before smoothing back his greasy hair and climbing aboard his motor cycle.

I cut through the tape and opened the parcel with interest. Inside the first layer, I found more tape and more brown paper, along with a covering note from R:

My darling J,

I haven't left yet, but already I miss you. Know only that you will be in my thoughts as I try to close this piece of business with all due speed. Here is the information I promised. Against all rules, I made a photographic copy – and broke several more to give it to you. If either of our outfits were to discover this contravention, I'm afraid it would mean certain trouble. Still, they have enough black marks against me already to fill a coal scuttle. What difference can another make?

I wish you all luck, and more love,

Forever yours, R

Beneath further layers I found a file. Opening it, I was confronted with a facsimile of my father's face and, beside it, his name: HUGH DAVID MONEYPENNY, LIEUTENANT RN; aka HUGH STERLING. I was almost shaking as I read what was written below. Along with a brief service record and copies of various commendations from his seniors and professors at Greenwich, I found the first black and white evidence of his involvement in Ruthless. The outline of the operation was there, in an extract from a document prepared for the Director of Naval Intelligence by his assistant, Ian Fleming: the names – both actual and operational – of the men involved, the equipment they took with them, even a script of the distress plea that my father was to broadcast from the radio of the Heinkel bomber after its forced landing in the channel. Everything concurred with Patrick Derring-Jones's* description of the course of events which led to Pa's capture.

The last page detailed the steps taken to trace the whereabouts of my father and the pilot, Miles Pitman, after the unhappy conclusion to the operation. It consisted of various enquiries, made via the Red Cross, to the Wehrmacht. Each met with a negative response. My father had apparently vanished. The last entry was one line,

---

* One of Hugh Moneypenny's fellow agents on Operation Ruthless – a mission to try to secure a German decoding machine, by crashing a captured German bomber in the English Channel. The plan, to overpower the crew of the German rescue launch and take their decoder, failed when they were confronted with a well-armed minesweeper instead. Two of the British crew managed to escape, while Moneypenny, the pilot, and a marine were taken captive.

dated February 15th, 1941: 'Informed family that Lieutenant Moneypenny presumed dead.' Such a short line;
such a catastrophic impact.

Reading it, I couldn't fail to recall my mother's desperation, the feeling that we had of being alone, on a rud-
derless boat in a stormy ocean. My mother never fully
recovered. I have never had a lasting relationship, while
Helena has attached herself, with the gritty determination of a barnacle, to a man old enough to be our father.

Appended to the file was a note in R's hand: 'Lieutenant
Hugh Sterling on list of officers resident at Colditz POW
camp on April 13th, 1945, three days prior to its liberation by US forces.'

I was filled with excitement. Here, at last, was the clue
I had been looking for. I jogged down to Kensington
library. In the military-history section I found two books
by a Major Pat Reid and one by Major Roddy Parks. I took
them all out and am already engrossed in *The Colditz Story*.
No mention yet of Hugh Sterling.

Saturday, 26th October

I finished the Colditz book last night. What an amazing
tale. What extraordinary men. At times, you get so carried
away by the adventure of it all, the ingenious escape
attempts and occasional successes, that it sounds almost
like boarding-school high jinks. Then you are dragged back
to the grim reality of life incarcerated in a forbidding
castle deep behind enemy lines. Many of the inmates
began to lose their minds; it's extraordinary that any
stayed sane. They were driven by the desperate desire to

escape. It was their duty as officers to find their way back to their regiments.

Reid did not write about Pa, but in Roddy Parks's book I found a passing mention of a Hugh Sterling. I started shaking. I wrote immediately to Parks, care of his publishers, to ask whether we might meet. At the moment, however hard I try, I can't imagine Pa in Colditz. If he was there, Parks will know.

Wednesday, 30th October

M called me into his office this morning, to ask whether I had heard from Eleanor Philby. When I assured him that he would know the instant I had, he asked me to convene a meeting to discuss the Philby situation. So it was that this afternoon I found myself sitting at his table, alongside Bill, Dingle [CME], and Bookie [CS].

'This can't go on any longer. Every day that he's there, he's giving away more secrets,' M said, banging his fist on the table. 'We can't afford to let it happen. Agent rings are being compromised all over Europe and the Middle East.'

'Sir, with respect,' Bookie began, 'the damage has already been done. He hasn't been into the Office for twelve years. We've kept an eye on him since then. He was given nothing of importance in Beirut, isn't that correct, CME?'

Dingle inclined his head, gracefully. 'Under your instructions, sir, I used Philby mainly for analysis – for which he had considerable flair. He knew none of our agents over there, even though, I must confess, I never believed in his perfidy.'

'Don't beat yourself up about it. It's not a matter of placing blame,' M said. 'He's a damned clever man – perhaps the most successful Russian spy of all time. As we're beginning to appreciate, hundreds of people died as a result of his actions – people who trusted us and risked their lives to help us.'

'We're offering him immunity?'

'It's that damned rock and hard place. We need him back and it'll humiliate the Russians if he comes. What will his life be like here anyway? It won't all be Oxford marmalade and cricket scores. He'll be reviled by everyone he counted as a friend. It'll be living punishment. It looks as if he's worked that out for himself. The bait's been dangling for long enough and he's shown no sign of grabbing it. Miss Moneypenny, do you think Mrs Philby will be able to persuade him?'

'I fear not, sir,' I replied. 'By all accounts they have a happy marriage, but he's already demonstrated where his loyalties lie. He abandoned his wife and children to go to Moscow. She's beginning to doubt that he ever loved her. My guess is that she will do anything now just to hang on to him. I don't think the power lies with her.'

'Doesn't sound like it. Thank you, Miss Moneypenny. So we have to come up with an alternative plan. Mr Philby *will* be coming home. Chief of Staff?'

'Sir. I've discussed this at length with CS. As we see it, there are two options. The first is to persuade him to come home of his own accord; the second, to enforce the persuasion, so to speak. Let's take the latter first. Kidnap is never an easy operation, especially from Redland. In this case, it will be triply difficult. We must assume that the Philbys are under constant guard. They will have minders outside their apartment, and whenever they leave they will be under surveillance. The KGB will have taken every precaution to prevent a kidnap attempt. That's not to say it's impossible. In anticipation of this eventuality, I have consulted both our station in Moscow and Special Forces. Through the good work of CS's men out there, we've managed to locate the Philbys' apartment. It's on an upper floor of a large block in a residential suburb of the city, some fifteen minutes out of the centre, near the Sokol metro station. On the advice of the commanding officer of the Special Air Services, I contacted our Cousins [the CIA] to ask if one of their birds [spy planes] could be targeted on this very address. They agreed and we are now waiting for detailed pictures and blueprints of the building. When we have them, we'll be able to start drawing up plans for an operation to extract Mr Philby.

'At the same time, we can continue to work on ways to persuade him of the benefits of returning home willingly – a reverse defection, as it were. So far, we have tried two approaches. The first was the offer of immunity through CME, in Beirut, which patently failed. The other is the on-going attempt to persuade his wife of the advantages of their return to this country, assuming further contact through Miss Moneypenny. This can be regarded as still in play, though we have no way at present of controlling this from our end. Which leaves us with a third action: we can try to make Moscow unattractive to Philby.' He paused.

'Yes, Chief of Staff. You have some suggestions?'

'This would be the work of Sov Section's planners, of course, but CS and I wondered how his Russian hosts would take to some well-placed rumours that Philby is – and always was – a double? That even now he's being run by London and passing back details of KGB debriefing techniques? They don't have to believe it, of course, but even a tiny seed of doubt in the minds of those on the fringes of the intelligence community could be cause for considerable embarrassment in Moscow and a reason to make Philby's stay uncomfortable.'

M looked around the table. 'CS?'

'The odds are against it, certainly, but it's worth a punt. I'll get on to drawing up outlines for both operations. Shall we call them, let's see . . . MARMALADE 1 and 2?'

'Fine by me. Good work, Bill. Thank you. Any other ideas, CS? CME? Very well then. We will meet again in one week to discuss further action. Thank you, gentlemen.'

Gentlemen? I was not asked for my ideas. In truth, I had none, just one question: what about Mrs Philby? What will happen to her? Will she be abandoned in Moscow this time, and left to the mercy of the Russians when her husband is 'extracted'? Poor Eleanor.

```
Q BRANCH REPORT 1963:III [abridged]
Q Branch has acquired a copy of the KGB's
main training manual. Entitled 'THE
FOUNDATION OF SOVIET INTELLIGENCE WORK' it
details the basic terminology, methodology
and tradecraft of KGB officers worldwide.
With careful study, this should enable
officers of this organisation to recognise
and thwart the actions of enemy agents. It
cannot be emphasised too strongly that it is
imperative that the KGB does not discover
```

that we have this manual in our possession,
lest they change their working procedures
accordingly.

A. KGB: TERMINOLOGY
Officers are always Soviet citizens and
referred to, in covert communications, as
WORKERS or CADRES. Whether working abroad
under diplomatic cover, or illicitly as an
ILLEGAL, their over-riding aim is the
recruitment of agents, known as
PROBATIONERS.
B. KGB: SURVEILLANCE TECHNIQUES
Directorate 7 - known as Semyorka - is
responsible for surveillance in Moscow and
is comprised of 1,000 officers. An additional
500 men and women from the Moscow Oblast
Directorate are involved in watching and
tailing alien diplomats, media, businessmen
and suspected spies. The minimum team number
for a surveillance operation is three,
working out of one car. In extreme cases, up
to three teams can be deployed for one
suspect. Teams are composed of men and
women, all competent drivers. They should
have in their possession various disguises,
including hats, spectacles, different
coloured coats and false moustaches, which
should be employed in rotation. Every team
member has a personal radio; the microphone
is hidden under the shirt or tie and the
transmitter concealed in a pocket. The car

contains a more powerful base station. Teams
work on an eight-hour rotation.

B.II: EVADING SURVEILLANCE

When embarking on a covert operation, to
meet a contact or agent, or deliver a
message or signal, the officer must first
undertake *proverka* (known to the Americans
as dry-cleaning), to ensure he is not under
surveillance. In optimal circumstances, this
should take a minimum of three hours, and
include multiple forms of transport. The
officer should never appear to show concern;
the aim is to make every action appear
natural. If a tail is identified, it is
standard KGB procedure to abort the
operation immediately. The officer should
ideally work with a partner, whose mission
it is to identify possible tails.

C. TRADECRAFT

DEAD LETTER DROPS: These should be clearly
designated in advance and located in an area
which both officer and agent have reason to
visit without suspicion, and out of eye
range of any possible watcher. A message
could be concealed in a rock in a park, or a
matchbox, fitted with a magnet, which could
thus be attached to the underside of a
bridge, for instance.

SIGNALS: These take two main forms: a signal
of personal identification, or a cryptic
signal posted at a pre-arranged site. The
preferred method is a chalk mark on a

lamppost, wall, notice-board or signpost.
This could be a cross, numeral or V inside a
circle; the recipient must be aware of the
meaning of the signal. It might signify that
there is something ready to be collected in
a dead letter box, that the dead letter box
has been emptied, a request for an urgent
meeting, or that the signaller intends to
leave the country the next day. Once
received, the message must be removed with a
damp cloth.

November

I soon dismissed the warning I had received from the senior history professor as a product of gossip and professional jealousy. He obviously had connections in SIS, in common with half of the middle-aged and middle-class white male academics at Cambridge. Someone, somewhere – probably within the Firm – had presumably tipped him the wink about the forthcoming publication of the diaries. Realising that they would cause a stir in the history world and bring attention to someone who was not in the club, he decided to try to intimidate me into pulling the book.

There was no way I was going to allow him to succeed. I had already learned a huge amount through my aunt's diaries, not only about her personal bravery, but also about her parents' – my grandparents' – strength and determination. I would not let them down.

More than any other Second World War prisoner-of-war camp, Colditz Castle has lingered in the public consciousness – a legacy of the books written by Pat Reid, Roddy Parks and later Airey Neave, and the films based upon them. Before I discovered that my grandfather had been an inmate, I regarded Colditz more as a movie backdrop for the now-legendary tales of derring-do than as a grim and gruelling prison, where men starved and lost their minds.

Jane Moneypenny must have been horrified when she discovered that her father had spent over a year under German guard in a cold and barren camp. There was perhaps an initial stab of euphoria at the knowledge that he hadn't died in 1940. But this would have been closely followed by shivers of despair at the suffering that he must have undergone there.

Although I never met my grandfather, I was brought up on stories about him: his sense of fun and good humour; his ability to 'read' the bush for any trace of animal activity. My mother always said that he could see a lion print and tell not only the age and sex of the beast, but when it had passed by, to within an hour. He taught my mother and aunt to ride and to shoot, and also how to creep up on the most fragile infant impala without causing alarm. My grandmother Irene, who also died long before I was born, was by all accounts a worrier: intense, passionate, fiercely protective of her children, she saw potential hazards around every corner. Hugh Moneypenny was her ballast, the silver lining in her every imagined cloud. When he disappeared, she was devastated and, according to my aunt, never recovered. She threw herself into her work, providing healthcare for native Kenyans, almost as if by alleviating their suffering she could atone for her own.

Everything I know about Irene and Hugh Moneypenny I learned from my mother and Aunt Jane, and from the few fading photographs they brought back from Kenya. Having never met them, I found it hard to picture Hugh's predicament in Colditz.

After reading the diaries, I went to the library and got out all the books about the castle's wartime incarnation, and once I'd devoured them I was filled with a desire to find out more. Since my father died nine years ago, I have had no living family. Neither side were prolific breeders; I'd no cousins, and the passing of time had taken what few great-aunts and uncles I'd once had. My family consisted only of the dead; it didn't seem too odd to want to know them better.

The week after my 'warning', I booked myself a ticket to Berlin. From there, I took a train down to Leipzig, where I was met by a jolly English import, who advertised his taxi tours on the Colditz Castle website. As we drove out of town and through the bland middle-European countryside, he waxed lyrical about the joys – predominantly economic and female – of living in the former East and asked why I was interested in the castle. I told him that my grandfather had been an inmate. 'Thought it must've been something like that,' he said. 'Don't get many women coming down here – certainly not on their own.'

We drove around a corner and over a bridge, and suddenly there it was, perched on a rocky crag to our left. My first thought was how small it was, like a castle from the Brothers Grimm. It was perhaps only a hundred feet from the lower ramparts to the river below. I had imagined it as a huge, forbidding fortress, its turrets permanently shrouded by cloud. We wound up cobbled lanes, and parked in front of the heavy wooden gates. Winter was already entrenched in southern Germany, and I pulled my coat belt tighter as we walked through the outer courtyard and into the prisoners' court. The guide was muttering statistics and stories that I already knew from the books, as we walked from the chapel to the cellar, up to a dormitory, and into the old canteen, criss-crossing the small, irregularly shaped courtyard that in winter never saw the sun, and which was the centre of the prisoners' lives.

The cold bit at my cheeks and fingers, and what had on first impression seemed almost disappointingly small began to take on a more forbidding aspect. I pictured the hundreds of men, far from home, huddled in this claustrophobic place. I was struck again by their ingenuity and resourcefulness and bitter determination to find some way to break free. They must have longed for their families, hundreds – in my grandfather's case, thousands – of miles away. It would have taken a brave man to withstand that deprivation. One of those brave men was my grandfather.

Wednesday, 6th November

The Philby group – or Marmalade as it is now officially known – reconvened this morning. As Eleanor's confidante and acting officer on that part of the operation, I was included on the list of invitees. As such, I suppose I must regard myself as one of the 'gentlemen'.

M was not in the best of tempers, clearly agitated by the lack of action. Despite my fears, and the flak he's been taking from all directions, he's still in his chair. I hope he stays there. These days, it feels as if we are balanced on the edge of a precipice, and if he falls or jumps, we will all go tumbling after.

We reported in turn. My contribution was short: still no word from Mrs Philby. There was brief speculation as to what that could mean. Was she prevented from writing abroad? Had she given up any idea of returning home? Was she happy and settled in Moscow? Had she confessed her relationship with me to her husband, and he presumably to his KGB controllers? Or did she merely have nothing yet to communicate? It was impossible to know, and short of initiating contact, which would be risky at this point, all we can do is wait.

My part in the discussion effectively over, I concentrated on making notes for the minutes. It's normally Bill's job, but I offered to do it and he accepted with relief. Bookie had brought with him maps of the USSR and Moscow, and photographs and drawings of the Philby apartment. First, he spread out the country map. 'Piecing together the bits of the puzzle, we are now fairly sure that Philby left Beirut on a Soviet freighter named the *Dolmatova*. She pulled out of port in a hurry on the night of January 23rd, leaving part of her cargo abandoned on the dock. According to her manifest, which', he paused, 'we made arrangements to view, she arrived five days later at her home port of Odessa. Now, that's a journey that should take no longer than two days. Our guess is that she made an unscheduled stop at a Black Sea frontier port to drop off Mr Philby at some place less obvious – possibly Mariupol, here', he pointed to a port in Ukraine, 'or Tuapse or Novorossiysk on the Russian coast if she took the eastern route. We have no way of knowing. From there, he would have been transported by air to Moscow, where we must assume he was first taken to a KGB clinic for a thorough medical. That would be standard practice.

By all accounts, he'd spent the previous months drinking himself stupid and they would want to ensure he was stone-cold sober and healthy enough to spit out all he knew without fear of his body collapsing.

'The first reports of his whereabouts in Moscow were here.' He rolled out a large-scale map of Moscow. Red Square was clearly marked in the centre. There was a star to represent the Kremlin and another for the Lubyanka. CS leant over and marked a cross at a spot by the river. 'This, we believe, was his first apartment. We have photographs of known KGB officers entering and leaving the building, though none of Philby himself. There was full-time security outside the apartment door as well as on the street. This ceased in the summer, at the time, we must assume, that he was moved to here.' He pointed to a spot on the outer edge of the map, four miles north-west of the city centre.

'This is a quiet residential suburb. The building, as we can see from the outside, doesn't look up to much.' He slid across the table a photograph, clearly taken from the air, of a huge, ugly grey block, situated at the furthest part of a semicircular cul-de-sac. There was a small, tree-lined park at the front, but it still looked run-down and forgotten. 'We do have a recent photograph of our man leaving the building.' He slid across a blurred image of a figure in a hat and heavy greatcoat, taken from a distance. 'Yes, I can assure you it is he. The boffins have run tests which prove it. Thanks to the Cousins, we also have a plan of the interior of the building. The Philbys' apartment is on the eighth floor, overlooking the square. We can see from the plans that it is spacious by Soviet terms – an expression, no doubt, of their gratitude.' He grimaced.

'Four rooms, all good size, four exterior windows. At the back, it opens on to a communal corridor which runs the interior perimeter of the building. There is a central staircase leading on to the lobby, which is attended at all times by a concierge. Unusually, in this building the concierge is a man and, we have to assume, KGB. Buildings of this type would habitually be run by an army of spherical babushkas.' He raised his eyebrows. 'Over to you, Bill.'

'Sir. We have shown these photographs to Special Forces and to our own Planners. They have drawn up a list of possible actions, which you have in front of you, but clearly a surreptitious infiltration by no more than two men is going to be preferable to storming the place. We'd never get away with the latter, for a start, and the political repercussions would be hideous – mass expulsions from the Embassy, that kind of thing. Best if we slip in unnoticed and slip out again with Philby.'

'Then what?' M asked. 'How do we get him back here?'

'That, I'm afraid, sir, is the rub. We can't bring a plane in and out unobserved. It'll have to be by road. We've drawn up several proposed routes across country to the nearest border, probably Berlin, using a relay of local agents along the way. From East Berlin, we should be able to smuggle him across the border in one of the usual ways. He's not a large man; he'd probably fit behind the front grille. Assuming, of course, that he's being co-operative.'

'What are the odds of success, CS?'

'Honestly, sir, the Planners have put them somewhere between 18 and 23 per cent. I'd say that's slightly on the bullish side. Worth the call, perhaps, but not a raise.'

M looked down. 'You need to work on improving those numbers. See how you can make the plans tighter. Now, what about the black propaganda?'

Dingle spoke up. 'CS has asked me to input on this one, sir. It's well known that Philby and I *were* good friends,' he stressed the past tense, 'presumably to the KGB too. They knew I was his Chief in Beirut. If he was a double, it would make sense that I controlled him, at least while he was there. What I need to do now is to attempt to send a message to him in Moscow that is secret enough to persuade the Russians that it's genuine, but not so secret that it escapes their notice. I'm working on the details.'

'The content?' M asked.

'You know the sort of thing, sir: that we're delighted he has succeeded in his primary penetration, and to start sending his product by the pre-arranged means, and so on. All in code, of course. We thought of using the Blue Star variation that we know – but we think they don't know that we do – was recently broken by Moscow.'

'Very good. Start composing the message and thinking about means of delivery, please. Let's progress both aspects of Marmalade and meet back here one week from today to discuss the next stage. Thank you, gentlemen.'

I stood up and capped my pen and left with the others. Maybe next week I should try wearing my trousers? I haven't worn them since that fateful night in Dorset – a fleeting window of intimacy cracked by the strange world we inhabit.

I wish R would come back. I hope he succeeds in what he's trying to do. Whatever the longer future might hold for us, I would like to think he was there, somewhere, in my tomorrows. I try not to dwell on the faceless army who may or may not be following me, intruding into the rhythm of my daily existence. I fail. They are with me at all times in my imagination.

Saturday, 9th November

James has gone to the Caribbean on the trail of Francisco 'Pistols' Scaramanga. I hadn't put two and two together when Bill ordered up the Scaramanga file for M straight after the 'incident'. It seems so long ago now. At the time, I found the event overwhelming. I was so horrified by James's apparent betrayal, by what could have happened to M – to all of us – that thoughts of the future were furthest from my mind. Yet M, who came within milliseconds of being squirted with deadly poison by his own agent, only minutes later was plotting his next mission. Does the man have a heart?

Scaramanga. Even his name sounds evil, like a witch's incantation. From what I have read about him – and that's more than I would like – he is a lethal killing-machine. It's all becoming clear, the reason behind M's decision not to punish James. I've wondered about it: the Old Man would never have been clement without good cause, even to his favourite officer. This, however, is a form of Russian roulette, with five loaded chambers. With odds like that, I would have jumped at a court martial. James, I'm sure, sees it differently. He came in for his meeting with Bill on Thursday – M's still refusing to see him – looking as fit and chipper as he ever has, and left for the Caribbean with a wink and a whistle and the traditional invitation to dinner on his return.

I pray to God he makes it. I read the report C.C.* wrote on Scaramanga after poor old Dickie was brought back from Dominica with a bullet hole in each knee. He still needs sticks to walk with, I hear, and misses the Office desperately. Pamela [CS's secretary] says he's found work as a freelance crossword compiler, but I can't imagine that provides much in the adrenalin department.

Scaramanga had a traumatic childhood in the circus, if I remember correctly, which ended violently after some incident with an elephant. He became entangled with the American gangs and has been killing people for money – and pleasure – ever since. He's now based in Havana, where Castro uses him for particularly messy jobs. In between times he roves the region, killing to order.

I remember his photograph: pale brown eyes holding no promise of character, a gaunt, brutal face framed by short reddish hair, long sideburns failing to disguise outsized ears set flat against his skull. It was the face of the Grim Reaper, and I can only pray for James's safe return.

Sunday, 10th November

I had just returned from a frosty walk with Rafiki this morning, when my telephone rang. An unfamiliar man's voice asked for me, then introduced himself as

---

* A former regius professor of history at Oxford, employed by M to oversee the analysts. Known to his colleagues as 'Lazy Five Brains', he specialised in pungent character assessments of both allies and targets.

Roddy Parks. Momentarily surprised, I thanked him for calling.

'You're Hugh's daughter?'

'Yes,' I replied. 'Hugh Moneypenny – Sterling, I mean. Did you know him?'

'I did. Great man.'

There was so much I wanted to know, but I couldn't think how to begin. He interrupted my hesitation to ask whether I would like to meet.

'Yes, please. Whenever would suit you.'

'How about in an hour? I'm in London. Would be happy to chat about a former classmate,' he chuckled. He had a jovial voice, which suggested that laughter was never too far away. 'Staying with a chum in Mayfair. How about the lobby bar at the Berkeley? We can have a Bloody Mary and a sandwich. Does that suit?'

I changed quickly into a tweed skirt and polo neck, pulled on my new short trench coat from Harrods and walked along the edge of the park to Knightsbridge. Questions were piling up inside my head and an inkling of hope, too, which I tried to suppress. Since the ups and downs of last year, I haven't let myself dream too much. Pa disappeared twenty-three years ago; it's been eighteen since the war ended. What are the chances of him being alive? Bookie, no doubt, would be able to assign some precise percentage to it – something like 6.379. I can't. My aim is not to find a living father, but merely to discover what happened to him. After years living with uncertainty, that would be a great prize indeed.

Roddy Parks looked exactly as his voice suggested. A dapper man in his early fifties, with a wide, friendly face and twinkling eyes above a neat moustache, he radiated energy and the aura of officer class. He jumped up from the deep armchair and clasped my hand. 'My dear Jane, what a treat. A treat indeed it is to meet Hugh's daughter. A Bloody for you?'

I thanked him and accepted. It is not my normal Sunday-morning practice, but he made you want to join in whatever was so enthusing him. I said I'd enjoyed his book.

'Thank you. Thank you, my dear. Wasn't easy to write. Day after day in front of that damned type-writer – almost made me long for Colditz. No such thing as a deadline there! Then that bloody Reid got in there first with his tales of home runs and what not.' He chuckled again.

Over the next hour, he talked about life in the camp, barely stopping to gulp back a succession of Bloody Marys. Very occasionally, just as I was about to ask about my father, he would slip his name into the conversation – as a participant in a particular escape attempt, as a leading light in the courtyard cricket team (I'd always believed that Pa loathed ball games) or as a player in the yearly the-atricals. When I tried to interrupt to ask more, he merrily barrelled on. They were obviously stories he'd told many times before and enjoyed re-telling. I got the same feeling of rose-tinted reality as I had when reading his book.

It was only after three large drinks that I was able to ask specifically about Pa. 'Arrived at the Castle spring of '44, as far as I can remember. He was in a poor state – pile o' bones. Don't know the details of how he got there – something about Warsaw, I think. He spent his first few months in the sick ward with pneumonia. Never had a chance to get really close before I was out. He was a good man, I do know that. Very good man. Didn't know his real name at the time, of course. Only found that out quite recently. He stuck to his cover story all the way. Most unusual. Don't know why he did that – must've been in Intel. All spies were zapped by the Gestapo. Still, brave thing to do – meant that he wasn't allowed letters from family, Red Cross packages and what not.'

'Did anyone know who he was?' I asked.

'Don't believe so. Otherwise I, or one of the others who made it home, would have found you, brought you up to speed. Hugh Sterling – I mean your father – got out, y'know?'

His words hit me like a punch to the belly. My shock must have been evident.

'I wasn't there, of course – back here in hospital – but I know all the stories of the latter days. Yes, he escaped a few months before liberation. He was heading north, I believe. It was the only way: the Swiss route was effectively closed off by those damned Hitler Youths, road-blocks every few miles, barbed-wire traps in the woods, everything they could do to keep us from getting out. Hugh must have been desperate. They had a radio in there, tuned into the BBC, knew the Allies were advancing and it was only a matter of time before the Yanks turned up with the keys to freedom in their well-tailored pockets. Yet he didn't wait. As far as I know, was never heard of again.' He looked at me. 'I'm sorry, m'dear. Not what you wanted to hear.'

'His name was on the register of inmates shortly before the Americans came,' I said. 'I've seen it.'

He gave my arm another squeeze. 'Means little, I'm afraid. Diddly squat. We used to change names frequently, just to bait the goons. We even had a couple of lads who pretended to escape, then hid underground for months. Every time someone got out, one of them would step into his place at *Appell* – that's roll-call – to make up numbers. Called 'em ghosts. Look, m'dear, if I remember correctly, your father's best chum was a chap called – what was his real name? He had a cover ID too, but I met him back here when it was all over and learnt his real name then. He was the one who told me about your Pa. Pitman. That's it . . . They came in together, if my memory serves me correctly.'

'Miles Pitman? The pilot?'

'That's the man. Last I heard he had bought a farm at the foot of Mount Kenya. Beans, I think it was. Could have been coffee, of course. Coffee beans – that must have been it! Ah, at the Castle, we used to dream about real coffee . . .'

He was off again, on a long series of reminiscences that flowed, one from the last, like a Japanese water sculpture. Watching him, I realised that the horror of a POW camp was the highlight of his life. It was when he was reliving the story that he was most alive. Between his fifth and sixth Bloody Marys, I discovered that he now ran a small pub in Lincolnshire. He had not married. He refused to let me pay for the drinks and hugged me goodbye with great warmth. 'Enjoyed it, m'dear. I'll have a quick squizz through my papers, if y'like. Sure I've got Pitman's address somewhere, if you're interested.'

I left him with a spring in my step, trying to prevent my hopes from soaring. At least I could banish the images of Pa dying in that forbidding castle from my mind. It's been a long road towards the truth about Pa, and every time it's looked as if I'm nearing my destination, I've hit another block. Maybe this time?

Wednesday, 13th November

At the Marmalade meeting, the plans to extract Philby from his apartment were debated at length. Last week, 009 had made his way to Moscow, via Berlin, and with the help of a couple of men, had managed to break into the Philbys' apartment on Saturday night, while they were at the ballet. Bill circulated 009's report:

We had learnt that the weekend concierge has a bladder problem, necessitating frequent visits to the gents on the first floor. Each visit takes an average of 4½ minutes. Using high—magnification night glasses, we were able to keep watch on the lobby from across the park. The targets departed the building on foot at 18.00 hours, accompanied by their security detail. At 20.13, the concierge left his desk and headed up the stairs to the first floor. I made a rapid entry to the building and had passed the first floor before he began his descent. Once on the eighth floor, I was able to locate the apartment. There is a chair outside the door, presumably normally occupied by the guard. There were three locks — all standard mortice — which I was able to open with little trouble and no trace. I have constructed a mould of the locks to enable the construction of copies for quiet access.

By flashlight, I managed to get a good look at the apartment. A floor plan is appended. I

exited the building at 21.47, at the signal
of 225, who was waiting outside with the
night glasses. The targets returned at
23.12, accompanied by their security officer.
He was relieved by a replacement at 24.00
prompt. The neighbourhood is quiet and we
noticed no external surveillance.

My assessment is that Phase One
(extraction) of MARMALADE is possible. One
agent would gain access to the apartment
while the targets are out and wait for their
return. His partner would deal with the
guard. We would have to be out before the
replacement arrives and sounds the alarm. I
await further instructions.

'Bit of luck about the bladder problem. Does this up the odds?' M asked. He turned to Bookie.

'Yes, sir, but the Planners still regard the exit from the country as the most risky component. However, we've drawn up more detailed options for this. I think, sir, we now have an estimated 43.7 per cent chance of success.'

'You're sure? 43.7 per cent?'

'Well, to be more accurate, 43.682, sir.' Bookie ghosted a wink at me as I looked at him, open-mouthed. M continued without a pause, as if it had been a well-trodden comedy routine.

'What do you think, gentlemen? Chief of Staff?'

'In my view, sir, it's too risky. The potential fall-out if it failed would cripple our intelligence operations in the Redland sphere for years.'

'Those Philby hasn't already,' M commented drily. 'CME?'

'I'm in, sir. I'd risk anything to get that bounder back to base.'

'CS?'

Bookie put his great mathematician's head to one side. 'It's not a banker, that's for sure. I'm afraid it's too close to call, sir. I'd hold back my money.'

'Which gives me the deciding vote. I say we do it. Next weekend. Same team: 009 and 225. Top secret. Give me the exit plans as soon as they're finalised. Thank you, gentlemen.'

Relieved that I wasn't required to vote, I'd got up to leave with them when M called me back and told me to sit down.

'You are doing well in these meetings, Miss Moneypenny. Good to have you aboard.'

'Thank you, sir.'

'That training we discussed: Bill's set you up on a basic skills and anti-subversion course at the Fort next week. Starts Monday. Send Miss Comely up to look after me, will you? With 009 in Moscow and 006 in Vietnam, she can't be rushed off her feet. Good luck.'

'Thank you, sir.'

How exciting. Can I tell the Powder Vine, I wonder? Probably not.

Friday, 22nd November

It's midnight and I can't imagine ever sleeping again. This has been one of those days that makes you question what it's all about. Is there a God? Justice? Hope? I feel emotionally drained, bereft, as though the curtains have been drawn on the future once and for all. I miss R. I want to be with him, or Helena, or someone.

It feels like a year has passed, but it was only four hours ago when my phone rang. I was in the bath, soaking out the exertions of the week down at the Fort. I let it ring for what seemed like ages, but it showed no intention of ceasing. Worried that Aunt Frieda might have had another turn, I raised myself out of the bath and made it to the phone before it stopped. Still dripping, I said hello. All I could hear on the other end was sobbing. 'Helena? What's wrong?' I asked.

'Turn on the wireless. It's too awful. I'm so sorry,' she gulped.

I let the handpiece dangle and rushed across the room to switch it on. I just caught the end of a sombre voice announcing '. . . died at 1.00 pm Central Standard Time. Vice-President Lyndon Johnson has left the hospital, but we do not know to where he has proceeded. Presumably he will be taking the oath of office shortly and become the thirty-sixth President of the United States . . .'

It didn't sink in at once. I picked up the phone again. 'What happened? Who's dead? It can't be true.'

'It is. JFK was shot in Dallas. What is going to happen to the world now?' Helena broke off again. In the background I could hear Lionel trying to comfort her. I put the phone down and went back to the wireless. I stayed glued to it for hours, listening to descriptions of the stand-off at the hospital before the President's body was removed and taken to Air Force One. Hundreds of police and agents sealing Dealey Plaza, where the shooting had taken place. Jackie Kennedy in her blood-spattered suit.

A solemn-faced Lyndon Johnson, his palm held aloft, swearing the oath of allegiance before a lady judge on Air Force One.

In my head, I saw the President's smile as he held my hand in his and welcomed me into the Oval Office. That was only fifteen months ago. He was so young, so vital. I honestly believed he could, and would, change the world. Now he's in a coffin. Who could have done such a terrible thing? Why?

Saturday, 23rd November

The nightmare has not gone away. I must finally have dropped off to sleep with the radio on last night, some time after hearing reports of the presidential plane arriving at Andrews Air Base. When I awoke, he was still dead and they were describing a small, ratty man named Lee Harvey Oswald being frog-marched to jail. Can one man really have pulled this off on his own? Seems unlikely.

I had been looking forward to this weekend – writing up my course notes; sorting everything out before Monday. I find I haven't the heart to do so now. It was a fascinating, full week, which now seems so trivial, like a game of cat and mouse. It can wait. I don't want to be alone. This morning, Hyde Park was virtually empty of all but the most committed dog-walkers, and even they seemed to drag their feet. The phone was ringing when I got in. It was Helena, asking me to come up to Cambridge for the night. She sounded almost hysterical – quite unlike her normal self. It can't be JFK.

Sunday, 24th November

I am on an emotional roller-coaster. Helena was waiting at the station when I arrived. I expected to find her tear-stained and ragged, but she was waving and appeared composed. She gave me an enormous hug. On the way to the house, we talked, inevitably, about the assassination, but I could tell that she was distracted. I turned to look at her. Beneath her frown, I could see a smile trying to break out. 'What's happened?' I asked.

'I'll tell you when we get there.'

Intrigued, I looked out of the window as we skirted down Newnham Road, past Ma's old college and then left, out towards Grantchester. It was a roundabout route, but Helena knows that it makes me feel close to Ma, if only fleetingly.

The home fires were burning. Lionel put down his pipe and gave me a warm embrace. He commiserated about the President, but even as he was doing so, I saw him give Helena a questioning look. Out of the corner of my eye, I glimpsed her shake her head and smile at him. I told them I'd had enough of the mystery and to please tell me what was going on. Lionel cleared his throat.

'My dear Jane, we wanted you to be the first to know, we have, um, er . . .'

'Set a date for the wedding,' Helena finished.

For a minute, I was struck dumb. I felt tears begin to trickle down my cheeks. I don't know why. After a seven-year engagement, I suppose I'd given up hope that it might some day be formalised into marriage. I rushed across the room to hug Helena. When we separated, we were both sobbing. Lionel looked embarrassed. Kind, dear, clever Lionel. I smiled at him. 'I couldn't be more happy for you. Well done. So when is it?'

'We thought about March 27th. It's a Friday. Could you make that?'

'The day after . . .?'

'Yes. It was Lionel's idea. He thought it would give us a reason to look at the end of March with joy, instead of sorrow. Do you think it's tasteless?'* Helena looked at me anxiously.

'No. I think it's perfect. Ma would have loved it. It's the most wonderful news. On top of everything that's happened. It's like a sign to look to the positive. I am sure you will both bring happiness into every life you touch.'

Yesterday evening, as dusk was falling, Helena and I went for a walk along the Backs. It was a beautiful, crisp evening and, for the first time in what seems like months, I didn't think about being followed. The early stars were out and the lights shone from within King's College Chapel. She told me how Lionel had woken up and said 'How about March 27th?' as if they were midway through the conversation. 'I didn't know, at first, what he was talking about. I honestly had given up thinking about it, but then he said, in his dear old way, "You know, for, um, er," and I did. Can you believe it? I suppose the tragedy must have sparked it off. Are you pleased for us? I hope so. It doesn't feel strange? You'll be my maid of honour, of course?'

---

* Their mother, Irene Moneypenny, was an innocent victim of rampaging Mau Mau warriors in what has become known as the Lari Massacre on 26 March 1953.

Of course I will. Old maid of honour. I found myself wanting to tell her about R, but it wasn't the time. Still no word from him. I know I shouldn't expect it, but I do miss him and I'm not sure, if it came to it, that I would be able to cope with the long, silent absences. I am so, so happy for Helena and Lionel. I only hope they don't take quite as long over the decision to have children. Right now, I can't imagine having a child of my own, but I would like to be an aunt.

Monday, 25th November

M walked straight past my desk this morning, as usual, as though nothing untoward had occurred over the weekend. I don't know what I was expecting – just some sort of acknowledgement of JFK's death. After all, we had met him together.* Or maybe a 'Welcome back'? Instead, he told me to convene a Marmalade meeting after lunch and to bring the signals in as soon as they arrived.

After a week away on the south coast, living in the land of make-believe, following pretend people around Portsmouth and changing hats and taxis in an attempt to avoid being followed myself, leaving secret envelopes under loose stones in the sea-wall, and rolling out of car doors in the prescribed manner – then returning to JFK's death and Helena's wedding plans – I had forgotten about the Marmalade mission. I had read no reports and decoded no signals. When you're at the Office day in and

---

* In the Oval Office, on 22 August 1962.

day out, everything seems urgent and crucial; but go away and you realise that the world keeps turning without your own little legs scrabbling on the treadmill.

The group duly assembled. The first sign that all was not well came from Bill's left eyelid, which was flickering as it has a habit of doing under a regime of sleepless nights and work-induced pressure. He had a thick pile of signals on the table in front of him.

M nodded at Bookie to begin. 'As you all probably know by now, Marmalade was not a success. Now is not the time for post-mortems, but I'll briefly run through what happened. We received information that the Philbys had tickets for the Tchaikovsky Conservatoire on Saturday night. 009 and 225 were fully briefed and equipped. They took up station as soon as they saw the targets leave their apartment building, along with their normal security escort.

'When the concierge went for his habitual break, 009 ascended the stairs to the eighth floor without incident. It was at this point that the plan began to break down. We do not have his report as yet, but from what I understand after talking to Moscow station chief, 009 had his newly minted key in the lock and was about to open the door, when he heard a sound coming from inside the apartment. He froze and listened some more. When he heard nothing, he opened the door an inch. The lights were off, but he had a strong sense that there was someone there. He was considering his next move, when the lights were switched on and two large men leapt towards him. According to Moscow station, 009 was extremely fortunate to get away. He ran down the stairs with the men close on his heels and managed to evade the concierge, who was fully armed, and get into the car with 225, who, on seeing the lights from outside, was waiting for him. While they raced across Moscow – two cars in pursuit – 009 reported what had happened.

'They managed to evade their tail long enough for 009 to be dropped at a safe house, where 225 changed cars and returned to the Embassy. There were, apparently, several vehicles positioned around the Embassy. He was stopped and questioned by uniformed KGB officers before reaching the gates, but, although regarded with suspicion, he had diplomatic protection and was allowed to gain entry. He sent his report at 02.00 GMT on Sunday.'

'Thank you, CS. Chief of Staff, any news from 009?'

'No, sir,' Bill replied. 'We presume he will head for East Berlin. I'm afraid we have to regard the route planned for the Marmalade extraction as compromised. He's a resourceful chap, though, speaks good enough Russian and, travelling alone, should be able to make it to the city. Then he's in familiar territory and able to make contact with us. I hope to hear from him within three days.'

'So what does this mean? It sounds as if the reception party at Philby's flat was expecting them.'

''Fraid so, sir.'

We all looked around the table. Marmalade has been a highly restricted operation, planned under conditions of tight secrecy. If it was penetrated, then it can have only been by a limited number of people. I felt a large, interior groan. In Bill's parlance, there were still unplugged holes in the sieve.

'Thank you, everybody. We will reconvene in a few days.'

I walked back to my office with a heavy heart. As I got there, M buzzed through on the intercom. 'Ask Miss Fields to come down please, Miss Moneypenny.'

Friday, 29th November

The Friday reports came in as usual. I was almost surprised to see them. It has been a week so far removed from normality that I wouldn't have been shocked to hear that all the field agents had been killed – or were taking leave to marry their secretaries. Such has been the nature of my troubled sleep.

M has spent much of the week in deep conversation with Dorothy Fields. As usual, when matters turn to moles, M reaches for Dorothy. Bill once told me that her brain is like a mechanised version of the Records room. You give her a name and she can draw up the relevant file and make instant connections. She was the one who dug up Prenderghast, and I know that she was looking into whether he had an accomplice in the office. Then Philby came along and I suppose channelled all available energies into salvaging what could be from the wreckage of our Soviet activity.

Yesterday afternoon, Dorothy came into my office and asked if we could talk. As I followed her down to the seventh floor, I thought again how innocuous she looked, with her ill-fitting dress and funny little cherry-topped hat. How appearances can deceive. She sat me down and called for coffee. While I was adding milk to mine, I felt her keen eyes assessing me. She said nothing, just sat there drinking her cup of black coffee and watching me sipping at mine. 'Coffee all right?' she asked formally.

'Yes,' I replied. 'Thank you very much.'

She laughed, a deep, jungle laugh. 'You're a bad liar, Jane. Thank you. I needed to know that. Now you can stop drinking it if you like. I know you can't stand the stuff.'

Startled, I looked up, caught her eye and started laughing myself. 'That's Kenya, for you. Too much coffee from too young an age.'

She started talking about her childhood, just over the border in Tanganyika. I hadn't known. Soon we were swapping stories of fishing for termites and long walks along dusty red roads. I have always been in awe of her: her adventures in Stalin's Russia, French Indo-China and Africa are the stuff of legend. But here she was, a large and friendly Mrs Tiggywinkle, acting for all the world as if she was at a WI coffee morning. I like her enormously. I hope we can be friends.

She turned the conversation neatly to the Marmalade operation. Her questions were adroit and succinct, but not remotely threatening. She wanted to know who I had talked to about it. When I replied no one, except M and Bill, she asked me a few more questions about my week at the Fort and whether it had come up in any context there. When I denied it, she thanked me for my co-operation. As I was walking out of the door, she asked if I had written to Eleanor Philby.

'No,' I told her. 'I wish I could, but I don't have her address.'

She smiled and waved.

This morning, as I was decoding the reports, I couldn't help but admire her skill at putting me at my ease, then finding out what she wanted to know without appearing to ask.

I was delighted to read 007's report. It was dotted with his usual humour and spiked with irreverence. For the first time since Tracy was killed, I felt he was fully the old James – brave and professional, with the faintest touch of mischief. He has been away for nearly three weeks now, and in that time has managed to take in most of the hotspots of the Caribbean. I don't want to be in M's room when he has to sign for James's expenses. Mr Scaramanga, it seems, has an uncanny knack of keeping just a step ahead of his hunter. According to his report, James arrived in Trinidad the day after a senior government official mysteriously disappeared on his yacht with his girlfriend. A man answering Scaramanga's description was observed leaving the country that same afternoon.

By the time James reached Caracas, the newspapers were reporting the murder of an oil-company head, who had been refusing to deal with Castro in Cuba. From Venezuela, fearing that his cover had been blown, he flew to British Guiana, where he is now waiting for a diplomatic passport.

'My new name is Mark Hazard,' he reported. 'Entirely appropriate, from Scaramanga's point of view. When I have received all the relevant documents, I will fly to Havana to wait. He is sure to return to his home at some point soon.'

Saturday, 30th November

I received a postcard from Roddy Parks, thanking me for meeting him and giving me Miles Pitman's address, a PO box number in Nanyuki, Kenya. I will write to him tomorrow.

December

My quest to find the hidden mole within SIS was failing to produce any concrete results. Rereading my aunt's diaries, I dug deeper for clues, compiling mental lists as to who it could have been. But I found no answers hidden in her pages, and, apart from what she had written, there was little evidence to suggest that a mole existed. After exhausting all conceivable sources within and without the Office, I went back to Bill Tanner. Again he parried my determined attempts to break through the barriers of discretion and discipline that I felt sure were holding back the truth. 'No mole,' he kept saying. 'It was the product of paranoia in a climate of fear. Careful, Kate. You'll get into trouble if you keep asking questions. You'll find no one on this side to admit to a mole.'

It was that precise combination of words that gave me the idea for a last angle of attack: if our records were closed or redacted, perhaps I would have better luck with theirs.

I already knew to expect little from the official KGB archives in Moscow: the few scholars who have been allowed access to them have been strictly supervised and limited in what they have been allowed to see. I had scoured – without success – the Mitrokhin Archives, the secret KGB records smuggled out by former KGB archivist Vasili Mitrokhin on his defection to the West in 1992. There, too, I found little in the way of hard information to help me. I needed to talk to someone who had been there, on the inside, at the time I was interested in. I needed to find a former KGB officer who was willing to talk.

Oleg Gordievsky is probably Britain's most celebrated Russian defector. He is to the SIS, what Philby was to the KGB. Over a period spanning eleven years, he provided our intelligence services with an unparalleled quantity and quality of product relating to the workings and day-to-day objectives of the KGB, which organisation he served for twenty-two years. I had read *Last Stop Execution*, his chilling account of what it was like to work simultaneously for the KGB and the British services. I knew he was living in England – I had heard him talk at a recent debate about the future of the intelligence services. But I had no idea how to find him. I sent an email to Ferdy Macintyre at SIS, asking if he could help me track down Gordievsky. If emails could simultaneously laugh and stick two fingers in the air, his response did.

It was, improbably, an old boyfriend who had once worked in Moscow – returning considerably richer, though with a premature mane of grey – who pointed me in the right direction. He introduced me to a former intelligence officer friend of his, who, over an expensive and well-lubricated lunch, let drop that he knew Gordievsky well. 'I'll set up lunch for us if you'd like,' he said. 'Oleg's fond of Chinese food.'

It was a cold winter's day in London, and I was nervous. I arrived early at the appointed restaurant, but both of my guests were already at the bar. They stood up to greet me, and I found myself looking down into the pale, bespectacled eyes of a legendary spy. He was wearing a grey jacket over an open-necked denim shirt, and drinking red wine. At first I found his accent hard to penetrate, though his English, I soon discovered, is excellent, and he has an extraordinary memory for names, dates and places. The two old spies swapped insider gossip about people I did not know, as I drank in the Russian names and the now-familiar acronyms. It was as if I had trespassed into a gentleman's club. For the duration of this lunch, at least, I was living in my aunt's world.

As we started to eat, and Gordievsky progressed from red wine on to beer, he dropped his stern façade and talked freely about his career as an agent working for the British. He was recruited in 1974 in Copenhagen, where he was working for the KGB from within the Soviet Embassy. Living in the West, he'd had an opportunity to see that the propaganda he had been drip-fed throughout his life was false. The grass was demonstrably and genuinely greener on the other side of the Curtain, he told me, smiling and waving his fork (he had rejected chopsticks) around the sumptuous interior of the new restaurant buried in the basement beneath the Dorchester Hotel.

His eyes had been opened to the faults and failures of the Soviet system, and he felt morally bound to do anything he could to contribute to its dissolution. Our mutual friend, the British former intelligence officer, interrupted him to comment that 'the information Oleg supplied when he was acting chief of the London rezidentura – particularly about Gorbachev's commitment to perestroika – almost certainly curtailed the Cold War.'

In spying for the British, Gordievsky had put himself in considerable danger. When his actions were eventually discovered by the Centre, he was recalled to Moscow, force-fed truth serum, and condemned to death. He was probably only weeks away from being executed when he activated a British-devised escape plan and fled over the border to Finland and from there to London. It was six years before his wife and children were able to join him in England.

'How are they adapting to life here now?' I asked. But it was the wrong question. Gordievsky's eyes grew opaque behind the thick lenses of his glasses. 'I do not know,' he said finally. 'I have had no contact with them for many years.' His commitment to the British, it appeared, had destroyed his marriage and severed his links with his children, as well as to his country. To this day, he is living under a Moscow death sentence. Unless things change, he can never return.

As we devoured the dim sum, he gave me a lesson in KGB tradecraft. The methods he described for evading surveillance were identical in most respects to those my aunt had read about in the Q Branch quarterly report decades before. I asked if he had met Philby. Regretfully, he hadn't, although one of Philby's closest friends in the KGB, the writer Mikhail Lyubimov, had been his superior in Copenhagen and one of the few men he respected in the organisation. From the moment he arrived in

Moscow, Gordievsky told me, Philby would have been under constant close surveillance and his flat would have been wired.

'And Eleanor?' I asked.

'Less so. She would possibly have had a team with one car to follow her if she went out. But, if she wanted to, she would have been able to shake it without too much trouble,' he told me.

Finally I asked the question that had been pressing at the front of my mind: did he know whether there had been a further Russian agent working in SIS after Prenderghast was exposed in the early 1960s? He looked me in the eye, drained his glass, and said, 'Yes – and I have told your services so.'

I felt my heart pound. 'Do you know who it was?'

'No,' he said. 'To the best of my knowledge, the identity of the agent has never been discovered.'

Sunday, 1st December

A postcard from R, at last. He's safe, thank God. I didn't know quite how much I longed to hear from him until I picked up the picture of Gaudi's cathedral and turned the card over to see his writing. There were only twenty-five words: 'I miss you and count the days until I can see you again. I hope and trust that will be soon. Take care, my love.'

I hugged the card to my chest and for hours couldn't stop smiling. I have been trying not to think about him, but it's been hard, not knowing where he is, whether he's safe or when he'll be back. What was he doing when JFK was killed? Sometimes, I wonder if he's thinking about me as I am about him. Now I know I have not been forgotten.

I looked closely at the postmark. Vienna. What was he doing there? Or indeed was he there, or had he given the card to someone else to post? Too many questions and no hope of answers. I took Rafi for a run in the park this morning and tried out some daydreams – of a simple, happy life with R and me in a thatched cottage in the country somewhere, cooking, reading, walking, laughing together. Could I do it – devote my life to pruning roses and warming his slippers? After the tension and excitement of Office life? It seems like an impossible dream and not one that's troubled me before. Driving an ambulance in wartime Cairo was the stuff of my childhood fantasies, not jumble sales at the WI.

In the meantime, I have those twenty-five words to live on.

Monday, 2nd December

I can't escape that prickly feeling that I'm being followed. Bill has assured me that our people are merely 'keeping an eye' on my back. This apparently involves driving past the flat from time to time, to see whether there are any suspicious cars parked in view of my front door. So far, they've picked up nothing, he says. But it's not when I'm at home that I feel it. It's going to and from work, on weekends, in the park, shopping, in cafés. I don't know whether the course has made me more sensitive or more paranoid about surveillance, but I'm constantly conscious of the possibility of it. As an exercise, I might enjoy it, but not this relentless, stultifying awareness. I enter shops with large glass windows when I don't have to, trying to catch sight of someone loitering outside. I take the tube rather than walk. I carry a spare hat and scarf and spectacles in my bag at all times.

Then I feel ridiculous, like the only one at a party wearing fancy dress. I can't say for sure that I've clocked the same face twice, because after a while, if you're searching, everyone starts to look familiar. I keep telling myself that herein lies the route to madness and for a few days I make a conscious effort not to look behind me. Then I catch sight of someone who, for some reason, looks suspicious and I start looking again. I can begin to imagine what it must be like for Eleanor, who must know that she is followed wherever she goes. Poor Eleanor. I hope it's not too ghastly, living in a hideous flat in a cold and grey city with long queues for a rare grapefruit. I hope that just being with Kim makes it all worthwhile.

This morning, I was convinced I recognised a woman on the bus. She got on at the same stop and sat a few rows behind me. I heard her asking for her ticket with a pronounced accent, which to my untrained ear could have been Russian or Slavic. Just as the bus was leaving the stop at Hyde Park Corner, I got up from my seat, ran downstairs and jumped off. She didn't follow. I stood on the side of the road, watching my bus turn down towards Victoria, cursing silently. Now I would be late for work. For what? Even if she had been following me, she surely knew where I worked by now and it wasn't as if I was heading towards some clandestine meet or had anything to hide. At best, she wasn't following me; at worst, I had broken a fundamental rule of surveillance evasion and shown consciousness of my tail. If that's what she was, then she will report back that I deviated from routine and they will redouble their watch on me. Damn and blast.

My ill temper was alleviated somewhat when I reached the Office and found a signal from Mary, full of surprise and delight at James's appearance in Jamaica. I had purposely held back from warning her that he was in the region – to stave off the disappointment she would have felt had his mission not taken him to Kingston. Fortunately for her, he picked up Scaramanga's scent at the airport while waiting for an onward connection to Havana, called the High Commission and got Goodnight. I almost blush to think about the reunion they'll be having tonight. The combination of James, alive and tanned, and a couple of rum daiquiris would be irresistible.

Aside from his presence out there – apparently in fine health – she had only bad news. Ross [Head of Jamaica Station] flew to Trinidad a week ago and she's not heard a peep from him since then. He was only meant to be scouting for Scaramanaga on 007's behalf and was under strict orders to keep a low profile and not to engage him in any way. If so, then why the failure to communicate? It's most unlike him. Mary sent out a Red Warning two days ago and was told to give him another week. Perhaps James will pick up some clue as to his whereabouts?

Wednesday, 4th December

M called me into his office this afternoon. 'Send this message to 007, wherever he is,' he told me. 'Mark it most urgent:

```
TOP REDLAND AGENT NAMED HENDRIKS IN
JAMAICA STOP AVOID HIM AT ALL COSTS STOP
WE HAVE HEARD FROM A DELICATE BUT SURE
SOURCE THAT AMONG HIS OTHER JOBS COMMA
HE HAS BEEN ORDERED TO FIND AND KILL
QUOTE THE NOTORIOUS SECRET AGENT JAMES
BOND ENDQUOTE HE HAS CABLED THE CENTRE
FOR YOUR DESCRIPTION ENDIT MAILEDFIST
```

'007's in Jamaica,' I told M. 'Station J signalled on Tuesday to say he had arrived safely. She didn't know where he was heading, at that point.'

   M didn't look up. 'Knowing him, straight into the dragon's den. We can but warn. Send the cable, please, Miss Moneypenny, then be a good girl and call down Miss Fields for me.' He didn't even have the grace to show concern for James's safety.

Thursday, 5th December

An urgent signal from Mary in Kingston, sent by Triple X, came through just as I arrived. It must have been the middle of the night over there. I got out my machine and started to decipher it:

```
MAILEDFIST EYES ONLY
TRACKED DOWN OHOHSEVEN LAST NIGHT TO THE
```

THUNDERBIRD HOTEL IN BLOODY BAY COMMA
ESTABLISHMENT OWNED BY TARGET SCARAMANGA
STOP EYE PASSED ON MESSAGE ABOUT HENDRIKS
WHOSE ACQUAINTANCE HE HAS ALREADY MADE
COMMA BUT DOES NOT BELIEVE HIS COVER HAS
BEEN PENETRATED YET STOP OHOHSEVEN
REPORTED THAT HEAD OF STATION JAY
COMMANDER ROSS WAS KILLED BY SCARAMANGA
IN TRINIDAD STOP TWO COUSINS INCLUDING
LEITER IN ATTENDANCE AT HOTEL STOP
URGENTLY AWAITING FURTHER INSTRUCTIONS
ENDIT GOODNIGHT

M banged his fist on the table when he read it. 'What is it about bloody Jamaica that we lose all our station chiefs? Meant to be a soft posting. Ross was a good man, served on one of my ships. Inform the High Commissioner, please, Miss Moneypenny. Contact his family – he wasn't married, was he? Thank God for that. Then send round the hat for a wreath, pick a date for the memorial service, all that kind of thing. Get Langley on the telephone for me – whoever's the highest ranking officer awake at this time. Send up Head of section C [Caribbean] immediately and tell Chief of Staff to come in too. We'll need to send out someone to hold the fort, and pretty sharpish, if I know 007. Whatever happens, there's sure to be a hell of a mess.'

I fear for James. With both Scaramanga and the KGB gunning for him, he's like a deer caught in the cross-hairs of a night-sight rifle. I pray for everyone's sake – James's, M's, Mary's, my own – that he manages to extricate himself. To lose him once was bad enough.

Friday, 6th December

I was woken early by a phone call from Bill, summoning me to the Office. I got there before dawn, just as M was arriving and shared his lift up to the eighth floor. Apart from a nod, he ignored me and instead talked to Fletcher about the effect of the damp weather on his stump. Apparently it itches when it rains. It was only when we got to M's door that he turned to me. 'Get the latest signals from Kingston and Washington, please, Miss Moneypenny. Decipher them quickly. Then you'd better join us.'

When I walked into his office, Bill, Bookie and Head of C were already waiting. I handed M the signals, which he read in silence. Then he looked up. 'Scaramanga is dead,' he announced. 'Along with a top KGB operative calling himself Hendriks, and a handful of mobsters from America. The result of a joint operation between us and the Cousins. Unfortunately, in the course of the party 007 was badly hurt. He was found unconscious in a mangrove swamp by a Jamaican police officer, next to Scaramanga's body. According to the report I have here, 007 sustained a shot in the right side of the stomach. It is suspected that the bullet was coated in poison. He was taken directly to the hospital, where he underwent an operation to remove the bullet. He has not regained consciousness, but the doctors say the bullet missed the abdominal viscera. He has been given an even chance of recovery, but he's got the best available medical care out there and he's a brave and strong man who has rid the world of an evil killer. He's come back from the dead before,' M gave a dry cough, 'and we must hope that he pulls through again.

'In the meantime, there is a considerable clean-up operation to undertake. Felix Leiter from the CIA was also badly injured. Apparently broke his leg – and we must assume it was not the prosthetic one he picked up as a result of a previous adventure with 007. The man will be limbless if he spends any more time with 007.' If it was an attempt at a joke, nobody laughed. M continued: 'Washington is awaiting a full report from him. Alec [Alec Hill, Head of the Caribbean Section, based in London], you'd better get on the first plane to Kingston to talk to him before anyone else does. Miss Moneypenny will organise your flight. We need to co-ordinate some sort of plausible story, otherwise we're going to have the Jamaicans on our backs, full of righteous fury that we've been operating on their soil without permission. Then there's the KGB to placate, not to mention the organisations of those other, er, gentlemen, who lost their lives. We need to avoid any possibility of retribution. If this can be sorted out, we can count it as a very successful operation. Thank you, gentlemen.'

I spent the rest of the morning sorting out aeroplane tickets and trying not to worry about James. After lunch, my phone rang. 'Jane, is that you?' asked a distant voice. 'I'm calling on the secure line from the High Commission in Kingston.'

Mary sounded exhausted and close to tears. I wished I could be there with her. 'How are you, Mary? How's James?'

'I've just come from the hospital. They say they're optimistic that he'll pull through. Apparently it was a miracle that the bullet missed his vital organs, but he's still unconscious and hooked up to wires and drips and all sorts of machines. He's a horrible, greyish-green colour. If it wasn't for his pulse beat on the monitor, I'd think he was dead. Oh, Jane, it's all ghastly. First Ross and now James . . .' She began to cry.

'Mary, you've got to pull yourself together. Alec is on his way out and there's not much you can do. James is in the best hands. We're all leaving the office in a couple of hours, and when we do, go home, take a pill and go to sleep. You're going to have a lot on your plate over the next couple of weeks and, when he wakes up, James is going to require all your energies.'

'Jane, you don't understand. I've just come from talking to Felix. He told me what happened. That awful Scaramanga had tied a dummy to the railway line in front of the train they were travelling on. It had blonde hair. It was meant to look like me. How can anyone be that evil?'

'Mary, it wasn't you and I'm sure James wasn't fooled. Go to bed now, please. You can take that as an order direct from M.'

I put the phone down and swivelled around to see M at his door, looking at me with raised eyebrows. I felt a blush rise. 'Sorry, sir. I hope you don't mind. That was Miss Goodnight. I invoked your name to get her to go home to sleep. I assure you I don't make a practice of it.'

'I hope you don't, Miss Moneypenny. In this case, however, you've done the right thing. Now go home your-self and thank you for coming in early.' He almost smiled – the first time in months that I'd even seen a hint of one. This news came not a minute too soon for the Old Man.

I got home and had a long bath. I wondered where R was and what he is up to. Will either of us ever truly be able to escape the blood and the adventure?

Sunday, 8th December

Thank God one of them is all right. I was in the Office this morning, as M had stayed in town for the weekend to monitor the situation in Jamaica, when 009 walked in, looking bedraggled but otherwise well. He went straight in to see M and Bill and, when he came out, he gave me a hug and said he was going on leave for a week and would I please come with him? When I laughed, he affected a look of hurt.

'You'll be missing out, Penny. Thought I'd go to the Bahamas for a spot of sun and swimming. You know the kind of thing – luxury hotel, white beaches, cocktails at sundown . . .'

'You're as bad as James,' I told him. 'Anyone would think you'd been reading the same book of chat-up lines. Now go away and turn those blue eyes on some gullible young thing.'

I was still smiling when Bill materialised at the door. 'He's a brave lad,' he said. 'Had a helluva trip out. First made his way to Berlin, where he was nearly caught trying to go through some new tunnel under the Wall. Got away in the nick of time. Seems like they've redoubled security on the checkpoints and no one's getting through in cars. So then he had to trek back across the whole country, on foot, in the back of lorries, by train when he could, to some Black Sea port where he managed to stow away on a series of cargo ships, ending up in Istanbul. Caught the first plane out yesterday evening. Looks in surprisingly good shape considering. Even the Old Man was impressed. Encouraging news, by the way, from Kingston. Sounds as if James is going to pull through. He's not out of the woods yet, but his vital signs have stabilised and the doctors say that, barring unexpected complications, he should regain consciousness in the next couple of days and make a full recovery.'

I will be able to sleep tonight.

Tuesday, 10th December

R is dead. I feel numb, furious, distraught, lost. I don't know what I'm doing or how to control my grief. I'm writing this almost as a way of holding myself together, and also to force myself to accept it has happened. Helena is next door, packing my things. R is dead. I don't want to believe it, but it's true – horribly, terribly, undeniably.

Yesterday morning, as I was getting ready for work, my doorbell rang. I opened it to find Bill. He took my hand and led me to the sofa. I knew it must be something bad, but it still hit like a thunderbolt. R was shot and killed late last night in East Berlin. He had been living there, under deep cover, since he left London, Bill told me. He had established good contacts in the Stasi and was trusted by them. He had just returned from a trip to Moscow, where he had positively identified Boris as Vladimir Ilyich Grushenko, stepson of Aleksandr Nikolayevich Shelepin, the former Chairman of the KGB. 'He'd found proof that he was the same man as James's "Colonel Boris" who had briefed him before his attempt on M's life,' Bill said. 'This Boris was also behind the scare tactics used against you and Hamilton in Dorset. Hamilton was certainly a target. Boris has risen to an important position as a result of his connections, but he's apparently unpopular within the KGB and regarded as a loose cannon. There's been talk of a drink problem.

'In his last report, Hamilton said that he'd learnt of a dossier being prepared by Boris's detractors, listing his numerous contraventions of discipline and operational failures. Through his contacts, Hamilton had been able to influence the content of the dossier. He was confident that Boris was close to being stripped of his position and thus his passport. He would no longer have been a threat.'

As I sat there, Bill's words seemed to flow over me. I tried hard to conjure up R's face, but all I could see was a single trail of footprints on a beautiful white beach in North Uist. I got up and walked over to my bookcase and removed the Spanish phrase book into which I had tucked my only photograph of him. I looked at us standing arm in arm in front of the Sagrada Familia, smiling at each other. The picture had been taken by a passing tourist, three days after we met, when I thought he was an architect and he believed I worked for the Foreign Office. So much has happened since then. What havoc did I wreak on this poor man's life? He wouldn't be dead if it wasn't for me. Boris came into my life, not R's. R only became involved when he tried to help me. Now, as a direct result of that, he's gone. I don't know what to do or feel. Guilt, fear, loss – a potent cocktail of them all is bubbling inside me as I try to stem my tears and the racking, painful absence of R in the future.

Dear, dear Bill stopped talking and looked at me with his kind eyes. He took my hand and squeezed it. 'I took the liberty of contacting your sister before I came here,' he said. 'She's on her way. Please take as much time as you need. M sends his commiserations. He says on no account are you to hurry back to the Office.'

I turned to look at Bill. 'What else can I do? What else is there for me? I have no other life.'

He took me in his arms and held me tight, stroking my hair. The doorbell rang. As soon as Helena came in, I started to weep. I think Bill must have left soon after. I cried for most of the day and Helena sat with me all the time. It was the first she'd heard of R. I never met his parents, or his sister. I don't think they even knew of my existence. We had hoped for some sort of future together, but now he's gone it's as if we had no past. At dusk, I was overcome with a feeling of desperate exhaustion. Helena gave me a cup of warm milk and put me to bed.

I woke at midnight and she was there on the bed beside me, wrapped in a quilt. My dear sister. As I was looking at her, she opened her eyes. 'Will you come with me to Kenya?' I asked.

'Of course. When?'

'Tomorrow – I mean today.'

She sat up.

'I'm serious,' I told her. 'I can't go to the funeral, meet his family, try to explain who I was and what he meant to me. What we had was private and I can mourn him privately. I need to go home. Please come with me.'

She nodded and said she'd call Lionel in the morning to come down with her passport.

He arrived before lunch. Our plane leaves this evening. I know I am running away, but it's the only way. I'm probably subconsciously searching for Ma and my lost innocence. I also know she's not going to be there, but at last I don't fear the memories. I just want to be under those African skies and to be able to grieve for R in a place that has nothing to do with him.

Wednesday, 11th – Sunday, 22nd December

This magical, beautiful, cruel continent. I feel myself surrendering to its siren call. Just being here has made my senses tingle. On the plane, Helena fell asleep holding my hand, and when we landed and the doors opened to let in that sweet and sour smell of heat and the tropics, I almost burst into tears – though this time they would have been tears of relief. I've missed it so much. I didn't realise. Why has it taken us so long to return?

Daisy was waiting at the airport to meet us, a decade and three children older, but still slim as a whippet and crackling with energy. 'I've got a surprise for you in the Land Rover,' she said, shepherding the older child in front of her, with the younger two clinging to each hip. I was too busy looking around me, at the flags and the bunting, strung everywhere in advance of the extended independence celebrations, to wonder what it was. Then, when we reached the car, my heart somersaulted. There, in the open back, was Moses, our old head syce. I'd known him for longer than I can remember. He looked after our horses and, after Pa went, took me for long rides into the bush. He'd been a father to me for longer than my real one.

He looked much older now, with opaque rheumy eyes which stared straight past us with no flicker of recognition. It was only when I went close up to him and said hello that a slow smile cracked his gloriously familiar face. 'Miss Jane, Miss Helena, karibu,' he said, standing formally in the back of the open pick-up. I jumped up and gave him a hug, which he didn't return, remaining stiff and, I imagine, embarrassed. Had he not had such inky skin, I'm sure I would have seen him blush. 'Mzé, I can't tell you how good it is to be home, especially now, with Uhuru.'* And it was home, I realised suddenly. A past home, maybe, but, despite the pomp and ceremony and recently planted rhododendron bushes, still wonderfully, recognisably home.

Daisy and Pieter, our old classmate and her childhood sweetheart – now husband – have taken over her parents' farm, near Karen. It was just as I had remembered in every detail, except for the new corrugated-iron roof, shining silver in the sunlight. Dogs were dozing on the porch, the bougainvillaea swarming over the fence and the song of small birds all around us. 'It's wonderful to be here,' I said. 'I can't tell you. I've been through hell, but this is just the antidote.' She smiled and led me into the garden. There was a rustling in the bushes and suddenly a warthog burst out and started trotting across the lawn towards us, tail held high. I turned to Daisy in astonishment. 'It's not . . . ?'

'No, sadly Winnie died, but the next best thing, her daughter, Clemmie.'

'I can't believe you've got her. Daisy, you are wonderful.'

---

* 'Freedom' in Kiswahili.

'We've got Tsarvo too. She's a bit old and stiff now and we pensioned her off years ago, but she survived the droughts and it appears was determined to see you again.'

After a joyful reunion with my old pony, and breakfast of fresh mangoes and pawpaws and bacon and eggs, I collapsed between cool white sheets for a couple of hours of rest.

That evening, it seemed as if the whole of Nairobi – black Nairobi, at least – was out in the streets, lining the roads to the airport and stadium. We saw Prince Philip being driven in the old Embassy Rolls, and waved and cheered with the crowds. At midnight, as the new yellow and green and black flag of the independent country of Kenya was raised and we sang the new national anthem, I felt lumps of pride and joy rise in my mouth, tinged with nostalgia. I wished Ma could have been there to see it. She would have been dancing and ululating with the Kenyan mamas.

Daisy seemed to be enjoying it as much as we were, but Pieter had stayed firmly at home, insisting he needed an early night as he had a full day's harvesting ahead of him. 'He's not so keen on the whole thing,' Daisy confided later. 'Along with most of our folk, he sees it as a one-way track to rack and ruin. He's probably right, but then again, as I've said to him, it's their turn now and surely they have the right to ruin their own country? He doesn't see it like that. Nor, I'm sad to say, do most of our friends. A lot of them have already jumped ship.'

That didn't surprise me. Daisy and I were always the only two msungus at the meetings of the student liberation group at university. We had such dreams then, of helping the country towards an independent future. Look at us now – Daisy a hard-working farmer's wife living in the house she was born in, and me a secretary in London. Hardly what we'd planned. Then again, Kenya made it to this point without our help.

After three days of rest and recuperation and long lunches with old friends who hadn't emigrated or disappeared up-country to escape the week-long marathon of Uhuru parties, Helena and I borrowed Daisy's Land Rover and drove along the dusty roads to our old farm. I was anxious to see as much of the country as I could. Somehow, as long as we were moving, I didn't dwell on R, though every corner, every familiar tree and kopje, was suffused with memories of Ma and Pa. It was almost as though they came alive here, where they belonged, while R was like a mirage, an optical illusion that melted into the dust whenever I tried to conjure his face.

It was wonderful having Helena there, beside me, sometimes talking for hours, sometimes sitting silently with our thoughts and memories. Visiting the farm was profoundly moving. The land was so familiar – the forest where we'd hunted monkeys, the rich red soil which turned to glue when the rains came, the lake where I'd sit and read for hours. Every place was peppered with stories of our childhood, but the new owners were away and none of our staff remained and it seemed, to me anyway, to have lost its soul. We didn't stay long, but headed north, towards Nanyuki and the cool foothills of Mount Kenya.

There had been no reply from Miles Pitman by the time we left London, but I remembered his PO box number and harboured great hopes of tracking him down. In the close-knit world of farmer-settlers, everyone knows everyone. We were staying with old friends of Ma and Pa's, on a beautiful ranch a couple of hours east of Nanyuki, where we'd stayed many times in our childhood. Their daughter had been Helena's greatest friend and now lived in another cottage on the farm with her husband, another childhood friend, and their children. As we had lunch with them the day after we arrived there, I couldn't help but reflect that, but for our parents' sudden deaths, this might have been our lot too. We would have lived each day amid the majesty and power of the African landscape. While our physical horizons would have been vast – there's nothing to touch a sunset out here, sitting on a hill watching the shadows creep across the unending miles of beauty before you – our mental horizons would have been stunted. The conversation has not changed in twenty years: the rains, the crops, the state of the roads and the natives. Politics in the outside world have no import here. Governments could change, spies defect and ministers resign and it would make no difference. I don't think I could live like that, not now, certainly not for ever. This trip has made me realise, though, that I need it from time to time, to remind me who I am and what I can withstand. Every day that I'm here, I feel stronger.

One evening, while Helena was out riding, I asked our hosts whether they knew Miles Pitman. Of course they did – known him all their lives. He'd returned after the war and bought a small farm on land adjoining theirs, just an hour's drive away. Good man, bit of a loner – his wife had bolted and nowadays he rarely left his farm. He'd be glad of a visit, they said.

The next morning, I got up at dawn and, leaving a message for Helena, drove over the escarpment towards Pitman's farm. It was a perfect African morning and, as I passed the waterhole, a family of elephants loped across the road in front of me, returning from their morning drink. I wished, for the thousandth time, that I had included Helena in my search for Pa. In the beginning, my expectations were so low that I didn't want to give her false hope. Then, when details started to emerge about his traumatic adventures, I tried to save her from anguish. Now, though, I would have loved it if she could have sat beside me on this miraculous drive. I pressed on, my stomach knotted in anticipation.

I soon found his house, a low brick cottage with a tin roof painted green. The lawn was neatly tended and there were frangipani bushes along the drive. The door opened before my knock: it is impossible to surprise someone in Africa – a plume of dust heralds your arrival from miles away. A small man was standing there, spry in khaki shorts, long socks and a well-pressed shirt fraying at the collar. 'I can guess who you are,' he said, taking my hand into his. 'You're the image of your father. Come in, please.' If he was surprised to see me, he showed no sign of it.

He didn't waste time with small talk either, just poured me a cup of coffee from the saucepan bubbling on the old iron stove, and began to speak. 'I received your letter only a couple of days ago,' he said. 'I've already started my reply.' He gestured at a small escritoire, standing in front of a pair of windows overlooking a dam. 'You can take it with you, but far better to talk in person.' He crinkled up his eyes and looked me up and down, like a dealer apprais- ing a horse, before a smile finally dawned on his wea- thered face. 'I've always wanted to meet you, and Helena too,' he said.

He led me on to the veranda, from where I could see Mount Kenya in the distance, its twin peaks etched into the clear morning sky. 'Look at that,' he said. 'Isn't it magnificent? Hugh and I were bound together by our love for this country. We got along from the first time we met, when the operation was still in the planning stage. You know about Ruthless?'

I told him as much as I'd learnt – that he and Pa had been taken on a German minesweeper after crashing their plane into the Channel. The other members of their team, Patrick Derring-Jones and Peter Smithers, had managed to escape. Pa was never seen again.

Miles Pitman gave me a sad smile. 'Not in England, perhaps. I spent the next five years with him, though, give or take a day or two. I owe him my life ten times over. When things got really bad, he would always pick me up and tell me that it could only get better. Your father was an incorrigible optimist.

'We had a rough time of it after we were taken in the Channel. We were all dressed as Germans, of course, which meant they could treat us as spies and shoot us on sight. That poor marine who was with us, he hit the water pretty sharpish with a hole in his chest. We knew we couldn't muck about, but Hugh, with his perfect German and his charm, managed to talk our way out of the executioner's sights and into a Polish Ilag – that's a camp for civilians. It wasn't as good as an Oflag; we weren't covered by the Geneva Convention and had to work and had no contact with outside. We were the only Brits there – no way of getting a message home. Hugh wasn't going to stand for that. He found the weakest spot in the defences and started to tunnel. Both of us were at it, every night for seven months. It worked, though – we got out and started running. Made it to Warsaw, where we were lucky enough to be found by a wonderful Scotswoman, Mrs M, the wife of one of the leaders of the Polish resistance. She looked after us for months. We were both in a bad state. Hugh had contracted pneumonia – the first of several bouts – and I also had chest problems. She fed us and got us back on our feet, and as soon as we were fit, we slipped out of the city, heading towards Bulgaria.

'We might have made it, but for one sharp-eyed guard at the border. He spotted something he didn't like in our papers – forged of course – and the next thing we knew, we were on a train headed for Colditz. This was January 1944. There was a big influx of British and American officers. Our names and ranks were taken. Hugh insisted on sticking to his pseudonym, as we had been instructed to over three years before, at the outset of Ruthless. It was a brave decision: the War Office had no record of any Hugh Sterling, they had never been initiated into Ruthless and had no idea of the pseudonyms of the participating officers. That is why no one knew Hugh was alive.

'There's not much I can tell you about Colditz that you won't have learnt from the books. It was cold most of the time and your father was in and out of the sick ward. It was cramped and grey and oppressive. We did our best to entertain each other, but time hung heavy. You can't imagine what a succession of days with nothing to do except wait for the next *Appell* and dream about home and a good meal does for one's spirit. That is why so many minds turned to escape. It was all that kept us from madness.'

'Roddy Parks told me that Pa escaped,' I said.

'Damn fool thing that was to do, too,' said Pitman. 'I told him so at the time, but he was desperate to get out and to let you know, somehow, that he was still alive. He wouldn't listen to us. He could be a stubborn old boy.'

I smiled, and nodded. My father's reputation for perseverance was legendary.

'We'd almost made it once before, he and I. Jumped out of an upstairs window during the changing of the guard and made a dash through the wire at the edge of the grounds and into town. We got as far as the Dutch border before we were caught. I'm afraid I gave the game away – I'd spent so much time underground tunnelling that my face was unnaturally white and my German wasn't up to much either. Hugh could pass for a native. Anyway, at the beginning of '45, we were all busy building that glider in the attic. It gave us something to do, while we were waiting for the Yanks. He was helping, but he had another plan of his own.

'He had devised a daring escape route. While we were rehearsing in the theatre, he got out through the kitchen and hid in the suspension of the bread delivery van. I was the only one he had told about it – there were informers, we suspected, even within our ranks. He said he was heading for the Protectorate [Czechoslovakia]. His escape remained undetected. For the next *Appell*, I organised one of the ghosts to take his place. He continued to do so until the day the Yanks came. Every day, I waited for Hugh to be brought back and, when he wasn't, my hopes grew for his safe journey home. I was convinced that when I got out, he would be there to greet me.'

His voice was breaking with emotion. He looked towards the mountain for a minute and, when he turned to me again, the resolve was back in his face. 'Hugh spoke about you all the time, my dear. I want you to know that. I am so sorry. When I came back here after the war, I meant to contact you, but it was a struggle getting the farm started. Then Connie left and, by the time I'd sorted things out, your mother had died and you and your sister were gone. I suppose I was waiting – waiting for the possibility of your father's return. I'd always hoped and prayed he'd be back. Hugh was a strong, clever man. I couldn't believe he wouldn't be able to get out. I've waited for his return every day,' he said. 'Perhaps it was you I was waiting for?'

His eyes grew misty as he fell into silence. I wished I could comfort him. I took one of his work-hardened hands in mine and we sat there, gazing out over the peerless view, our thoughts joined in a brave and frightened man running for his life in a strange and hostile country. I had, I realised, come to the end of the line. The likelihood of being able to follow his tracks any further was minimal. I needed to face up to the reality that Pa was lost.

Wednesday, 25th December, Christmas Day

Home again. Since receiving M's cable, typically terse – PROMONEYPENNY IMPERATIVE YOU RETURN SOONEST SIGNED MAILEDFIST – I have been involved in a constant flurry of logistics. At first, we were told the flight back to London was full. After an appeal via what is now the Consulate, they found one seat. Helena urged me to take it – saying she would be happy to spend another night in

Nairobi. I had a brief fantasy of packing her on to the plane and walking out into the bush with a goat's bladder of water and a small hunting-rifle and disappearing for ever – the thought of returning to London and the reality of life without R was too horrible to contemplate – but an emergency summons by M is not to be ignored. I persuaded Helena to bring her bags to the airport just in case, and in the event, after using my eyelashes and best Swahili on the newly promoted BOAC duty manager, another spare seat miraculously emerged.

Helena fell asleep straight away, with her head on my shoulder, but it was never going to be a possibility for me. Too much was churning around in my head: what Miles Pitman had told me, what M was going to tell me, what I wish I had told R. I wish I had been straight with him from the beginning – told him about the Office and worked it out together. Of course I can't think about it rationally now, with mists of what might have been obscuring what was. Perhaps if we had talked about it to each other and examined what our work meant to us, instead of each grasping on to it as an emergency lifebelt, then maybe we would have found a path to a future together? It is too late now and regret is a selfish, destructive emotion, but I can't banish the 'what ifs' from my mind.

Kenya was wonderfully cathartic. As the sun shone, I felt strength and resolve seep into my bones. Lying on the dry grass, looking up to the cloudless sky and listening to the symphony of birdsong, I felt, for a time, perfectly content. I was back in a world at once familiar, yet full of the excitement of the unknown, and I felt free. I resolved to look to the future with optimism and without fear, to carpe the diem and make the most of it – laugh when I can and love if I can and, if a man like R never enters my life again, to thank the stars for my friends and colleagues and for my wonderful sister.

Spending that time with Helena was a privilege and a pleasure more than I can say. She is dear and funny and sensitive, listening without complaint as I gabbled on and on about R and my now-useless regrets. Lionel will be the most blessed of husbands. I still wish I had told her about meeting Pitman, but, despite that, I feel closer to her than I have in years – certainly since she moved to Cambridge and met Lionel. That reaffirming of our sisterhood, particularly in the face of another bereavement, was a gift for me more valuable than any jewels. I hope she feels the same.

A car was waiting for me at Heathrow. We said an affectionate goodbye, before I was driven the short distance to Quarterdeck.* Hammond showed me to the library, just as he had a year ago, when M dropped the thunderbolt that James had disappeared in Japan. Bill was waiting, standing by the window looking out to the forest. As the door opened, he turned and then rushed across to give me a warm embrace.

'Can't tell you how much I've missed you, Penny. We all have. The Old Man especially. We had a job to find you,' he chuckled. 'Had half the new Kenyan government and all their game trackers working on it. Still, it seems to have worked. You're here now and you look well.'

I thanked him and wished I could return the compliment. While I was delighted to see him, his face was pale

---

* M's country house, a pretty Regency manor on the edge of Windsor Forest.

and his eyes tired. It dawned on me that I hadn't thought of the Office at all while I was away and that I had no idea what had happened. It is a peculiar parallel universe we inhabit, where the dramas of the world are enacted behind a screen of security. On the blind side of this screen, where the vast majority live, nuclear destruction could have been threatened and averted, lives lost and saved, coups thwarted, secrets traded, without a hint of it seeping into the wider consciousness – or indeed mine, half the world away in Kenya. It was a strange thought.

I asked Bill what the meeting was about, but he just raised his eyebrows and told me to wait for M. When he emerged through the door, dressed as usual in a suit and spotted bow tie, and went to stand, ramrod straight, with his back to the fire, I could only just suppress a smile. In the space of a day and a night, I had travelled from the Kenyan bush to this bastion of English masculinity in the grounds of Windsor Castle. All without a bath.

M dispensed with the formalities, instead brandishing an envelope. It was addressed to Helena in Cambridge and had a Russian postmark. 'From Mrs Marmalade,' M announced, before I could wonder how he had come by it. He passed it across to me. The envelope had been opened already. I reached inside and pulled out a card. There was a picture on the front of St Basil's Cathedral. I turned it over to read the back. 'Moscow cold and snowy. I hope your sister is well. Wish you were here. Love E.' I handed it back to M.

'She needs help,' I said. 'That was the signal. He doesn't want to leave and she can't persuade him to go.'

'We understood that much,' he replied, drily. 'So, are you prepared to go?'

My surprise must have shown. M was looking at me intently, as if trying to gauge my inner thoughts, while Bill assiduously switched his gaze to the window when I turned to him. 'Me?' I asked.

'It's you she's asking for,' said M. 'She trusts you. The question is, are you willing?'

'Of course, sir,' I said, almost without thinking.

Bill cleared his throat and I turned to see him glaring at M.

'Sir, with respect, I maintain that this is not a good idea. Miss Moneypenny is known to the KGB. For God's sake, they tried to recruit her last year and she shot one of their officers,' he burst out, in a rare exhibition of emotion. 'She's probably on their hit list. Is it worth the risk for the minor chance that Philby might be persuaded to come back to London, where he knows damn well he will be reviled and vilified? On top of all this, she has suffered a huge shock recently . . .'

'What relevance is that?' I asked, suddenly riled by Bill's insistence on treating me like a fragile flower. 'Sir, if you think I should go, I will have no hesitation in doing so.'

M walked across to the window. 'We gave Mrs Philby our assurance that we would help. We cannot go back on that. As to whether Miss Moneypenny herself goes – that is up to her. I agree that it will cause additional risk, but we should be able to offset most of that with a decent legend. The Centre won't be expecting her, which is in her favour, and we can easily disguise her absence from the office, as long as this is kept a top-secret operation, strictly NTK [Need To Know]. I'm not prepared to permit a single leak. On the benefit side, she has already established a relationship with Mrs Philby. How likely is it that anyone else could even gain access to Philby's wife, let alone gain her trust?' He looked at Bill. 'We need to get him back, if we possibly can. A woman is never going to be put under as much scrutiny. We should be able to get her into Moscow with little trouble. Is that not right?'

Bill nodded.

'Very well, Miss Moneypenny, as I have said before, if we can manufacture the appropriate cover for you, are you prepared to go?'

'Yes, sir.'

On the way back in the car, Bill tried to remonstrate with me, but all I could think of was that I would be getting away again – away from the lingering memory of R and the demons of guilt that visit me in the night. 'I'm going, Bill,' I told him, as the car turned into Ennismore Gardens. 'I'm going for Eleanor. Now it's up to you to ensure that I'll be safe out there.'

It's late now and I haven't slept for two nights and I can't imagine how I will sleep now. My brain is turning at such speed that I fear it will hit a corner and career out of control. It's Christmas night and I've got no tree and no presents. I realise that, for the first time in weeks, I'm alone.

Monday, 30th December

At last, a glimmer of good news in the morass of bad. James is almost back on his feet. The business with Scaramanga and the mobsters was sorted out between us and the

Cousins with the minimum of diplomatic manoeuvring – and scant observance of the strict truth, I understand. Felix Leiter kept his leg and left Jamaica a week ago, after a solemn face-saving ceremony at James's bedside attended by the Commissioner of Police and a Supreme Court Judge, in which they were awarded the Jamaican Police Medal for 'gallant and meritorious services to the Independent State of Jamaica'. Another piece of lettuce to add to the Commander's pocket-wear.

This morning, M called me into his office and dictated an 'Eyes Only' herogram to James at the hospital. After acknowledging receipt of his report, he continued:

```
YOU HAVE DONE WELL AND EXECUTED AYE
DIFFICULT AND HAZARDOUS OPERATION TO MY
ENTIRE REPEAT ENTIRE SATISFACTION STOP
TRUST YOUR HEALTH UNIMPAIRED STOP WHEN
WILL YOU BE REPORTING FOR FURTHER DUTY
QUERY
```

As I took down his words, I couldn't suppress a smile. The olive-branch had been offered, with no conditions attached. James was back in the game. M continued:

```
IN VIEW OF THE OUTSTANDING NATURE OF THE
SERVICES REFERRED TO ABOVE AND THEIR
ASSISTANCE TO THE ALLIED CAUSE COMMA
WHICH IS PERHAPS MORE SIGNIFICANT THAN
YOU IMAGINE COMMA THE PRIME MINISTER
PROPOSES TO RECOMMEND TO HER MAJESTY
QUEEN ELIZABETH THE IMMEDIATE GRANT OF A
KNIGHTHOOD STOP THIS TO TAKE THE FORM OF
```

THE ADDITION OF A KATIE TO YOUR CHARLIE
MICHAEL GEORGE

I looked up. 'Sir, he's not going to take it,' I said. M looked at me. 'You think not? Write that he must cable his acceptance immediately and add something along the lines of "This award naturally has my support and entire approval and I send you my personal congratulations." Then we'll have to wait and see. If you care to have a wager on it, I'll put five shillings on him accepting. Chief of Staff, incidentally, agrees with you, but he's yet to put his money on the table. No doubt CS would be on for a punt too.'

It was a rare sign of humanity from M – evidence that, beneath the gruff exterior, he was truly delighted by James's return to the fold. I was happy to accept his bet, for the pleasure of seeing his face light up with a hint of mischief. This afternoon, we received a reply, which I deciphered on the Triple X before taking it in to M. I passed it to him without saying anything and watched as he read it to himself. The expression on his face didn't change until he got to the end and emitted a short, bark-like laugh. 'Scottish peasant, eh? One with Krug tastes.* Well,

---

* Bond's response read, 'REFERRING YOUR REFERENCE TO AYE HIGH HONOUR EYE BEG YOU PRESENT MY HUMBLE DUTY TO HER MAJESTY AND REQUEST THAT EYE BE PERMITTED COMMA IN ALL HUMILITY COMMA TO DECLINE THE SIGNAL FAVOUR THAT HER MAJESTY IS GRACIOUS ENOUGH TO PROPOSE TO CONFER UPON HER HUMBLE AND OBEDIENT SERVANT STOP EYE AM A SCOTTISH PEASANT AND WILL ALWAYS FEEL AT HOME BEING A SCOTTISH PEASANT AND EYE KNOW COMMA SIR COMMA THAT YOU WILL UNDERSTAND MY PREFERENCE AND THAT EYE CAN COUNT ON YOUR INDULGENCE ENDIT OHOHSEVEN'.

you and Bill obviously know 007 better than I do. Haven't got any cash on me at the moment. All right if I give it to you tomorrow?'

Of course I nodded my assent, even though I know, when dealing with an Office wager, tomorrow rarely comes.

1964

January

I had no idea that my aunt had been to Moscow. She never made any allusion to it, and I never asked. I don't know where my mother thought her sister had disappeared to at the beginning of 1964, in the months running up to her wedding, but presumably Aunt Jane had made up some story. I am sure my mother would have been terrified if she had known that her only living close family member had crossed the Iron Curtain.

From a post-Cold War vantage point, it is not easy to grasp the fear in which the Soviet Union was held in the 1960s. Just over a year before my aunt's visit to Moscow, the world had come to within a whisper of nuclear war, with Russian and American missiles pointed and primed against each other across the battlefield of Cuba. The Soviet Union and its satellites kept their activities strictly under guard, releasing to the West only the propaganda images they meant us to see. For most people over here, Moscow meant long lines of tanks and limitless armies of soldiers goose-stepping their way across Red Square. It meant Yuri Gagarin beating Alan Shepard into space, and Soviet women athletes powering to the top of the Olympic medals podium. It meant

Stalin and his purges, the labour camps and the vast acreage of frozen steppes.

In my aunt's time, employees of the intelligence services were prevented from visiting Communist countries, unless specifically ordered to do so. Yet the greater part of their work involved a minute dissection and analysis of the comings and goings in the Soviet sphere. The Eastern Bloc comprised the enemy, and was at all times assumed to be plotting to overthrow or undermine the democratic structures of the West. Like all her colleagues, Miss Moneypenny had read countless intelligence briefings relating to all aspects of Soviet life; she had listened to the stories of agents who had returned from undercover missions into Eastern Europe, and had attended the memorial services of her colleagues who had been caught there without permission. But nothing had prepared her for the possibility that she would one day have to cross that physical and ideological frontier herself.

Monday, 6th January

I was summoned this morning to see Head of Q in his basement burrow. I knocked on his door, which some prankster had covered with warning notices: 'DEPARTMENT OF DIRTY TRICKS!' 'BEWARE, UNEXPLODED BOMBS!' 'SHOCK HORROR – HIGH VOLTAGE FENCING!' 'QUIET, BOFFIN AT PLAY!' Very Q Branch humour.

'Enter, good doctor,' called a voice. Puzzled, I stuck my head round the door. 'No, it's Miss Moneypenny. If it's a bad time, I can come back.'

Head of Q chuckled. 'Miss Moneypenny you were, but now you are Dr d'Arcy, scholar of Byzantine art, spinster, aged thirty-five. Interests: religious art, Marxism, Persian cats and younger men. How does that sound?'

'I hate cats,' I said. 'If it has to be an animal, how about chinchillas or Shetland ponies or something less snooty than Persian cats?'

Head of Q chuckled. He's always been one of my favourite people here – his air of distracted intelligence masks great kindness and a childlike sense of humour. He goes through agonies whenever an agent is injured – or worse. I think, more than almost anyone, he was devastated when 007 disappeared and, when he did his Lazarus trick, Dr Desmond [McCarthy] was foremost in promoting a spirit of forgiveness.

He gestured for me to sit down, then reached into his filing-cabinet and extracted a file. 'This hasn't been easy, you know. We've been working under extreme time pressure and I'm not used to being kept in the dark about a mission. However, if M and Bill say this is how it has to be, then who am I to pry?' He looked at me, expectantly, but apart from a smile, I kept my counsel.

'Well, we'd better get on then. There's a lot to get through. M wants you off inside two weeks, which is cutting it a bit fine. We've got to get this legend established, equip you and find a route into Redland. None of that's easy. The Planners are handling your entry, but the rest is up to me.

'The main challenge has been to find you a cover that fits and is plausible enough to get you into the sphere and keep you there. For Moscow, we can't just issue you with a new passport, give you a Universal Exports* business-card and send you on your way. The Reds are too damn suspicious for that and I'm sure they've known about UE for years. Over-staffed too – they check out everyone and everything. No, we agreed it would be best if you assumed the character of a real person, a known sympathiser. Not many of those on our files – certainly few your age and general appearance, more's the pity.' He gave another of his high-pitched giggles. 'However, I've managed to fish out a beauty for you. Dr Rose d'Arcy, graduate of the University of London and the Courtauld Institute. Wrote some rather inflammatory articles linking art to Marxism for the *Spectator* and the *Left Review*, got herself noticed by our chums over there, possibly even recruited – though I doubt it somehow: too bombastic – and, after a warning word in her ear by our people, took flight in the middle of the night to settle in East Berlin. That was seven years ago, and would have all been very well, but for the fact that, in a fit of misguided idealism, she threw away her British passport. Now her mother's ill and she wants to get back over the border to see her. East Germans won't let her. They fear, probably with good reason, that she'll do a bunk and broadcast to the world how dreadful it is to live in a poor and dismal Communist state, where nothing works and everyone is being watched by some-one else.

'By one of those great strokes of fortune, she mentioned her desire to see her Ma to one of our people over there – and there aren't many of us, so it was a piece of luck

---

* The cover organisation used for years by British secret-service agents working abroad.

indeed. He duly reported back and, bingo, we've got her in our pocket.' He beamed at me.

'So,' I said slowly, 'you've got to spirit her out somehow and slip me into her place.' Inside, I was shaken by the mention of East Berlin. R had been killed there. To me, it seemed a city of evil. Head of Q hadn't noticed my unease. He was fiddling with some unidentifiable gadget piece as he continued.

'Clever girl. It's not going to be an easy operation. They can't know she's gone, but if we do the change-over almost simultaneously, no one should be the wiser, particularly if you leave the city immediately. We're setting up this end. One of ours has gone up to Scotland to meet Ma d'Arcy – damn silly name: sounds like a Gyppo fortune-teller, if you ask me – and she's on board. Given us photographs and all sorts of background on her darling Commie daughter. Look here, not bad for a Red, is she?'

He handed me a photograph. The face of a young woman stared at me with direct brown eyes, knitted brows and a look of determination on her face. She had high cheekbones and rich chestnut, tangled hair and was strangely beautiful. Had R met her, I couldn't help wondering, before dismissing the thought as absurd.

'Yes, it's an old photograph. If we give your locks a bit of a tint, drag you through a hedge backwards and wipe the smile off your face, it won't be a bad likeness. Good-looking girl. We should be receiving some more recent photographs sometime soon. Our man in East Berlin is busy making her acquaintance and, by all accounts, she's not doing much resisting.' He chuckled again.

'Agent 734. Handsome son of a gun. Run along now and study the file. Buzz me if you've got any questions. We'll test you next week, when you come down to be equipped. By then, hopefully, the Planners should have done their bit, the Doctor will be on board and you'll be ready to go. It's not easy, slipping into someone else's clothes. I do wish I knew what you're up to, dear girl. Please be careful.'

I gave him a hug and left. As I read the file this evening, it seemed at the same time more possible and yet more preposterous. Would I seriously be able to pull off being an art historian? I speak very little German, for a start, I've never been to Berlin and I have no desire to do so now, after what happened. I don't have a clue about religious art and I loathe cats. Then what happens when I get to Moscow? Since the plan was first mooted, Boris's face has kept slipping, unbidden, into my mind. I push it away, telling myself that Moscow is a huge place, that I'll be there under an assumed identity, that the chances of running into him are virtually zero, but that doesn't banish the fears. In Berlin, will I be visited by R's ghost? I suppose I will have to trust M and Head of Q and Bill. Anyway, what's the worst that could happen?

Thursday, 16th January

The last ten days have been extraordinary. I wake up thinking about my alter ego and, after a day studying her file, looking at photographs, reading her school reports, childhood diaries, letters home, as well as her more recent published work, I go to bed rolling her name around on my tongue. I eat and sleep Rose d'Arcy. Thanks to the Q Section barber, I now have her hair, rather like simulated unkemptness. I look in the mirror and feel like my younger self, unfettered by responsibility and maturity. I have learnt an extraordinary amount about Byzantine art, more than I thought I wanted to know, and the more I learn, the more I appreciate it. When I get back, perhaps I'll treat myself to a trip to Istanbul? R and I often talked about going together. I still find cats faintly insidious, though, having borrowed Pamela's for the week, I can put up a good enough show, if tested.

I find it hard to believe I'm going. The mechanics of my entry to Moscow are from a childhood spy game rather than the real, dangerous world of Cold War espionage. The Planners assure me that getting across the Wall into the East will be a piece of cake; it's the reverse operation for my 'mirror', as Dr Desmond insists on calling her, that will prove more testing. The success of my penetration will hinge on her successful extraction. If it works, it will be a straight exchange – the German-speaking academic for the English secretary.

734 has apparently made excellent headway. Dr d'Arcy is co-operating fully with the plan to get her out, though she's no idea that I'm coming back in her place. Under his instructions, she has booked a train ticket to Moscow and a hotel room when she gets there. She obtained the relevant visa 'for artistic research' with little trouble, 734 reported. Reading between the lines, she has fallen under the spell of his youthful physique. Once in the West, she'll be flown directly back to Brize

Norton and, from there, taken by helicopter to her mother's home near Inverness. I've no idea if – and, if so, how – she is planning to return. I, on the other hand, most certainly plan to.

I can't help but feel excited about it, though I still dread Berlin. This total immersion in the mission has been a partial distraction from the absence of R, though I still think about him constantly. I'm looking forward to seeing Eleanor again, assuming I can make contact. I will: M has told me that there is no room for doubts. I relish the thought of adventure, of starting again in a strange place, as a different person. Most of all, I suppose, I'm looking forward to feeling useful.

That is not to say that I have no fears. Some nights, as I lie in bed, I start shaking uncontrollably; I dread to think what my neighbours imagine I'm doing.

In exactly two days, I will be on my way across the Berlin Wall, travelling against all sensible traffic. Helena and Lionel came up last night, to say goodbye and pick up Rafiki; he'll enjoy the semi-rural break. They pointedly asked no questions about where I'm going, though I could see Helena aching with curiosity. She satisfied herself with a quip about my new 'hair un-dresser' before begging me to make sure I'm back for their wedding. I will be, I pray. Now I'm as ready as I can be. I have my hairbrush camera and invisible, heat-reactive ink. I have a long list of signal sites and fallback plans for evacuation, written in tiny writing and rolled up in cotton wool in my sponge-bag.

All I need is rest.

Saturday, 18th January

The car arrives in half an hour to take me to the airport. I hardly slept last night. R's face kept trespassing in my dreams. Bill grabbed me as I left the Office and tried to persuade me not to go. He said he knew it was too late, that it would probably just increase my fears, but that he had to try. 'Jane, Jane, is there anything I can do to change your mind?' he pleaded.

I told him that M would call that sort of talk sedition and that it could cost him his job.

Bill looked suddenly sad. 'In the end, what's the job?' he asked. 'Set against everything else, it's just a great big game.' I was surprised: I had never before heard him utter even a word against the Office. Then he seemed to catch himself. He smiled and embraced me hard and then held me out in his arms and looked serious.

'Please promise me that you'll take care of yourself. No unwarranted risks, no rash bravado. You're more important than ten Philbys. I'm not going to let anything happen to you. Do you understand?'

I just nodded, but I'm not sure I did.

Monday, 20th January

There is no turning back. I'm on a train bound for Moscow, clad in the clothes and character of Rose d'Arcy. The events of the last two days hardly feel real; if it wasn't for the almost audible beating of my heart, beneath the layers of grey and brown wool, imbued with the scent of another woman, I would think I was in a dream.

193

I arrived in West Berlin on Saturday afternoon, just as dusk was settling on the city. I was met at the airport by an agent from Station WB, who introduced himself as Fred and drove me into the centre. At first glance, there was little to tell that this bustling, apparently affluent metropolis was essentially an island in the East. The roads were full of new cars, the broad avenues lined with shops, their lights blazing multi-hued in the approaching darkness. There was nothing to distinguish the people walking along the pavements from the streams of workers leaving offices in London, Paris or New York.

I commented on this to Fred, when he turned to look at me and said, 'Just wait for it – only a couple more minutes.' Before I could ask what 'it' was, we rounded a corner and there in front of us, topped with rolls of barbed wire and covered in graffiti, was the Wall. I don't know what I was expecting. I've seen it in so many pictures, but I suppose I still thought of it as somehow wall-like, with bricks and cement, not this hideous, monolithic concrete barrier, tall and smooth and forbidding. There was a small crowd of protesters on the Western side, holding banners and chanting. Several women were prostrated against the Wall, weeping. On the other side, I could just make out the drone and dust of huge bulldozers and wrecking-machines, bludgeoning down houses and apartment buildings.

'This is Bernauer Strasse,' Fred told me. 'For the first weeks and months after the Wall went up, people on the other side would leap out of second- and third-floor windows in an attempt to get here. The people on this side held out huge blankets and piles of mattresses to help them, but many were still killed. Now those buildings are being knocked down. This barrier, over-night, separated wives from husbands, mothers from their children. Apart from the fortunate few who made it over, they will slowly become strangers to each other, divided not only by the Wall, but by politics, ideology, a different way of living. Did you know, on the other side, there are no maps of the West? The city, for them, ends at the Wall; beyond, there's only blank paper. It's a potent symbol of life behind the Iron Curtain. Looking forward to your trip?'

I tried a half-smile, which withered before it reached my mouth. 'What time do I go?' I asked.

'We're planning on 1700 hours tomorrow, as long as we get the go-ahead from 734 on the other side. We've decided the easiest way is a straight swap. We take you over with the passport you're travelling on and get you an evening visitor's pass. We deliver you to a safe house to wait while the photographs are swapped, then she'll get your pass-port and an escort out, and you'll receive her documents, plus a bag of clothes and books. You will not meet. She will have no idea of your presence here. Does that sound good to you?'

I nodded, even though I knew the question was only a polite formality and the thought of losing my British passport filled me with disquiet. 'In the meantime, we've booked you into a nice guest-house just off the Kurfürstendamm, where you can get some rest. You can't bank on sleeping much tomorrow.' He must have read the look of doubt in my eyes. 'I've got something to help you tonight. A special present from Head of Q. Before that, though, you'll want to eat. There's a host of restaurants near your hotel, and if you want any company . . .' He let the offer hang in the air, until I thanked him and said I'd rather be on my own.

We drew up outside a tall building. He carried my small holdall into the lift cage, pushed the button for the third floor and held out an envelope. 'Well, I'll say cheerio then until tomorrow. A room is booked under your name. There's some cash in here, along with the sleeping-draught and my contact numbers. Please do not hesitate to call me at any time, day or night. I'll report your safe arrival to HQ and, if I don't hear from you before then, I'll be back here to meet you at 1400 hours tomorrow to run through the procedure once more. In the meantime, please try to rest.' He shook my hand, then clanked shut the lift door and sent me on my way.

With the aid of a grain of Seconal, I slept better than I have for months. It was already light when I woke and after a cold shower my head felt miraculously clear. I ate breakfast, picked up a map from the front desk and set out for a bracing walk. I had intended to stay fairly close to the hotel, but I found myself being pulled back towards the Wall. It was a magnetic compulsion I couldn't fight, as if I was being drawn to the last place where R was alive. I jumped in a taxi and asked to be taken to the Tiergarten, near the Reichstag. As we drove up the central avenue, I could see it ahead of me, masking all but the pelmet of the Brandenburg Gate. I got out and stood gazing at it once more, wondering at the demented logic that had split not only this city, but the world in two. This Wall is what the Office is all about, it drives our thoughts and our plans, and fuels our fears. I was about to cross it. Somewhere on the other side R had been killed. I realised I didn't know exactly where.

The afternoon briefing sent my heart shooting into my mouth, where it stayed as I was picked up in the car of an off-duty American army captain. 'Look like you're out for an evening of sightseeing,' he drawled. 'I come over often and they rarely check me, but if they do, I'll say you're my friend and as long as they don't take it into their tiny bureaucratic heads to check your identity somehow, it should be plain sailing.' We were driving up Friedrich-strasse. Ahead I could see American flags and two tanks flanking a boom. 'Checkpoint Charlie,' my companion announced. 'Busiest route from West to East. Kiss your ass goodbye!' I raised my eyebrows a fraction and tried to look in the mood for a party as, with a salute and a smile, we were waved straight through the American gate. We then drove across a bare gash of earth, possibly fifty yards wide – No Man's Land. Ahead, with the wall looming on either side, were the East German guards.

This time our reception was chilly, despite my companion's attempts at jocularity. The soldiers were sharply uniformed and accompanied by an officer in long boots and a greatcoat, who barked out a series of questions, his breath exploding in mushroom clouds of smoke in the cold night air. He poked his torch through the window at me for what seemed like an age, the beam caressing me up and down in an almost indecent fashion. Inside, my stomach was squirming as I battled to fix a smile on my face. He barked an order and, with a lazy salute, the American handed over my passport and a form I assumed to be a visitor's pass. These he studied with concentration, alternating glances between me and the photograph in the passport. Then the officer asked another question and my companion gave a quick retort, put his hand on my thigh and leant over to plant a kiss on my lips. The soldiers at the window burst into mirthless laughter. Even the officer smiled, gave a ghost of a wink and waved us through.

We sped off and it was only once we were well clear of the gates that the American drew the car to a stop and turned to me. 'Please accept my apologies, ma'am. Can't say it wasn't a pleasure, but still it was beyond the bounds of polite behaviour. That Stasi fellah was giving me the willies. I thought for a minute he was going to haul us out of the car and interrogate us. Fortunately I managed to defuse the situation.'

'What exactly did you say?' I asked.

'That, ma'am, I'd prefer you didn't know. We're through, which is the main thing. Now I'm just going to have to hold thumbs that he's off duty by my return trip. After the look he gave you, he's not likely to fall for a substitute. We're going to drive around a bit, stop here and there, as if I'm pointing out the sights, then, when I'm absolutely sure we're not being tailed, I'll deliver you to the safe house.'

'Dry-cleaning?' I asked.

'Spot on,' he replied.

An hour and a half later, I'd had opportunity enough to compare East with West. The gulf between them, represented by that monstrous Wall, could not have been more glaring. This side, there was no bustle and no bright lights – other than the powerful searchlights trained on the Wall and the barricades of wire and tank traps layered a quarter of a mile into the city. There was little traffic on the streets, and what there was belonged to the army. People seemed to trudge along the pavements, muffled in dark coats, hats pulled hard over their faces. When a tank trundled past, few raised their heads to look. There were no open shops, no restaurants, just the occasional dingy café or beer-hall. In less than two decades since the war's end, what was once a great and united city had divided into soot and diamonds. It was extraordinary that the two could coexist, so similar in formation, yet so far apart.

Eventually, we drew up outside a small bar on a quiet street on the outskirts of the city. My American had explained that it was owned by dissidents running a covert escape line to the West. 'I don't know how long it'll last before they're turned in,' he'd said. 'In this country, your neighbours and friends are all possible spies. However, we should be OK for tonight.' He escorted me through the bar and up the back stairs to a small room, with a bed in one corner, on which were laid out an assortment of shapeless garments – Rose d'Arcy's I assumed. He told me to change quickly out of my clothes, which he would deliver to my 'mirror' together with my doctored passport. Someone would be back for me in a couple of hours. 'Once I'm safely over the border with my charge, you'll be in the clear,' he said. 'Your guys are handling it from there.'

A kind-faced old German woman brought me a cup of tea and motioned that I should rest. I lay down on the narrow cot and closed my eyes. Sleep was never going to be an option. I still felt my heart beating overtime and my muscles were coiled with tension. Images flicked behind my eyes like a slide-show; fragments of imaginary conversations I would have as Rose d'Arcy crowded unbidden into my head. I willed myself to relax, but the next hours,

I knew, would be crucial. If they didn't manage to get my doppelganger out safely, my future hung in the balance. The plan was so tightly strung, it allowed for no deviation.

Eventually, I heard footsteps on the stairs, followed by a soft knock on my door. I leapt out of bed to open it a crack. On the other side, I saw a smiling young man. He was dressed like an East German, but his voice, when he asked for 'Dr d'Arcy', was as English as Assam tea. He came in and introduced himself as '734 – but you can call me Jem'. Then he looked me up and down, leant forward to ruffle my hair and stood back again and nodded. 'Not a bad likeness,' he pronounced. 'Not bad at all. Wouldn't fool her friends, but hopefully you won't bump into any of those where you're going. For the purposes of your trip, you tick all the right boxes. Just keep your mouth shut at all times. The good Dr d'Arcy speaks atrocious German, but at least she has the rudiments of a vocabulary.'

'Is she through all right?' I asked.

'Yep, just received the all-clear. I was worried myself for a while. She's quite a fire-cracker, liable to go off the deep end at the slightest provocation.' He smiled. 'Do her good to go home for a while and learn some manners. Now, I have your train tickets. It's a thirty-two-hour journey from here to Moscow, which includes a couple of hours' wait at the border while they re-gauge the carriage wheels for the Russian tracks. That's when you're most at risk from the border guards prowling up and down the train. However, your papers are in order, you've got a valid visa and, since your trip originated in the Bloc, you should be OK. Still, I'd pretend to be asleep just in case – it'll give you an excuse to grunt if they try to question you.'

Nothing he said was new to me. The Planners had briefed me thoroughly before I left, but I still listened with due attention. There was no room for mistakes.

Wednesday, 22nd January

I made it. The train journey passed without incident, or real sleep. My compartment was situated inconveniently over the brakes, which made a sharp rattling sound like a machine-gun discharging its load whenever we slowed down. I was lucky with the border: the East German check was perfunctory and when the Russian guard came in and barked some orders, my travelling companions produced their papers and I followed suit, my eyes half shut. The documents didn't seem to cause him any disquiet and he made no move to search my luggage or engage me in conversation, which I'd been dreading, despite all the precautions. I drank endless cups of weak Russian tea from the crone presiding over a steaming samovar at the end of the carriage, and bought some more bread and cold meat from the shifting cast of ladies who jumped on the train at the stops, and walked up and down the corridors selling their wares. I thought of James: it was less than a year ago that he'd been on a Russian train, still convinced he was a Japanese fisherman. So much has happened since then – to him and to me.

Eventually, as dawn was breaking, we started drawing into the city through the drab outskirts, where clusters of uniform buildings huddled beside hulking factories spewing smoke and steam into the dove-grey morning. As we slowed, I could make out small, box-shaped cars, their headlights glowing a dull yellow, scurrying along broad thoroughfares. People huddled into heavy greatcoats and fur hats tramped the snow-covered pavements. With a last steamy hoot, we pulled into Rizhski Station and I followed my companions on to the platform. Even though I was well prepared, with layers upon layers of wool and sheepskin, the cold was like a sharp slap to the face, biting into my nose and cheeks and searing up my nostrils. It was at the same time excruciating and invigorating and I silently thanked Rose d'Arcy for her long johns, huge scarf and gloves.

There were taxis waiting at the entrance to the station. I found a relatively cheery-looking man and handed him my piece of paper bearing an address written in Cyrillic script – Hotel Sovietsky, chosen by Q Branch for its discreet location, a few miles away from the city centre and conveniently close to the Philbys' apartment. 'It's a small hotel by their standards, built at the behest of Stalin in 1952,' Head of Q had told me, 'and used by him to put up visiting dignitaries from around the region. We thought it might be better to hide you in the glare of the spotlight, so to speak, rather than try to disguise you as a tourist. There's no danger of you bumping into anyone familiar. It's reasonably priced and comfortable enough.'

It is indeed, and more so. For a small hotel of only 100 rooms, it was built on a grand scale. The ceilings are magnificently high, there are large portraits of Stalin on every wall and the corridors smell of polish. After checking in, I walked up the marble staircase to my third-floor room. It was spacious and mercifully hot. Large windows looked over a small park, in which I could see barrel-shaped old women, small children strapped to their fronts with patterned scarves. To my left ran the busy Leningradsky Prospekt, the main route to Russia's old imperial capital, and in the distance, I could just see one of Stalin's legendary skyscrapers, the Seven Goddesses.

As day breaks on my second morning here, I feel strangely happy. Moscow is far from the grey behemoth of my imagination. Yes, it's huge and powerful, but it's also beautiful in parts and the people shyly courteous.

I caught the metro – in itself an artistic experience – down to Red Square. The sun caught the multicoloured domes of St Basil's Cathedral as I stood outside Lenin's mausoleum, gazing towards the river.

I spent the afternoon at the State Tretyakov Gallery, an extraordinary red-brick and white-enamel palace, jammed full of Russian paintings, from the earliest icons to the present day. It would, I surmised, have been Rose d'Arcy's first port of call. For a few days at least, I plan to do nothing that might give anyone who might be following me any reason for suspicion. All day, I fought the impulse to check my tail. I am, in effect I suppose, engaged in a marathon exercise of dry-cleaning.

Sunday, 26th January

My first clandestine contact, and I'm sure as I can be that I wasn't followed. I got up early, slipped into a church service near Red Square and stood among the chanting women. From there, I went into GUM, the state department store – a magnificent nineteenth-century stone edifice, marking the entire eastern edge of Red Square, with internal glass and steel galleried corridors lined by state-owned stores selling little, but attracting long queues. I looked in glass windows all the way, checking for a tail. I sat in a small café for a while, bought some paper from a stationer's, caught the metro back to the Tretyakov and sat in front of a particularly fetching icon, which I started sketching. Then I went to the loo and slipped out and jumped into a passing taxi. My rendezvous was the statue of Peter the Great, towering over the tip of the island in the river opposite Gorky Park. I was to look for a man wearing a navy striped scarf. I arrived in good time and tried to keep myself warm by stamping my feet while appearing to look interested in the monumental statue. It seemed like an age. I didn't want to check my watch, but after my cheeks started to singe in the cold, I got out my handkerchief and managed a quick glimpse. It was fifteen minutes past our appointed assignation. I found my pulse quickening. Following my instructions, I aborted and reverted to Plan B.

I walked quickly to the nearest metro station, trying to work through the implications of his no-show. At best, he wasn't sure he was 'clean' – as Head of Station S, he was sure to be under intense surveillance at all times – but what if he failed to make our next meeting? What if he'd been caught and compromised? After a few days of feeling free in Moscow, I felt the tension return. He was my life-line. Without him I was stranded in this vast and over-whelming city.

I emerged from the metro at Kiev Station and walked quickly north along the river to the Ukraine Hotel, one of the Seven Goddesses. As I approached, it loomed larger and more overwhelming – vast, splendid, a terrifying symbol of Stalin's appetite for power. Inside, it was mercifully warm. I unmuffled myself and sat down to drink a warming cup of tea in the first-floor bar. I was still fairly sure there was no one on my tail. Once feeling had returned to my fingers, I walked towards the lift and pressed the top button. Emerging at a small staircase, I climbed into a glass-sided pergola, its double doors leading out on to the viewing platform. Everything was exactly as it had been described to me. I was still a few minutes early, but the view on every side drew me back out into the bitter cold.

It was magnificent: the sky was a watery blue and the river frozen into silver stillness. I felt as if I could see the entire city – golden domes, steely skyscrapers and the steam from tall cooling-towers wafting across the rooftops. I was the only person there and, for a while, my worries evaporated as I walked around, drinking in the view. Suddenly, I felt a presence at my elbow. A man about my height, with a frost-tinged moustache, said softly, 'It's cold enough here to freeze cream.'

'As long as it's chocolate, I'm happy,' I replied, word perfect.

He smiled. 'Sorry about the no-show earlier. It took me longer than I expected to shake my shadow. Now, we haven't much time – they'll be looking for me. London will be delighted to hear of your safe arrival. I've had a handful of signals from M's Chief of Staff asking for news of "Seville" – damn funny code name if you ask me. He knew damn well that our meet was scheduled for today, but seemed anxious all the same.'

'You can report back that I'm well and smelling the orange blossom. Send him my love and tell him to stop fretting.'

'Will do. Next, I have to inform you that "Colonel Boris" is currently in Moscow, based at the Lubyanka, and you should steer clear and exercise extreme caution. We have a report placing him in East Berlin on December 9th.'

I felt my teeth clench and prickles of sweat spring up under my thick coat. It could have been no coincidence: somehow he was involved in R's death. The anger must have shown on my face.

'Are you all right?' my companion asked. I nodded.

'He has not, however, been spotted anywhere near Marmalade. Is that clear?' I nodded again.

'Over the past week, we've been led to assume that Marmalade is unwell, as he has not been accompanying Mrs Marmalade on her trips to the Central Post Office. The Planners regard that as your most likely meeting-point. She normally goes on a Wednesday and a Saturday around 11.00 hours. You are to arrive at 10.30 hours and request to open a PO box in your name. That will give you a reason to be there. If she turns up, you're to proceed according to your instructions. Is that clear?'

'Yes,' I replied. 'Thank you.'

'Very well. You know you are to contact me only in case of emergency or if you have something important to report. We'll be keeping an eye on the signal sites. You remember them?'

'They're etched on my brain,' I said.

'One final thing: CS's secretary wanted me to tell you that 007 was fighting fit and enjoying a good night's sleep in Jamaica, if that makes any sense?'

I couldn't suppress a quick grin at the thought of Mary fussing over the invalid. How long would he be able to take that?

'All that remains is to wish you all the best of British.' He flashed me a quick smile before slipping back through the doors and disappearing into the bowels of the hotel.

Wednesday, 29th January

I went to the Central Post Office, an unprepossessing utilitarian block at Chistye Prudy, north-west of Red Square, and duly opened a PO box in the name of Dr Rose d'Arcy. As a result of my lack of Russian, it took well over an hour to complete the formalities. I kept a surreptitious eye out for Eleanor, my heart beating a little faster each time the door swung open, but she never came. Eventually, when I could string out my business no longer, I left. I felt as if I'd been stood up on a hot date – I had been looking forward to seeing her more than I can say, not only for the sake of my mission, but, I'm forced to admit, for the company. I think of myself as reasonably brave, and better than most at solitude, but this is testing my limits. I have so much time alone with my thoughts and there is only a certain amount of energy I can devote to the mission. R keeps slipping uninvited into my dreams – and nightmares. The pain of missing him is unabated.

With the exception of my brief brush with Head of Station S, I haven't spoken English to anyone for over a week. What I would give to be able to pick up the phone and have a quick chat to Helena, or Bill. I've picked up a few words of Russian here and there and, with the aid of a chart translating the Cyrillic alphabet, am able to find my way around quite well now. But I've never felt so utterly foreign before and so stupid, unable to communicate in anything but the most basic form. I'm also constantly aware that I stand out as an alien. Despite my East German clothes, strangers stare at me wherever I go. Do I have a strange scent? Do I hold myself differently? I know my features are not typically Russian, but there is such a range of faces and forms in this vast land that I should be able to meld in as long as I don't try to say anything.

If I feel like this after a week, what must Eleanor feel after four months, with her Harrods coat and American gloss? Presumably she is watched wherever she goes, not only by strangers, but by the KGB. I look for her on every street corner, in the metro, in galleries or churches. I long to hear how she is. I wonder if she is expecting me? I wasn't given her address; all I know is that it's not far from my hotel.

I was heading back towards Red Square when I saw a metro station ahead. Even with my imperfect recognition of the Cyrillic alphabet, I could recognise the word 'Lubyanka'. I looked to my right, up to a vast grey and pale brick building covering the entire block. The windows were small and impenetrable. Was Boris at one of them, watching me, waiting to make his move? Was Greville Wynne, the British spy, incarcerated behind another? I felt the back of my throat constrict with instinctive fear, and half ran down the street. Boris still haunts my thoughts.

If she conforms to routine, Eleanor will be at the Post Office on Saturday. It seems a long time from now. What if she's ill? What if they've moved their box? I plan to go each day, just in case.

Friday, 31st January

Hallelujah! We've made contact. I was posting a letter this morning, when I heard the unmistakable tones of an American accent. My heart started beating wildly. Slowly, I steeled myself to turn around in a calm fashion and with a combination of relief and excitement saw her there, at the counter beside me, standing next to a plumpish, attractive woman in a fur coat.

I knew my lines, but all of a sudden I was scared, afraid that I would somehow fluff my part and blow the operation. I took a few deep breaths and walked along to where they stood. I waited until Eleanor looked around. 'I'm sorry,' I said, before the surprise could register on her face. 'I heard you speaking English and wondered if you could help me with something.' With an effort visible to me, but hopefully not to her companion, who was looking curiously on, Eleanor collected herself.

'Of course,' she said, 'whatever I can do.'

'I'm new to Moscow and I've lost my map. Could you possibly tell me the best route to the Tretyakov Gallery from here? I'm not used to approaching it from this direction.'

Eleanor glanced behind her, towards the door, and in my peripheral vision I could see a burly young man in a suit waiting there, looking at us – her security escort.

'I'd be happy to show you,' she said. 'It's one of my favourite places in Moscow. I go often.'

'I do too,' I told her. 'Most afternoons. I'm studying early Russian icons. Sorry, I should have introduced myself. My name's Rose d'Arcy.'

'Eleanor,' she replied, 'and this is Melinda,' she said gesturing at her friend. 'Rose needs directions to the

Tretyakov Gallery,' she added, somewhat unnecessarily. 'Come downstairs with me and I'll point you in the right direction.'

As we turned to leave the building, the young man followed, just within earshot. Eleanor gave me detailed directions and I thanked her. 'Perhaps we will bump into each other there someday?' I said.

'We're bound to,' she replied, with a ghost of a wink and then, after a quick glance to each side, she silently mouthed the word 'tomorrow'.

I didn't even feel the cold as I walked the few blocks to the gallery. Inside, I was singing. The waiting part is over.

February

The diaries were beginning to take over my life. I was so engrossed in my aunt's adventures that my day-to-day university activities felt increasingly like a chore. I resented every minute I spent away from them; her world seemed infinitely more exciting and important than mine. I decided to do something about it. At the end of the Michaelmas term, I requested – and was granted – a sabbatical. I had conceived a secret plan of my own: to travel to Russia in my aunt's footsteps, convincing myself that it was necessary in order to be able to check the details of what she had written, the geography of the city, the street and place names.

As soon as my sabbatical started, I moved up to London, leaving most of my belongings in storage in Cambridge. I'd been informed by the bursar that my rooms would be used by a visiting professor in my absence, and I had rented out the Grantchester cottage. I intended to base myself at the London flat of the wife of another colleague, who taught at University College London during the term and spent most weekends and holidays with her family in Cambridge.

In London, I buried myself in the National Archives and the British Library, reading everything I could find about Philby and the Cambridge spies. I started planning my trip to Russia. I was delighted to discover that the Sovietsky was still operating as a hotel, and that the Tretyakov Gallery was open for business.

It was as I was leaving for the library one morning that the letter from my department head arrived, informing me of my peremptory dismissal. I was shocked – by both the content of the letter and the tone in which it was written. Humiliation soon turned to rage. I'd always thought I was on fairly friendly terms with my boss; how could he have done this without giving me the benefit of rebuttal, or even a chance to explain? In the strictest terms it was true that I had contravened the Official Secrets Act, and it was therefore within their power to terminate my employment. But not like this. It was not as if I was threatening national security. Everything my aunt wrote of was more than four decades in the past.

I felt not only anger, but a sense of displacement. I was born in Cambridge, my father taught at the university for more than forty years. The city has always been a part of my life. I went to school and university there, and, despite numerous wanderings, have always been drawn back to the only home I've ever known. When my father died, it had seemed natural to move back into our old cottage and pick up where he left off. Now it felt as if I had been orphaned all over again.

My first instinct was to get on the first train from King's Cross and go and plead my case. I hadn't heard from Trinity, which presumably meant that I was still a member of College. Perhaps they would help me? I made myself a cup of tea and reread the letter. Suddenly I saw what had happened: it wasn't the university that had initiated this action, but my aunt's former colleagues at the Office, who for some reason had put pressure on the department to dismiss me.

Perversely, the letter made me more determined to forge ahead. But that would mean finding somewhere else to live. I needed to cut the umbilical cord with Cambridge, and had no desire to embarrass my friends. I looked through the property pages and, as luck would have it, chanced upon a tiny garret in Rutland Gate for rent, just over the rooftops from my aunt's old flat. If I leaned far enough out of the window, I could see Hyde Park.

It wasn't home, but it would do as a stop gap, as I forged ahead with the research for this book.

Saturday, 1st February

Somewhat to my surprise, I woke up thinking about the Powder Vine. I wonder if they have any idea where I am or what I'm up to? The official line is that I'm on leave, but I can't believe that story will have lasted longer than a single lunchtime group lipstick application and, once the seed of doubt had been sewn, Janet and Pamela will have been on the scent like a pair of blood-hungry hounds. I'd wager a couple of bob that they've worked out exactly where I am now, and probably what I'm up to. There is very little office activity that escapes their notice – and if they know, who else does? Has the 'sieve', for want of a better name for our suspected office mole, caught wind of my mission?

Who could it be? However often I review the cast of my colleagues, I can't see a plausible traitor among them. Then again, I failed miserably to recognise the cut of Prenderghast's jib. Thank goodness for Dorothy Fields! If anyone can track down the bad apple among us, it will be Dorothy.

In the run-up to my meeting with Eleanor, I feel suddenly vulnerable. Up to now, it's been an adventure, albeit a high-octane one with thrills aplenty and its fair share of scares. I've always felt that there was a way out: if the going got really tough, I could flee through the snow to the Embassy and they'd see me home safely. Now that I've met Eleanor, however, we're both vulnerable. In the eyes of the KGB, we're spies. Come to think of it, they would not be wrong. If they – and I'm fully aware that 'they' is a loose term encompassing any number of private informers – guess our true purpose, then there could be no escape. I'm putting not only myself at risk, but Eleanor too. At best, she'd be deported, separated from her Philby, who would no doubt also suffer the consequences. At worst . . . I cannot bring myself to think about the worst. The image of that tall grey building, ringing with the screams of thousands, haunts me.

Perhaps it's the wait that is setting my imagination aflame? Since our meeting in the Post Office, I've been barely able to sit still. I went back to the Tretyakov yesterday afternoon, searching out possible places to meet – quiet spots, out of the sightline of the many guardians who stare, stone-faced, at the exits. Last night, I treated myself to dinner in the hotel's grand dining-room, a splendid, double-height room, with a painted ceiling and a stage at one end. I ate a surprisingly good beef stroganoff, washed down with several glasses of vodka, the effects of which, I am sure, are still with me. I love the way you can trace its path from throat to stomach. When I get back to London I will buy some. If. . . Perhaps I'll learn to make a Martini according to James's oft-repeated recipe: 'Three measures Gordon's Gin, one of vodka, half a measure of Kina Lillet, shaken until ice-cold, with a large thin slice of lemon peel.' If I never hear it again, I'll remember it until my dying day.

What comfort it gives me to think of the familiar in this strange place.

Four more hours until the earliest I could plausibly hope to meet Eleanor. Soon time to set out. I pray she makes it. The minutes are passing too slowly. I wonder what she's feeling now. Whether Philby will let her go? Whether she'll manage to leave her escort behind? Head of S said that they didn't keep her on a tight leash – and occasionally let her go out unattended. It's cold today – the temperature dropped ten degrees overnight – but there's not a cloud in the sky and the sun is shining. If I couldn't see people from my window, on the street below, hunched into themselves, visibly battling the cold, it would pass as a perfect winter tableau. I had better wear as many layers of clothes as I can reasonably fit under my coat. My coat? Rose d'Arcy's coat. Increasingly, I forget I'm not her. Then I can start dry-cleaning – today I must not be followed.

Sunday, 2nd February

The extreme cold made my journey to the Gallery more torturous. My planned route took in GUM, where I stood in line to buy a new fur hat – not mink but water rat, cheaper and, from a distance anyway, barely distinguishable from the real thing. It has a low brow and side-flaps, which I can tie under my chin, so now it's only my nose and upper cheeks that bite when the wind blows. At one point, I feared I might have an unwanted shadow; there was a hat I thought I recognised, following me from shop to shop, and I thought I caught sight of it again, skulking on the opposite side of the gallery as I came out of the Ladies. My heart beat a little faster.

I caught a taxi to the Pushkin Museum, where the hat, at least, was nowhere to be seen, and after three more metro journeys – each to small churches – I had calmed down sufficiently to persuade myself that 'the hat' had been merely curious at the rare sight of a foreigner. The problem for me is that so many Russians look similar – medium height, with prominent cheekbones and pale, deep-set eyes. I can only really identify them by their clothes and this is made harder by the weather, with its universal disguise of heavy coats, hats and scarves. I shall just have to trust that my circuitous route and established afternoon visit to the Tretyakov have dulled 'their' interest – if indeed it was ever more than a product of my heightened imagination.

After a few more sights, and a quick, stand-up bowl of *pelmini*, little meat- and cabbage-filled parcels of thin dough that I've developed quite a taste for, I arrived at the Gallery at one. I peeled off my layers and left them in the basement cloakroom, before heading to the icon rooms on the ground floor, steeling myself to smile at the guardians as I passed. After such assiduous attendance, I trust they are beginning to regard me as part of the furniture. I'd brought my pencils and sketch-pad with me; I just have to hope no one looks too closely at my risible attempts at a likeness. Thank goodness the religious artists of those days painted in the two-dimensional. I settled in the third room, where there was a large bench facing a picture that I am particularly drawn to – a seventeenth-century Virgin of Vladimir growing out of a vast bush of thorny roses emerging from behind the red Kremlin walls. For some reason, it reminds me of Eleanor.

I drew and tried not to look at my watch. I was early, I knew. At best, I could hope she would arrive at two, but it might be any time up to four. The minutes crept by.

By two, with the anxiety prematurely rising, I'd sketched the Virgin and Child and was embarking upon the saints and bishops surrounding them.

At three, I was feeling distinctly sick and my knee had started jigging of its own accord, making the drawing even harder.

As four was approaching, I'd convinced myself that this was what most people thought of as 'afternoon' and that she had probably not set off from home until well after lunch.

There were few visitors, but any time someone walked into the room, I'd feel my stomach contract as I forced myself to look slowly up from the page. The inevitable disappointment had me constructing new and plausible excuses for her late arrival.

As the minute hand slid by half past four, my seat was numb and my picture as finished as it was going to be. I stood up to stretch my legs. I walked to the end of the room and, as I turned back, I heard footsteps. My heart stopped for an instant, as I dared to hope . . . and then there she was, emerging into the room, wonderfully, delightfully familiar. She stopped as she saw me, as if caught in car headlights.

I walked towards her and attempted a natural smile. 'Excuse me, but didn't we meet yesterday in the Post Office?' I said. She looked around. There was no one else in the room, but it still felt necessary to follow the charade. In this country, one cannot discount even the walls having an acute sense of hearing.

'Yes, Miss, um, d'Arcy, wasn't it?'

'Dr actually, but please call me Rose,' I replied.

She came to sit on my bench and for a minute there was silence, after which we both started talking at the same time. Then stopped and laughed.

'It's very good to see you again,' she said, with genuine feeling. 'Do you like these magnificent paintings?'

'Indeed I do, but to tell you the truth, I've been sitting here for hours, I've finished my work and could murder a cup of tea.'

She brightened visibly. 'An excellent idea. I know a small café not far from here.'

We collected our coats and, as she was putting hers on, I could see clearly that she had lost weight. Her skin was pale and dull and there were frown lines on her forehead that I'm sure weren't there just a few months ago. It wasn't until we walked out and she had looked several times behind her that she started talking.

'Oh, Jane, I can't tell you how happy I am to see you. I prayed you'd come, but I didn't hold out much hope.' She looked straight ahead, but her voice was breaking and I could see a slight welling in her eyes. 'Thank you so very much.'

'I'm here to help if I possibly can,' I told her. 'Let's find somewhere warm and noisy to talk and you can tell me all about it – but please remember to call me Rose and please don't look behind you again. If we're being followed, it's much the best thing to ignore it, act as if you don't care.'

'I do, though,' she said. 'You can't imagine how awful it is. We're accompanied or followed almost wherever we go: Kim's to all intents and purposes under twenty-four-hour surveillance. I'm sure there are bugs in the flat. I've tried to ask him, but he just shrugs.'

She led me into a small café, full mainly of women, and, after finding a table at the back, went up to the counter to order tea. 'I even hate the goddamn Russian tea,' she said as she returned with two steaming glasses filled with a pale liquid. 'It tastes of dish-water and they look at you as if you're mad if you even mention the word milk. Kim, of course, maintains that it's an acquired taste.' As she looked at her cup, a veil of sorrow crossed her face.

'How is he?' I asked gently.

'He's Kim,' she replied, 'and then again he isn't. I was so excited about seeing him. The plane flight seemed like hours and then we were touching down on a small airstrip surrounded by tall birch-trees. There were only about twelve passengers and we were on this bus, heading to the terminal, when it stopped halfway across the tarmac and I was ushered out. It was quite dark by then, but I could just make out three men standing there, all in hats and long, dark, greatcoats. I didn't recognise him at first – I'd never seen Kim in a hat before, he'd always maintained he didn't believe in them – but then he said "Eleanor" and I just flew into his arms. It was so good to see him. I was carried along on the euphoria of a newly-wed. I should have realised that it was not just the hat that was different.' She paused to sip her tea.

'When we arrived at the flat, there was champagne on ice. He'd made it as comfortable as he could for me, but it was still small by Western standards and dark and so hot. There's no way to regulate the heating here, you know,' she said. 'The level's set by the state, just like everything else, and pumped into the apartment. All we can do is to open the windows and let the cold air in for a while, until it gets unbearable and we have to shut them again. It's such a waste. For the first few days, we talked and talked, constantly. He wanted to hear all about the children and what had happened since he left.

'I told him everything, of course. It was when I admitted that I'd picked out the photograph of his friend for your Chief that Kim changed. His face went white and he looked pointedly at the light-fitting, as if to remind me to watch what I said. Then he ordered me to write down exactly what had happened in detail. "Do you realise that you've compromised a valuable agent?" he asked. I begged his forgiveness, but he was angry for days. I think he was probably scared. He's been having terrible nightmares.

'In the meantime, I busied myself with the flat – trying to turn it into a home for us – and gradually he calmed down. It's been hard figuring out how everything works, it's all so different here, but I was willing and eager at first to give it a chance. Of course, Kim's whereabouts are a great secret. He's been given a Russian name – Andrei Fyodorovich Martins – see, I can hardly pronounce it – and he's having Russian lessons. We both are, but I'm having trouble getting the hang of it.'

I succumbed to an urge to touch her arm; she looked so sad, and so empty, it was as if she was desperate to pour out everything that had happened. In one short year, her life had been turned on its head, inside out and then shaken. At the beginning of last year, she was married to the man of her dreams, who she thought to be a British journalist, living in Beirut with his children and hers; now she's thousands of miles from her daughter, in Moscow, with no friends apart from her husband, who has been revealed to the world as a traitor. I had a sudden, almost physical pang for R.

'For a while, I thought everything was going to be OK,' she continued. 'We met the Macleans – that was his wife I was with at the Post Office – took a trip to Leningrad on the train, went to the ballet from time to time, and on occasion we're even allowed out without our minders – though I have little doubt they follow us anyway. Most mornings, Sergei, who is Kim's case officer, comes to the flat and they lock themselves away in his study for hours. I suppose he's being debriefed, but it always puts Kim in a state afterwards. He gets frustrated and snaps at me. One day, I asked whether he had to do it, and he looked at me rather sadly. "Of course I do," he replied. That's when I made my great mistake.' She paused and looked down into her tea.

'I asked him, "What is more important in your life: me and the children, or the Communist Party?" He answered without hesitation: "The Party, of course." I felt so foolish. I should never have asked. I had no idea. I'd never met a committed Communist before. Despite everything, despite the harsh reality of here, it's like he has to hold on to his belief.' I squeezed her hand tight under the table. I was suddenly afraid that she was going to cry and, if there was anyone spying on us, it would be like waving a red flag – or perhaps that should be a Union jack?

'Eleanor, I can't tell you how sorry I am,' I said. 'I can only begin to imagine what it's been like for you, but I'm afraid we really can't do this here. It's too risky.'

She collected herself. 'Of course, silly of me – and you a stranger too.' She gave a dry laugh. 'I'd better get back to Kim anyway, as he'll be beginning to wonder where I've gone. I rarely go anywhere without him, but his pneumonia has been playing up recently and he's been ordered to stay in bed.'

As we walked to the metro, she grabbed my arm and said, urgently, 'Please help us. Kim has no intention of leaving, but he has to. He won't see that he's a burden to the Russians now that he's here, a burnt-out agent with nothing more to contribute. I'm afraid of what will happen when he's emptied his brain to them. They won't allow him into KGB headquarters, or give him a rank or a job. He's already finding it frustrating and it can only get worse. He refuses to see it. He puts on an act that he's happy here and loves the cold. He even claims to find the goddamn queues for food a challenge. He's a very proud man. I need your help to persuade him. Look, please come to dinner on Wednesday. Kim should be better by then. I'll tell him I made friends with you at the Gallery. He'll have to run it by the minders of course, but it should be all right. I'll call you at the hotel. It's only one stop from us on the metro. I'll meet you at Sokol Station.'

With that promise, she vanished through the metro doors. I waited outside for as long as I could bear the cold, trying to see if she was being followed, but there was no way of knowing.

Poor Eleanor. I feel for her with every bone and every sinew in my body. She knows, whether she's admitting it to herself or not, that even in terms of her marriage hers is a reckless mission. If Philby were ever to discover her connivance in it, he would not forgive her. She must love him very much.

Wednesday, 5th February

Dinner at the Philbys. Despite myself, and against all my better instincts, I couldn't help but be charmed by him. I can quite see why he has such an effect on women. He comes across as shy, with a stutter and a boyish desire to please, which, allied with old-fashioned gentlemanly manners and a sharp and erudite mind, is unquestionably appealing. When he's talking to you, he focuses every ounce of his attention on what you're saying. It's wonderfully flattering. In a funny sort of way, he reminds me of Bill.

The flat was better than I had imagined. Approaching its grim façade from the outside, I felt a strong sense of déjà vu. I almost looked around to see whether I could spot 009 sitting in a car across the cul-de-sac, his night glasses trained on the eighth-floor windows. Inside, they had made it their own. There were plants everywhere,

Eleanor's paintings on the walls, a blue wicker sofa in one corner of the living-room and matching green armchairs and another sofa on the other side, with a huge, heavy, silver-plated electric samovar on a small table beside it. Most noticeably, there were piles and piles of books. After we were introduced, Philby apologised for them; 'I inherited them from GGGGGuy Burgess,' he explained, seeming to luxuriate in the freedom to mention his old friend's name. 'Sadly just missed seeing the ppppoor fellow before he died.' He showed me Burgess's armchair, a high-backed plum-velvet wing-tip, and, in the bedroom, his carved wooden bedstead: 'GGGGGuy always insisted it had once belonged to Stendhal,' Philby said. 'Knowing him, it had no such gggggrand provenance. He was always a romantic. Bbbbbut I'm forgetting myself. I'm sure you'd like a drink?'

He almost skipped across to a makeshift cabinet on the far side of the room, from which he drew out a bottle of brandy. 'We like something I call an Orange Blossom – brandy and orange juice. Would you care to try it?' I nodded my assent. The rest of the evening passed pleasantly. Thankfully, he didn't question me too closely on what I was doing here, due in part to Eleanor's well-timed announcement that dinner was ready. I managed to scrape through his earnest questions about the relative merits of early Russian painters, I hope, though it felt hideously like I was back in the school exam hall.

He had cooked a delicious hot curry, even grinding his own spices, he told me with pride. 'I thought it must have been ages since you last had a good curry,' he said. 'They don't make them on this side.' I realised in time that he was referring to the years that Rose d'Arcy had spent in East Berlin, not just my two short weeks in Moscow. From one or two other comments, I guessed that he knew more about my legend than I'd revealed to Eleanor. I had clearly been checked out by his handlers – and passed their test. It was not altogether welcome news: I was now on their radar, and would have to exercise extra care.

After dinner, when Philby suggested a game of Scrabble, I accepted with alacrity. Scrabble always reminds me of Aunt Frieda and those first few months in London. Helena and I were like ships adrift in an unfamiliar ocean, and it was in great part the nightly games that helped to anchor us in our new life. Aunt Frieda is an excellent player, but Kim Philby would have dismissed her in his sleep. Still, I acquitted myself without shame and the good, competitive game created a bond of respect between us. Eleanor was quiet throughout, but when I was getting ready to leave and Philby suggested that I join them and the Macleans on a trip to the ballet on Saturday, she flashed me a look of pure encouragement.

I walked back to the metro station with my mind buzzing and excited. Now, I wonder whether it was wrong to have warmed to Philby to such a degree? I struggle to remind myself that he betrayed his country, and mine, for thirty years. Men and women died as a result of the secrets he gave away. Many were innocent. M came to within a screen's breadth of becoming one of them. Philby systematically lied to his friends, his employers, his wives and children, for the benefit of a regime he never really knew. He left Eleanor in Beirut without a clue as to where he was going. He has torn her from everything else she loves to bring her here now, for his own sake. His charm is legendary – how else could he have achieved what he did? I must not be taken in.

Friday, 7th February

I was walking away from the Post Office, when I caught sight of Philby going into the Savoy Hotel. He was arm in arm with a woman and they were laughing. I assumed it was Eleanor and was about to hail them, when I recognised her as Melinda Maclean. Instead, I burrowed into my scarf and hurried on my way. Perhaps they were meeting Eleanor there?

Sunday, 9th February

A very strange and disturbing evening. I arrived at the Philbys' building at the same time as the Macleans, who, it was clear from the start, were not on good terms. They hardly talked to each other, and when they did, it was in barely suppressed snarls. I did not warm to either: he was vastly tall and patrician in appearance, with an air of unsuppressed arrogance, while she wheedled and whined like a typical spoiled American. Both Philby and Eleanor were unfailingly courteous to them both, but I sensed that, but for their extraordinary circumstances, they would not have been natural friends. Melinda flattered Philby mercilessly and I could only hope it was his manners that prevented him from dissuading her. If Donald noticed, he didn't care, although I suspect Eleanor did.

The Bolshoi was a wonderful experience. The Theatre itself is beautiful, grand and imposing from the front in a way that our Royal Opera House fails to be. As we walked through the columned portico and into the lobby, a pleasant-looking man in his early forties approached us and handed Philby an envelope containing our tickets. Philby smiled and thanked him, whereupon the man melted back into the darkness. I assume he was Sergei, or another of Philby's KGB minders. The thought made me shudder, though he barely gave me a second glance.

The unease, however, melted away as we entered the auditorium. I almost gasped aloud at the splendour of the crimson and gilt balconies, curving towards the central stage. We had a box on the grand tier, with an excellent view. The ballet itself did its surroundings proud. I have always loved *Giselle*, with its heartbreaking tale of love that endures beyond the grave, but the Bolshoi gave it an extra resonance. The ballerina dancing the lead seemed to jeté and pirouette with every ounce of her soul, portraying both innocence and passion with the utmost veracity. By the interval, I had forgotten the unease of the early evening and wanted nothing but to praise and admire the spectacle we were enjoying.

A discreet knock at the door revealed the same man we had seen earlier, this time with a waiter in attendance, bearing a bottle of iced vodka, some tumblers and a plate heaped with caviar. Philby clapped his hands with glee and thanked him. Certainly, the way he was being treated portrayed no lack of generosity on the Russian side. If Eleanor's fears were true, I had yet to see evidence of them.

I was enjoying the vodka and our magnificent surroundings, when I caught sight of a man in the opposite box. I felt my heart pound. I could have sworn he had his opera-glasses trained on us, though he swung around when he saw me looking at him, before fading back into the gloom at the back of his box. It was purely instinct, but I was suddenly convinced I recognised him. Eleanor caught my look of shock and asked if there was anything wrong. I tried to make light of it. 'Of course not,' I replied. 'I thought I'd seen a ghost. Perhaps Giselle's spirit lives in the Bolshoi?' She frowned. I don't think she was convinced.

Through the second half, I couldn't stop thinking about it. He was too far away for me to have made out any of his features and I'm sure it must have been just my overactive imagination at work, but there was something, a feeling that just wouldn't go away. Even the ballet's spell failed to take away the bitter aftertaste of my fear.

Nevertheless, I clapped and cried with the rest of the audience during the well-deserved ovation, and when Sergei led us out of the side entrance, I caught no glimpse of those pale eyes that had been haunting me. Keen to make an evening of it, Philby suggested a drink at the Metropol Hotel, but I excused myself and, thanking them profusely, caught a taxi back to the sanctuary of my room at the Sovietsky. I lay awake for hours, trying to convince myself that I'd been mistaken.

Tuesday, 11th February

I have the feeling that I'm being followed. I haven't managed to catch anyone in the act, but wherever I go, I feel the prickles in my back. It started the day after the ballet, when I forced myself to make my usual afternoon visit to the Gallery. Following the rules I had learnt back on my course at the Fort – it seems like a different existence, when R was still alive and Kennedy too and I thought I was playing games on the south coast – I jumped in the last carriage of the metro, just as the doors were closing: I was sure I saw someone leap in the next door along. I couldn't be certain; the metro is a busy place, full of rushing people, and I didn't catch a clear sight of him. I realised that the best I could do would be to stick to my usual routine and do nothing to raise their suspicion.

I telephoned Eleanor to say thank you and, although she sounded pleased to hear my voice, I nevertheless detected a slight reticence in hers and she failed to suggest another meeting. I can only stay calm and wait and hope that she contacts me.

Monday, 17th February

I found an envelope pushed under my door when I got back yesterday afternoon. My name was written in capitals, but I recognised Eleanor's hand. Inside was just one line: 'Meet me at Sandunovsky Banya, Neglinnaya Ulitsa, 7 p.m.' It was already 5.30, which didn't give me much time to take evasionary precautions. Still, I did what I could: metro to a café, then taxi, tram and back on the metro to Teatralnaya, from where I walked past the Bolshoi Theatre and up a side street by a Georgian restaurant. It was dark and intensely cold again. It took me some time to find the entrance to the baths, hidden one street back, to my right, but at least I was fairly confident that I wasn't being followed.

The gruff lady minding the reception at first tried to send me away, only relenting when I managed to persuade her that I was meeting a friend. With a grunt, she gave me a towel and pointed towards the ladies' changing-room. There, thankfully, I found Eleanor, already stripped to her towel. She looked relieved to see me. 'I've found an empty banya,' she said. 'Get ready and follow me.' She walked around the corner and opened a door. Hot steam came billowing out as we slipped in. When my eyes adjusted to the gloom, I could see that we were in a small, marble room, with a large, steaming tub in the corner and benches to either side.

'Melinda brought me here soon after I arrived,' she told me. 'It was the only place I could think of where we wouldn't be overheard. Look, I don't think it's safe for you here any more. Since that night at the ballet, Kim's had a stream of visitors, all KGB, I assume. Apart from Sergei, I didn't recognise any of them and they weren't introduced. He doesn't say what they've been talking about, but I thought I heard your name being mentioned today. Your real name, that is – but I can't be sure.'

I sat back, suddenly cold in this bath of hot steam.

'I'm scared,' she went on. 'I don't know what's going to happen. I wish I had never started this. Perhaps I should have gone home to the States and never come?'

All I could do was comfort her and try to keep my composure, though I felt every bit as unsettled as she did. My mind was racing. What should I do? Was this the signal to implement my escape plan? If so, would I be leaving my friend in danger?

'You could have been mistaken. It might not be as bad as we imagine,' I said, at last. 'I'm fairly sure that no one's searched my room at the hotel, and I haven't noticed anyone following me.' It was not the time to mention my fears. 'How about if we give it another couple of days and I'll try to contact London to ask for advice? If they pull me out, do you want to come with me?'

She looked stunned. 'What, and leave Kim?'

'We can't take him against his will. It's not the way our service operates,' I said, conveniently forgetting the kidnap attempt just a couple of months before. 'If you want to come, however, I can certainly try to make the arrangements.'

She shook her head. 'I couldn't leave Kim on his own here. I couldn't. He's my husband . . .'

I patted her hand in an attempt at reassurance that I didn't feel. 'The offer's there. Please think about it.'

There was a knock on the door and we both started. We opened it to find a large lady in a white smock, holding a small forest of birch sticks in her mutton fists. She barked something in Russian. I looked at Eleanor, but she just shrugged. 'Is it time for my torture?' I asked the lady, who glared back, unable to understand a word I said. She shut the door behind her and motioned me to lie down on the bench. I tried shaking my head, but she just stood in front of the door, pointing at the bench.

'A beating with birch sticks is meant to be good for the circulation,' said Eleanor. 'I haven't had it myself, but I'm assured it's got health benefits. Besides, I don't think you've much option.' A small smile was playing at the corner of her mouth and she looked as if she was trying her best to suppress full-blown laughter. 'It's the speciality of the house,' she said. 'I'm going to change now. Relax. You might enjoy it.'

I lay down on my stomach as instructed, while the mountainous lady came up to my side, put down her sticks and then, to my horror, stripped off her top. She climbed up on the bench and, straddling my back, began pounding her hands into my shoulders, kneading me like a huge mound of dough. It was all I could do to stop howling, but each time I tensed, she dug the base of her palms in harder. I tried to calm my rebelling muscles; then, just as I thought she'd stopped, I felt a sharp slash on the back of my thighs. Then again: slash, slash. She was whipping me with the birch in what felt to be a frenzy. The sting was becoming unbearable. Surely this was not normal? I cried out for her to stop, but she didn't. I didn't want to turn over, for fear she'd hit me in the face. I had to do something. If I didn't, and quickly, I thought I might faint. In a flash, an image of James came into my head and I remembered him relating his misadventures in an upstate New York mud-bath. It gave me strength. As fast as I could, I rolled to one side and threw myself off the bench. I leapt to my feet and, not waiting to see what the torturing mountain was doing, flung myself at the door. Thankfully it opened outwards and I pushed through and into the merciful cool of the corridor.

Eleanor was waiting in the changing-room. 'Was that good?' she asked, but she must have seen something in my expression, as her face recomposed itself into concern. 'Jane, are you all right?'

'I don't know,' I replied. 'I don't know if that was par for the course and I'm made of weaker stuff than the average Russian – or whether I was being given a warning.' I turned round to try to look at my back, and heard Eleanor gasp. I was covered from shoulders to ankles in red welts, which felt every bit as bad as they looked. 'We must take you to a doctor,' she said. 'Get something to put on them.' I shook my head. 'I just want to get back to my room. I'm sure they'll have gone down by the morning.'

I spent the whole of today lying on my front with the window open. It was freezing, but at least soothed my back. I went over and over yesterday's events, seeking some sort of explanation, some sort of truth. What should I do? It was only this evening, after a cool bath, that I felt able to get up, but even sitting is painful.

Wednesday, 19th February

I got back to my room, after forcing myself to visit the Cathedral, and sensed immediately that someone had been there. Nothing was visibly out of place, but there was a faint smell that didn't belong to the maid – and I'd left after her, in any case. I went first to the drawers, but the hairs were where I had placed them and my things were in perfect order. Then I turned to the inner surface of the cupboard handle, where I had sprinkled talcum powder. There was a smudge. Someone had been in my room. I swallowed the lump that had appeared unbidden in my throat.

I sat down and took a few deep breaths. I could have been mistaken, or perhaps the maid had returned for some reason? There were a number of innocent explanations, and in any case, I had nothing to hide. I suppressed my initial urge to contact the Office.

Thursday, 20th February

I woke up this morning unwilling to leave my room, but when I opened the curtains, I saw that it was snowing outside – soft, large flakes of white, white snow. It was a signal that the temperature had lifted. I was suddenly infused with energy. I layered on my clothes and rushed outside. In the small park opposite, I picked up a pinch of fresh snow and put it on my tongue. It brought back vividly the day, in my mid-teens, when Ma had urged Helena and me to climb that little bit further up Mount Kenya, promising us we would see snow if we did. She was right and, to two unworldly Kenyan girls, it was a miracle.

For want of anything better to do – until I heard from Eleanor, at least – I caught the metro back to the Tretyakov. I was becoming rather fond of the icons, with whom I'd spent considerably more time than with anyone else over the past few weeks. I was walking towards the Virgin when I saw, sitting on my regular bench, Kim Philby. He turned as he heard me come in. 'Dr d'Arcy, my wife said you were often here.' I was struck dumb. I had not the least idea why he might have sought me.

'Perhaps I could buy you a cup of tea?' he asked.

I nodded. He told me to fetch my coat and meet him inside the metro station in fifteen minutes.

He was waiting when I passed through the doors. With his arm under my elbow, he steered me on to the train, taking care, I noticed, to check who might have followed us. We got out two stations further on and jumped in a taxi, which took us to a small Georgian restaurant in a part of town I was not familiar with. 'Have you tried Georgian cuisine?' he asked, as we were led to a table in the corner. Apart from the waiters, who hung discreetly back until they were called, we were alone.

'You might be wondering why I want to talk to you,' he began.

I said I was.

He leant forward. 'I think I've made a terrible mistake. Eleanor is clearly unhappy here and it's my fault. I have, somehow, to make amends. I don't know how much you know, but I'm sure you're not who you're purporting to be, which means that, in all likelihood, you're from the Office. Am I correct?'

I just raised my eyebrows. 'I don't know what you're talking about, Mr Philby.'

'Whatever you say, I've been in this business long enough to know a British agent when I see one. Don't worry, I'm not going to reveal your secret to my friends here.' He looked down. 'Quite the reverse. As I said, Eleanor's unhappy and we've got to get out of here. You probably know that I was offered immunity by Dingle in Beirut, shortly before I took off?'

I did my best to look flummoxed, but he continued. 'I turned him down and I'm regretting it. I know I've made my own bed and I'd be prepared to lie on it if it wasn't for Eleanor. She's making herself ill staying here, but I know she won't leave until I do. You've got to help me to get out. Once I'm gone, they'll let Eleanor leave; she's still an American passport-holder and they promised me they would never hold her here against her will. I believe them.'

He stopped and looked at me. I was momentarily stuck for words. What if it was a trap? I could not walk straight into it. 'I'm an art historian,' I said carefully, 'not a travel agent.'

He gave a brief laugh. 'I don't expect you to give me an answer now, or even admit to your true calling. All I'm asking – pleading for – is that you inform your friends at the Office of our conversation and submit my request. We can meet again here in five days to discuss their response. Are you willing to do that?'

I inclined my head slightly and gave what I hoped was a blank look. 'It's always a pleasure to have tea with you, Mr Philby, and as you said, the Georgian cuisine is excellent. How could I refuse?'

He called for the waiter and paid the bill. As we stood up to leave, he leant forward. 'Look, Dr d'Arcy, Rose, whoever you are, I'm putting myself at considerable risk to do this. Even meeting you would be considered a hanging offence, if they knew who you were. I'm doing it for Eleanor and if you have any sympathy for her, you'll help us. Be careful, though. If my friends here know what we're doing, we'll all be in severe – and I mean severe – danger.' With that, he held open the front door and ushered me out.

Friday, 21st February

I woke early this morning and kick-started the prescribed routine for sending an urgent message to the Office. First,

I wrote an anodyne note on a postcard of St Basil's. Then I dipped my pen into the invisible ink and, in tiny letters, began to write between the lines, sketching my conversation with Philby and his request to come home. I mentioned my strong suspicion that I was being followed – and asked for instructions. When I was finished, I carefully unrolled the cotton wool in my sponge bag to reveal the details of the dead letter box I had been told to use. I spent the next four hours criss-crossing Moscow, to all appearances sketching the metro stations. When I was fairly sure I was clean, I hailed a taxi and asked him to take me to Gorky Park. I found the skate-hire shop I was looking for and, after asking for skates in my size, took them into the cloakroom to change. I put my shoes, as instructed, into the top right-hand cubby-hole, then sat down and started slowly putting on my skates, waiting for the room to empty. I was just lacing up my second skate when the last inhabitants left, a woman and child, skipping up and down on her blades in excitement. Looking around carefully, I went back to the shoe holes, reached up and carefully slotted my envelope into a gap above the top shelf, pushing it in until it didn't show. Then I set off for the ice.

The cold, fortunately, gave me the excuse to come in after half an hour. The evening was beginning to draw in, providing the cover I needed to finish the job. I walked quickly back across the bridge to the metro station, exited by GUM, ran up the stairs to the Ladies and, locking myself in the furthest cubicle, drew a cross in white chalk on the wall above the door. As I had been told, it hardly showed. With relief, I flushed the loo and went downstairs to a café, where I bought a small meat pie, which

I forced myself to eat. The signal site would be checked, I had been told, each morning and then I would be contacted.

Tuesday, 25th February

The last few days have been unbearably tense. I'm sure I'm being followed, but am doing my best to act as though I haven't noticed and to keep to my routine. I have changed my mind about Istanbul: I don't care if I never see another icon. Right now, all I want is my own flat, Helena and Rafiki – and I'm not convinced I will ever see them again.

Sitting in the Ladies at the Tretyakov, due to meet Philby in two hours, I am steeling myself to set off. It's well below freezing-point again, but if I catch the metro and then walk across Gorky Park, I should be able to lose them. They've been using cars, I'm sure – I've noticed a mustard-coloured Volga on several occasions. There are probably others, but my sense is that they are less assidu-ous when I'm on foot.

For a huge city, Moscow has become intensely claustro-phobic. I feel as if I am surrounded by eyes, boring into me from all directions, and yet I'm dreadfully lonely. Sometimes, I wake in the morning and wonder whether it's not just a bad dream. I wish it were.

I met Head of S on Saturday night, outside the Bolshoi Theatre as the ballet crowd was dispersing. I don't think we were spotted. I told him in detail what Philby had proposed. He looked thoughtful – and concerned – and said he would contact London for instructions. This morning, a note was slipped under my room door. It said to bring the Marmalade back to Oxford, but to exercise the utmost caution in doing so.

The coda had Bill's signature all over it. Dear Bill – what I wouldn't do to see his friendly face now.

I can't help but think of R. Now I can begin to imagine what it was like for him in Berlin, the days and weeks before he died. It was my fault. I as good as killed a good man – not an innocent one, I know, and one who had made a choice to work for a clandestine organisation. He knew the risks, but still, he wouldn't have raised the ire of Boris had it not been for me.

Boris: where is he? I feel his presence around every corner.

Thursday, 27th February

We leave in three nights. The plans are nearly set. Philby insisted we travel overland, by train to Leningrad and then north to the Finnish border. He says that's our only chance. We leave on the midnight train and should not be missed until mid-morning the next day, if all goes as we hope. To give us an extra few hours, Eleanor will stay in their flat that night. The next morning, she has made an appointment at the American Embassy to discuss her forthcoming planned trip home to see her daughter. Sergei knows she is going; it should not cause suspicion. Not until she fails to leave the Embassy compound, by which time we should be almost at the border.

I have the address of a safe house in Leningrad. A taxi-driver will meet us at the station and take us there. Agent

859 will be waiting to escort us to the meeting-point just this side of the border, in the woods near Vyborg. Head of S insists it will work like clockwork, but I don't think even he believes that. Still, if we can trust Philby – and I suppose we have to, though there are times when a look of uncertainty crosses his face – it is our best chance of escape.

If we can trust Philby.

March

I did my best to persuade myself that it was a relief to have lost my job, and instead buried myself in my aunt's words, living through and with her the cold Russian winter of 1964.

Two weeks after New Year 2006, I boarded a plane for Moscow. Apart from that brief trip to Colditz, it was my first time behind the old Iron Curtain. Previously, I'd always been drawn to the south or west: Africa and the Americas. The grey former Soviet states had held no appeal. But now I was excited. Reading my aunt's diaries had pitched me into that world, and I longed to see at first hand what she had seen, to go to the same places, experience what she had. It was not only that: retracing her footsteps made her come alive again for me, and right then, living alone in a small flat, divorced from my Cambridge life, I needed her.

Moscow was not what I had imagined. As the taxi emerged from the outer ring into the city centre, I was struck by how busy it was, and how grand. In the dusk, Stalin's Seven Goddesses twinkled with fairy lights. We followed the river past the Kremlin on our right, the Bolshoi Theatre on our left, then GUM stores, which dwarfed Harrods in both size and grandeur. The taxi driver was a large, jovial man, proud of his city but nostalgic for the old, Communist, ways. 'Since market economy, we are very poor, have to work very hard,' he said. 'Was not like that before.'

The Sovietsky was just as my aunt had portrayed it. The walls were still hung with portraits of Stalin, and the corridors still smelled of polish. Only the air of menace was absent. Today in Russia, a foreigner is to be welcomed, not followed. As I crossed the city, by metro and by taxi, nobody looked at me and I did not feel out of place. One of my first stops was the Tretyakov Gallery, which I wandered around unnoticed, to my delight finding the Virgin of Vladimir among the ground-floor icons, emerging from a rose bush just as my aunt had described her.

I had been warned that Russia was about to enter a cold snap, and on my third day there, as huge neon signs announced that the mercury had sunk to minus 25, I felt the icy wind sear up my nostrils and through my eyeballs. It was, according to the *Moscow Times*, the coldest winter for more than forty years. My aunt was there forty-two years ago. It was an oddly comforting parallel. With her fortitude as inspiration, I continued to plunge from the overheated interiors into the freeze outside, tracing the routes she had walked and the places she had written about. I went to the Bolshoi Ballet and up to the top of the Ukraine Hotel. I took the metro to Sokol station and walked around the dreary streets behind Leningradsky Prospekt, comparing each apartment building to the description of the Philbys' in my aunt's diaries, in the hope that I might stumble upon it.

One night I had dinner in a Georgian restaurant with a friend of a friend who had spent the last six years in Moscow, reporting for the *Sunday Times*. When I told him that I was interested in the Philbys, he asked whether I wanted to meet Mrs Philby.

'Mrs Philby?' I asked, temporarily stunned. In my head, Mrs Philby was Eleanor, and I knew she wasn't in Moscow.

'Rufina, Kim's fourth wife. A lovely lady. She still lives in their old flat near Pushkin Square. I'm sure she'd be happy to meet you.'

He gave me her number, and the next day I called her. A Russian voice answered, and when I started speaking in English and explained who I was, she switched languages and invited me to tea the following day, giving me detailed directions to her home. It was not the same flat that Philby had lived in with Eleanor, but smaller, and closer to the centre.

I still managed to get lost, and arrived half an hour late and freezing. She could not have been more welcoming. Now in her mid-seventies, she is attractive and clearly intelligent. She showed me to a tall-backed armchair bequeathed to Philby by Guy Burgess, and pointed out the old-fashioned wireless on which her husband had listened to the BBC each morning while drinking his tea.

The flat was comfortable and lived in, filled with Philby's books – thousands of them, many inherited from Burgess – and the rugs and pictures that had been brought over for him from Beirut: the same ones that had adorned his Sokol apartment, where my aunt had met him with Eleanor. Rufina appeared to be devoted to his memory; the apartment, if not a shrine, was a tribute to her husband, and she seemed happy to talk about him, as if by so doing she could keep his memory alive. They had had a very happy marriage, by all accounts. She was thirty-eight and working as an editor at a publishing house when they were introduced by Ida, the Russian wife of another former British spy, George Blake. 'He always claimed to have decided that day that he would marry me,' she said, with a smile.

For two hours, she reminisced about the husband who had now been dead for as long as they had been married. Many of the things she told me matched what my aunt had related in her diaries: the terrible nightmares, the constant surveillance, and his love of cooking – especially hot curries.

'Did he ever tell you that he had tried to leave?' I asked.

She shook her head. 'He knew it was impossible. His life was here, and there was nothing he could do to change that. There were things that frustrated him, of course – he would have liked to have been of more use. But this was his home, and he was happy here.'

Sunday, 1st March

The last few days in Moscow were the most anxious of my stay. I met Philby once in a café and Head of S, late at night, in an underground bar off Tverskaya. On neither occasion did I spot surveillance, but I felt it there always, like an unblinking eye, even when I was alone and locked into my hotel room.

As the date of our escape approached, it appeared increasingly preposterous. Was it even faintly conceivable that I would be able to travel hundreds of miles, through a strange and hostile country, infested with secret informers reporting to a feared and omnipotent KGB? I, who apparently had 'foreigner' emblazoned on my forehead, accompanied by Kim Philby, Moscow's prize poodle, proud symbol of its supremacy over the West?

Fear and uncertainty rushed over me in waves of desperation, interspersed by bursts of phoney bravado. This was not a game – nor even an adventure. Why had I accepted M's challenge? Why hadn't I disappeared into the bush in Kenya at Christmas, or married a bean-farmer when I was twenty-one and never come to London?

Then I remembered R. I could not capitulate to the forces that had destroyed him.

The night of February 29th was cold and clear. I packed my small holdall and checked out of the Sovietsky. Despite everything, it had been a good home to me, quiet and comfortable. Even Uncle Joe's putty features, staring down from every wall, had become benign in their familiarity. Still, I will not miss it. There is nothing about Moscow that I will miss – not the cold, nor the food, the scared and beaten people, the watching eyes behind every wall, tree or window.

I caught the metro to Leningradsky Station. It was smaller than I had expected, just ten lines, all bound for Leningrad. My instructions were to meet Philby in a small café on Platform 1 at 23.30. Our train, the Kraznaya Stella – Red Arrow – left at five minutes before midnight. My heart was pounding as I walked down the platform and into the familiar clamour of steam trains, snorting like giant dragons preparing for flight. I couldn't escape the feeling that I was walking into the enemy's lair. I willed myself forward. I had long since passed that mythical point of no return; I had no other options but belief and hope.

There was no one in the café when I arrived, just two rough-faced men in heavy leather donkey-jackets, talking to a large lady behind the counter. They fell into a watching silence when I walked in, stripped bare by the lime glow of fluorescent lights. I sat at a table in the corner, praying that Philby would arrive. What sort of predicament was it when my fate rested in the hands of the greatest traitor of a generation?

Five minutes passed in a grudging succession of slow seconds. Finally, the door opened and a small figure slipped through, almost swallowed by a heavy Astrakhan-collared greatcoat, a fur hat and scarf. I would not have recognised him had he not walked towards the table and beckoned me out. 'Keep your hat on at all times when we're not in our compartment,' he said in a low voice. 'Without it, you stick out like a sore thumb. And don't say a word.'

I nodded and followed him down the platform. It was still bitterly cold, despite the steam and smuts billowing out from the train chimneys, fiery sparks flying like particles of pumice from an erupting volcano. The air around us smelt of hot oil and coal, and each time the valves were released, to a full-bellied whistle, I felt my stomach contract. There were men standing on the platform, dressed in ankle-length black leather coats and heavy boots. They stared as we passed. I willed myself not to look back.

Philby handed our tickets and a bundle of papers to the guard at the end of our carriage, who studied them carefully for what seemed like an age, before handing them back with a nod and leading us down the carriage. Philby had booked a first-class compartment under his Russian name. I travelled on Eleanor's Russian papers. As soon as we had been shown in, he closed and locked the door behind us. 'We're here for the next nine hours,' he said, producing a bottle of brandy from his bag. 'Better make the best of it.' He pulled down the blind and slid into the bench on one side of a small table, motioning me to sit opposite. 'We've made it over the first hurdle. If you believe in God, you'd better pray the rest passes smoothly.' He poured the brandy into two tooth-mugs, handed one to me and raised his. 'To successful escapes,' he said.

'To safe returns,' I replied.

We sat for a time, looking at each other as the engine gathered steam. As the wheels began to move, in their first hesitant rhythm, the sounds of a band playing the Red Flag were piped across the station. I noticed Philby stiffen, before he shrugged his shoulders and gave a wry smile.

'I suppose it's goodbye to all that,' he said.

'I hope so,' I replied. 'Are you sorry?'

He appeared to contemplate my question. 'Yes,' he said finally. 'I was twenty-one when I became a Communist and I did so from the purest of motives. I believed it was the only way to counter the Fascist threat, and dampen the avarice of an increasingly self-interested West. It was simple and so beautiful, in theory. When I joined our friends here, I knew it was for life. I committed my soul,

my mind and my body to the Movement. I never antici-
pated that I would turn tail and run.'

'So why have you?'

'I told you. For Eleanor.' He grabbed the brandy bottle
and poured himself another glass, which he drained in a
single gulp.

'I'm not sure I believe you,' I said finally.

He gave his shy smile. 'Did you bring Scrabble?'

'No.'

'Are you planning to sleep?'

'No,' I replied, looking out of the window as the dim
lights of the city started to recede and we were swallowed
by darkness.

There was a knock and we froze. 'Turn away, or
put on a scarf or something,' Philby hissed, before
getting up to answer it. He opened the door a crack
and I heard a deep voice asking a question in Russian.
Philby said something, and the question was repeated.
Then he appeared back in the cabin and reached for
our papers. I could hear my pulse drumming a tattoo
in my ears. There was another exchange of words,
after which Philby called back, 'Darling, I think the
gentleman wants to check that you're here. Are you
decent?'

I had slipped my night-dress on and wrapped a towel
around my head in a makeshift turban. I lay down on the
narrow bench with the blanket over me. 'Come in,' I
called back.

The door opened a little more and I saw a large face
with a thick moustache and watery green eyes, emerging
out of a khaki serge uniform. He gave me a terse nod and
quickly retreated.

Philby came back in and, with a shaking hand, refilled his glass and lit another cigarette. 'That was a bit hairy,' he said. 'Luckily for us, he was regular police, not KGB. Still, the old ticker skipped a couple of beats. Another brandy for you?'

I sat up and nodded. There seemed little chance of sleep for either of us, and no point in pretending.

'Why did you join the Office?' he asked.

There was no reason to lie. 'I needed a job,' I told him. 'Both of my parents were dead and I had a younger sister to look after. My father had been in the diplomatic service – or so I thought – and I was put up for an interview by the head of the secretarial college.'

'What do you mean, "or so you thought"?'

'It transpires he was in intelligence too.'

'What happened to him?'

'He disappeared in the war. We were told he was dead.'

'He wasn't?' Philby had picked up the doubt in my voice and matched it with gentle concern in his. Alone with my thoughts for so long, I felt myself wanting to confide in him.

'It seems not – not at that point, anyway. He is dead, but I don't know how and where.'

'That's tough,' Philby said gently, reaching across to touch my hand.

I was fighting to hold back the tears. At once, I wanted to blurt out my fears and regret, but at the same time, I was conscious, deep down, that I was being played by a supreme intelligence officer. I managed to pull myself together, smiled and took a sip of my drink. I didn't want him to touch me.

We sat in silence for a while, accompanied by the rhythmic puffing of the engine and the occasional shuddering hiss of brakes. Then he started talking again – about himself, about Communism, how he and Eleanor had met, and of his two previous wives.

'I'm a romantic,' he said at one point.

'Yes. You'd have to be.'

He drank more and more, his eyes beginning to glaze over, his speech becoming increasingly indistinct. Just as I thought he was about to keel over into sleep, he looked at me and said, his stutter back in force, 'She nnnnever even learned to rrrread the nnnnames of the metro stations, you know. I'm sorry, old ggggirl. Nothing ppppper-sonal. Hhhhhad no choice.'

'What do you mean?' I asked, but he had fallen on to his side and was snoring softly. It was past four in the morning. I lay back on my bunk and closed my eyes, but his words kept circling in my head, like hungry sharks. Who was he talking about: me or Eleanor? Why was he sorry: for what he had done or what he was about to do? I knew inside it was the latter. I thought about jumping out of the window. I lifted the blind and saw the ice on the glass and the fleeting shimmer of moonlight on the trees as we whipped past. There was no escape.

The night passed slowly, my wakefulness punctuated occasionally by shouts from Philby – cries of pain and anguish and anger. Eleanor had said he was prone to nightmares; I suppose it was not surprising.

I was still awake when there was another knock on the door. I got up to try to wake Philby, but he wouldn't move. The knock came again, this time accompanied by a woman's deep voice. I could just make out the word

Leningrad. We were approaching our destination. I left it a minute, before opening the door and scurrying down the passage to the bathroom, where I splashed my face with cold water. I talked to the terrified face in the mirror: 'Stop imagining the worst. You are not Philby's prisoner. It has all been set up by M and Bill. We are being met by our side. It will be all right.' I stared at myself, forcing determination back into my brain. For a moment, I looked almost Russian.

I soaked a towel and carried it back to the compartment and squeezed it on to Philby's neck. He sat up with a start, saw me there and frowned, before reaching for his cigarettes. The train started to slow. He quickly put on his jacket and smoothed his hair.

'A taxi will be here to meet us, is that right?'

'Yes,' I replied.

'Come on then – hat on, scarf on, wrap up. We're in beautiful Leningrad. An architectural feast for the eyes. Not what it once was, of course, but still magnificent.' As he ushered me out of the train, he didn't once look at me.

Monday, 2nd March

Leningrad was even colder than Moscow – a damp cold that seemed to seep through layers of clothing to bury itself deep in one's bones. As we walked along the platform, we were approached by a huge man in a leather cap, blowing clouds of steam. 'Come,' he said. I looked at Philby, who nodded tersely, and we walked towards a maroon Volga. We climbed in and without another word, the driver sparked up the engine and set off.

I looked out of the window at the roads, covered in snow. It was past nine, not yet fully light. The pale aura of the sun, just peeping over the horizon, dusted the buildings in a soft lilac and made me feel, for that instant, as though I was floating through a dream. I wished I was: there was something about the reality that made me feel profoundly uneasy. We drove over a bridge, and to either side I could see huge clouds of steam rising from the frozen River Neva.

'Sewerage,' Philby grunted.

We drove along broad avenues, lined with neo-classical palaces, painted yellow, green and blue, but I was once again in the iron grip of fear and beyond the call of beauty. All I wanted was to get out of the city and run for the border as fast as we could. The driver pulled up outside a small house on a narrow street not far from the river and gestured towards it, but stayed in his seat as we struggled to open the doors and get out. I couldn't see a street sign, and could only hope he had delivered us to the safe house. As soon as we were clear of the car, the driver gunned his engine and sped off. Philby gestured for me to knock on the door, as he stood behind me, scanning the street in each direction.

I walked forward and gave it two sharp taps. From the other side, I heard an answering rat-tat and the door was pulled open. I was greeted by a blond man, about my height, wearing a dark polo neck and flannel trousers. 'Name's Gerry. Glad you made it,' he said, in the unmistakably English tones of Oxford and the Guards. I felt a groundswell of relief. 'I was getting a tad worried. Bit of an incident at the border, been driving day and night to make it on time, but here I am. You must be the fabled Mr

252

Philby.' He stuck out his hand and as I turned to look at Philby, I noticed his eyes briefly narrow. 'Jolly good,' Gerry continued. 'Tea, anyone?' I could have kissed him. He led us up some stone steps to a set of double doors. Producing a large ring of keys, he opened up and ushered us in.

There was a comfortable sofa across the hall and I could already smell coffee brewing. After asking for warm milk instead, I went down the corridor to the loo, where I was shocked to see my drawn reflection staring back at me. I washed my face and as I was heading back to the hall, I caught the rumbled low notes of a quiet conversation. It stopped abruptly as I rounded the corner. Philby looked up at me.

'Plan's changed a little, it seems, on the orders of the Office. We're to rest up and set off at dusk.'

'Won't the Centre have sent out the search parties by then?' I asked.

He shrugged. 'Nothing we can do about that. Best we all try to sleep.'

Gerry came back with my milk and, after a couple of sips, I felt waves of tiredness slide over me. I stood up and excused myself. He pointed to a door, behind which I found a bed, lay down and fell instantly asleep.

Tuesday, 3rd March

It was pitch dark when I woke, and my head was pounding. I must have been asleep all day. I couldn't read my watch in the blackout. What was happening? By the density of the darkness, I could see it was long past dusk.

I tried to sit up, but my muscles felt leaden. What was wrong? Then I remembered the milk; it must have been drugged. Where was Gerry? Where was Philby? I tried again to sit up, but my legs wouldn't move. I reached down and felt, to my shock, that they were bound to the bed. I tried to call out, but my mouth was dry and all that emerged was a strangled croak.

As I was struggling to loosen the binds, I heard the quiet squeak of rubber-soled shoes, then the unmistakable scrape of a bolt being drawn. I turned in the direction of the noise, to see a sliver of grey light gradually widening, until it was blotted out by a dense shape. 'Gerry? Philby? Who is it?' I called.

There was no reply. Suddenly the lights flashed on. I shut my eyes, temporarily blinded. I opened them, and as my vision started to return, the shape solidified into focus. The features hit me hard, a jolt which spread through my body. I closed my eyes again, as I heard my name being spoken in the unmistakable, pedantic, richly accented voice of my nightmares:

'Jane Moneypenny.'

I opened my eyes to see his, pale and lifeless, staring at mine from only a few feet away. He was wearing a smart navy suit and, on his lapel, a small pin displaying the gold and red enamel shield and sword of the KGB. My stomach gave a dry heave. I swallowed and try to calm myself. But for the eyes, he could have passed for an affluent city banker. Those dead eyes and the smell: I could almost smell the cruelty he exuded, just as he, presumably, could scent my fear.

'Boris,' I said at last.

He gave what passed for a laugh, a hollow-throated cough.

'This time you have no gun, and no friend to protect you.'

I shivered. 'Thanks to you,' I spat. At the mention of R, anger and adrenalin hit me.

'Your friend was meddling where he had no right to. It was the Centre's will that he should be eliminated.' He smirked. 'It was my pleasure to carry out their orders.'

I tried to sit up again, straining my legs against the ties, but they were too tight. I looked across to see Boris, his face twisted in a half-smile, sitting there calmly looking at me.

'What do you want now?' I asked. 'Where's Philby?'

His smile broadened. 'Did you really think the good and loyal Comrade would want to return to the country he dedicated his life to destroying? To be held in contempt by those who were once his friends? No, my dear Miss Moneypenny. He was following our orders from the start. It was I, personally, who thought up this plan. I knew who you were. I knew your plan. Were you so stupid, or so arrogant, as to believe you could walk into our country and extricate a Hero of the Red Banner from under our noses? Ha!' He gave a derisive laugh. But I was thinking of Eleanor. What would become of her?

'Did you think you could brainwash one of our best men and kill the head of our service on his home turf?' I asked. 'You weren't very successful there.'

He shook his head. 'Ah, the good and obedient Commander Bond. From what I hear, he nearly succeeded. Well, some I win and some I lose . . . This one I will win.'

'What do you want from me?'

'Thanks to Comrade Philby, we have compiled a very interesting dossier on the workings of your "Office". Very interesting indeed. However, it is not complete. My

255

superiors are aware that our Comrade has not been inside your office for thirteen years. While we are sure that little has changed in terms of procedure – we know that you British do not look to your own security with the rigour that we do – there are certain current administrative methods and practices that you, as personal assistant to the man you call M, are ideally placed to inform us about.'

'Why would I do that?' I asked.

'Because if you don't, you will never see your home again – that lovely apartment in Ennismore Gardens that I had the pleasure of visiting. And,' he added with a sly look, 'you will not live to see your sister married.'

My stomach churned – Helena. How did he know?

'Untie my legs, please, and we can have a proper discussion,' I said finally, with as much dignity as I could muster.

He shook his head. 'No. I like seeing you lying down. Perhaps I should bring in my loyal compatriot Comrade Ludmilla from the Sandunovsky Banya, to ease your tension with a little more of her special brand of massage? I believe you enjoyed that.'

My thoughts jumped again to Eleanor, this time tinged with doubt as I remembered that hint of a smile when the monstrous Ludmilla had arrived with her birch sticks. Was Eleanor part of the plot? I quickly pushed the thought aside: Eleanor had come to us straight from Beirut, genuinely confused and frightened. Her actions all along had done nothing to dispel that impression. No, it was she who was being played, every bit as much as I was. My thoughts veered back to the Office – the sieve. Had we both been betrayed by our Office mole? Who? Who among my colleagues, my friends, had known?

I shook my head to clear it, as the implications of what he had said became plain. There could be no pay-off. Once I had divulged what I knew, there would be no going back, no wedding, no Powder Vine, no M or Bill or James. I would die at the same hands as R had. It was small comfort. I started to shiver, but then I was flooded with a sudden feeling of freedom. There was no point in telling him anything, therefore I had only two options: to escape somehow, or to die. For the sake of my sanity, I needed to concentrate on the former.

Our exchange continued for what felt like hours, Boris threatening and cajoling me, promising violence or escape. I parried as best as I could, appealing to his better interests, warning him of the retribution the Office would seek if I were to disappear. It was harrowing, and exhausting. I was still lying down, tied to the bed. He was standing over me, huge and all too real, from time to time pausing to take a deep swig from his hip-flask before dousing me with alcoholic fumes. At no time did he touch me. He didn't need to – his eyes were as menacing as a whip and chain.

'Where were you meant to meet your people this evening?' he asked in a wheedling voice, after a long line of questions about the Office. I shook my head.

He frowned. 'No ambush, I assure you.'

We sat in silence for a minute before he suddenly changed tack. 'I know where your father is,' he said. 'I can take you to him, and then you will tell me.' It was a quiet statement, but it hit me like a force-ten gale. I willed myself not to pay any attention; they had used Pa as a lure before.

My mouth was parched, my neck ached from the effort of raising it, and my legs had gone numb. Worse still, my bladder was at breaking-point. There was no way I would give him the pleasure of that humiliation. More to buy time and in the hope of relief than because I believed he was telling the truth, I agreed. He untied me, and slowly I managed to unfold my aching limbs and hobble down the passage to the bathroom.

I felt better once I'd splashed freezing water on my face. I sat back down on the loo to think. I can't pretend that there wasn't a tiny bit of me that ached to believe him, while my rational side warned me not to fall for the cheapest of interrogator's tricks. The quest to find the truth about my father had taken me down blind alleys before, with frightening consequences. But it was still hard to cure the habit of hope.

Strangely, I was no longer scared. My head had cleared and I concentrated on the trials ahead. There was a chance – a small one – that one of our Watchers might have seen Philby when he was back in Moscow and informed London, who would send out a rescue party. Gerry would have raised the alarm – if he was in a position to do so, of course, though that seemed unlikely on reflection. Presumably, the safe house would be the first place they would look, if they could get to Leningrad. But was this our safe house? I had no way of knowing. In case it was, I had to leave some sort of sign to show that I was alive. I racked my brains for what it could be and where to leave it. Then I remembered something we had been taught about Illicit Entries at the Fort: when searching a property, always check the lavatory cistern for evidence of recent occupation. I would leave a trail that shouted 'Miss Moneypenny'. I had my handbag with me and quickly got out a few coins – pennies would have been best, but roubles would suffice. I lifted the lid and slipped them in. It wasn't much, but to the right person, it showed that I'd been there.

Boris banged on the door. I took a deep breath and let myself out. 'Hurry,' he said, taking my arm. 'We have to leave before first light.' He steered me towards the front door, where a large, uniformed man was standing guard. 'Where's Gerry?' I asked.

'You mean Viktor,' he laughed. 'Your agent 859 was unavoidably detained before he got to your "safe" house – which, incidentally, is just around the corner from here.' He laughed again. 'Viktor passes as a real English gentleman, does he not? He's Dutch by birth, went to Cambridge and there became convinced of our cause. He has escorted our friend Philby back home.'

Cambridge, I reflected, had a lot to answer for.

Flanked by Boris and the guard, I walked down the stairs and out into the freezing pre-dawn. The guard unlocked the door of a car and climbed into the driver's seat. Boris ushered me into the back before getting in beside me. I shrank to the far edge of the seat, wanting to put as much space between us as I could. He barked some instructions and we set off.

It was only an hour later, as the first pale fingers of dawn started to feel their way over the horizon, that I was able to work out that we were heading north, into the Arctic Circle. To our left, I saw the frozen sea, shimmering silver through the pine-forest. My mind was darting in so many directions that I found it hard to concentrate. I was conscious, however, that we were driving away from Moscow, and that at no point since I'd woken had Boris contacted anyone. It struck me then as odd. Where was he taking me?

After another hour on the road, the light was getting stronger. Boris had taken several swigs from his flask and I could smell the brandy fumes on his breath. He leant forward to talk to his driver again, pointing. We were driving through a small town on a hump overlooking the sea. As we passed the railway station, I made out a name I recognised: Zelenogorsk. We were on the route towards the Finnish border – the same road that Philby and I should have taken. There were people on the streets, young men with twisted peasant faces, spherical women wrapped in scarves like Maryoshka dolls, their stockings concertinaing around their ankles. They turned as we passed; any car, it seemed, was a spectacle for the people of Zelenogorsk. After another mile, we swung suddenly down a rutted track into the forest to the right, and drew up outside a wooden farm-house, painted green. There was a mule tethered in the barn and smoke curling from the chimney.

Boris got out of the car and shouted. The door opened and a middle-aged woman stuck her head out. She started when she saw Boris and quickly disappeared again, like a cuckoo marking the half-hour. A few moments later, a man walked out, straightening his thick wool jacket. He also looked frightened, and saluted and bowed in one awkward movement. Boris barked at him and the man backed away, still bent double.

'We can stay here while it is light,' said Boris. 'It will be warm, at least.' Something about what he said puzzled me, but I couldn't work out what. He pushed through the front door into a large room, furnished with rough wooden chairs, a large table and two benches, covered with thin cushions. Shortly afterwards, the woman appeared, with some dark bread and cold meat on a wooden board. I realised I was hungry. 'We can rest here,' said Boris, 'and this afternoon I will show you something.'

It was then that I realised what had struck me as strange: why would Boris, a high-ranking KGB officer, need to stay off the roads in daylight? So we both had something at stake. There was room, perhaps, for manoeuvre.

I took the blanket the woman had offered, wrapped it around me and sat on a chair near the fire to think it through. It couldn't have been Boris's operation from the start; Philby would never have been party to some cowboy mission to capture me. That wasn't his style. No, either Philby had been genuinely prepared to escape – in which case he would be in deep trouble now – or Boris had hijacked an official KGB mission. The latter was more likely. If so, what would their plan have been?

My guess was that they would have intercepted us near the border, at our rendezvous with the reception party. They would have brought us back to Moscow, possibly parading me as a propaganda victory, before locking me up in the Lubyanka like Greville Wynne, or using me as a bargaining chip for one of their spies currently in a British prison. If we had kept to the schedule, we should have been at the RV point by now. Boris was playing a spectacularly high-risk game. Already in disgrace following his failed mission to turn me last year, he probably thought that he had a chance to rehabilitate himself by getting me to divulge potentially important information about the inner workings of the Office. He had little hope of success – knowing what little I did about the KGB, any unauthorised activity was treated as a serious offence, even if it was undertaken by the stepson of a former KGB chairman.

He said nothing to me throughout the day. I sat and stared at the fire, letting my thoughts fly freely. I settled, for a while, on Eleanor, wondering where and how she was. I could only hope that she wouldn't be punished for her role in this escapade – that Philby's participation would have protected her. It dawned on me that she was probably the reason he had agreed to string me along. It would make sense of his behaviour: I was the quid pro quo for a blind eye being turned on Eleanor's collusion with the enemy. I hoped so, both for Eleanor's sake and because I felt some sympathy for Philby. Beneath it all, I saw him as an essentially decent man, whose path had been determined by deeply held – if misconceived – beliefs which now entrapped him.

I thought about the Office. If I never returned, who would take my place? Maybe Pamela? But I doubted she would leave Bookie voluntarily. She was in love with him as surely as he was with her. I just hoped that he recognised it and would someday do something about it. Then, perhaps, he could start to work on his gambling problems. Surely not Joanna. I couldn't imagine M putting up with her painted fingernails and trip-tripping high heels. My thoughts drifted to James. He must be back from Jamaica by now. I hoped he had not left Goodnight's heart in very many pieces. Mary is a good girl and deserves a faithful husband.

Helena and Lionel – just over three weeks until their wedding. That was my greatest sadness, that I surely would not now be there to celebrate with them. I prayed they wouldn't cancel. Helena needs the security of marriage and she has been patient for too long.

I thought about R and what could have been – the waste of his life and the time we could have spent together. I thought about my father too. I'd been involved in the search for so long, obsessed by the slightest possibility that he might be alive somewhere, that I'd lost sight of what that would have meant. He would have to have been incarcerated for nearly a quarter of a century – or, if he was free, he had washed his hands of his family. Neither alternative was tolerable. Better, surely, that he was dead? It was a stunning revelation, another liberation in this extraordinary day.

My day passed painlessly. It was as if, with the threat so imminent and real, the fear had taken flight. There was little I could do and even the concept of my death no longer frightened me. I had delivered myself into the hands of fate and, although I would fight beyond my last scrap of remaining energy, I was not scared of the consequences.

As the light started to fade, Boris roused himself. 'Come,' he said, 'I have something to show you.' He led me outside and down a small track and into a wood. The last vestiges of daylight filtered through the pine and birch trees, throwing violet shadows on the snow. The only sound was of our feet crunching through the icy crust. There were no footprints ahead of us, yet Boris walked confidently, as though he had been there many times before. I suppose I could have tried to run, but I knew he had a gun. And where would I run to?

We slid down a steep bank to a frozen stream. There was a rock to one side. 'Sit there,' Boris said. He then stood beside me and pointed at the opposite bank. I couldn't see it at first, just the slender trunks of silver birch, standing in serried rows, blending into the snow-covered earth. Then I followed his finger and made out a smaller, upright shape, which my eyes had initially passed over as a tree stump. It was also covered in snow, but what I had initially thought of as branches, extending to either side, I now saw were too regular, too straight. It looked like a cross.

'Your father,' he said.

I felt a sharp jolt in my stomach, but I sensed it was the truth. It was as if I had been here before; it felt strangely familiar and almost comforting. Unbidden, tears came into my eyes and suddenly I was weeping – not with sorrow, but relief. I'd found him, at last.

When my legs regained their strength, I stood up and jumped over the stream to the cross. I crouched down and gently wiped off the snow. I touched it, and for that short instant I was with him again. I smiled through the tears and stood up, silently offering a prayer to my father. I told him that Helena was getting married, about my job and life in London, about Ma. I assured him that he was always in our hearts, and asked for his help in escaping my predicament.

I turned to Boris, who was stamping up and down in the cold. 'Now you will tell me where you are to meet your people. You will tell me and I will take you there,' he announced. I felt too emotionally drained to refuse. There was just a chance that he was telling the truth. In the weakness of my gratitude, I gave him what he had asked for.

He smiled briefly. 'Come now. We have to go.' I followed him. He was walking fast, looking from side to side, clearly anxious. He strode on through the icy forest and, when we reached the farmhouse, called for his driver and hustled me into the car. As the engine was started up, the old couple came out to watch. I looked at them and waved, willing them to recognise me as my father's daughter. Had they known Pa? They looked like good people, in debt, for some reason, to Boris. Suddenly, I needed to know. I opened the car door, jumped out and ran towards them before Boris could stop me. 'Please,' I said. 'Hugh Moneypenny. Hugh Sterling – did you know him? Hugh. He was my father, my *otietz*. I am his *dotchka*.' As I said it, I saw the light of comprehension in their eyes. I heard Boris, behind me, opening the car door and shouting angrily. The old man grabbed my arm and pulled me with him into the house, up the crooked wooden stairs and into a small room. There was a narrow bed in the corner. He dragged it out and pointed to the wall behind the bed-head. There was something carved on it, some letters. I crouched in front of it, as I heard Boris's heavy steps on the stairs. Then I was weeping as I realised what I was reading, a set of initials: H I J & H M '45. Hugh, Irene, Jane and Helena Moneypenny and the date – five years after we'd been told he died. The last time when our small family had been united, if only in his thoughts.

In another second, Boris was there and pulling me back down the stairs before I had a chance to ask the old man any of the myriad questions that were circling my mind. We were in the car and driving away before I had even been able to say *spasiba*.

We drove off into the snow. Night had fallen and the roads were empty. I sensed we were still heading north, in the direction of the border and our meeting-point. I still did not understand why – and what was going to happen. Why had Boris taken me to Pa's grave – if indeed it was. Why did he want to go to the border? I prayed I had not betrayed our people, but all that really mattered was that I'd found Pa, at last. Boris had still made no contact with anyone and, without back-up, he surely posed little threat? I hoped not. I turned to him, with a torrent of questions pressing to be asked, but he just shook his head and fixed his eyes ahead, his shoulders tense and hunched. At some point soon, I knew he would have more questions for me and I tried in my head to compose plausible answers that would satisfy his superiors without compromising the Office.

Then the driver said something to Boris and pointed at his rear-view mirror. Boris swivelled in his seat and shouted at the driver to speed up. I tried to look behind, but he pushed me back roughly in my seat.

'What is it?' I asked.

'We do not know,' he replied. 'Probably nothing, but hold tight.' The car lurched to the right, down a forest track. The lights were switched off and we came to a stop. Boris turned round and, from behind, I heard the sound of a car passing on the main road. Boris exhaled audibly and ordered the driver to get back on the road.

'You see. They are looking for me,' I said, more to convince myself than him.

He gave a bark. 'I almost wish it was so . . .' He let his sentence hang in the air and I realised that I'd been right: Boris was being hunted by his own side.

We will talk when we get to a safe place,' he said, as we continued to drive into the darkness.

I kept quiet. My chances of escaping, I realised, were almost non-existent. Boris would not let me go; I was his insurance against both sides.

We drove on for another hour. Then Boris signalled for the driver to slow down, and asked me to describe, again, the meeting-point. It was a small clearing off the road, five miles before the border town of Vyborg. The track would be marked by a large rock.

Then there it was, a grey hump lit by our headlights. I just had time to register that there was no snow covering, when we swung to the right. I heard the click of the safety-catch being released on Boris's gun. Then there was a sudden flash of light and a bang. The car swerved violently to one side, crashing through the trees. Boris and the driver were both shouting. I held on tight to the door-handle. Then, with a lurch, the car catapulted forwards into a ditch. I banged my head against the seat in front, and the next thing I knew I was being dragged out of the car. I heard another shout; there was a flash and the unmistakable whip-crack of a shot being fired.

I looked around, but all I could see was our car on fire. My first thought was that we had been hijacked by the KGB. I started to crawl away – anything seemed preferable to the top floor of the Lubyanka. It was freezing and my clothes were soon soaked through from the snow. Just a few yards away, I could hear the sounds of a struggle, and as my eyes adjusted to the darkness, I could see, backlit by the burning car, two figures grappling with each other.

I watched, transfixed, as the men rolled over each other, exchanging punches and emitting strangled grunts. The driver was nowhere to be seen. Then, with a final effort, the smaller man pushed the larger against a tree, hitting his head, and he sank to the ground. I thought, fleetingly, that I must get away, as the smaller figure got up and started running towards me. He was dressed in black, wearing a balaclava. I struggled to my feet, preparing to run. I didn't know where I would go – just away from him. As I turned, I heard my name being called.

For a minute, I wondered whether I was dreaming. He called again, and the voice was wonderfully, gloriously familiar – 'Penny? Are you all right?' – and I knew it was truly him. I summoned up all my energy.

'Bill? What the devil are you doing here?' I asked, my voice a small croak.

Then his arms, wet and cold, were squeezing me tight. 'Thank God you're all right. Heard you were in a spot,' he said. 'Thought I'd come and give you a hand.'

'You shouldn't have. I was quite on top of things,' I replied, half-laughing, half-crying as I buried my face in his shoulder.

'I never doubted that. I was in the neighbourhood. It was the least I could do.'

He led me towards a car and sat me in the front seat where, miraculously, I found a thermos flask. 'Help yourself to some tea,' he said, after switching on the engine. 'It's probably cold by now, but it's got plenty of sugar in it and will do you good. I should go and see to him.' He nodded in the direction of the figure by the tree.

'It's Boris, you know,' I said.

He nodded. 'I feared as much.'

'What are you going to do with him? He brought me here.'

He smiled. 'Dear Penny, I won't let him get you again. But I'm not going to kill him in cold blood and I can't leave him where he is.' He disappeared into the darkness, re-emerging minutes later with a large figure slumped over his slim shoulders. I wondered, briefly, at his bravery; this was a new Bill. I had never thought of him as a man of action before, despite his impressive collection of wartime medals.

'There was another man, the driver,' I said.

''Fraid we'll need one of your CFF's* for him,' Bill said. 'Had no option. It was a hell of a risk ambushing the car with you in it, but I knew I'd be outnumbered. Thank God you're not hurt,' he said again. 'Now, let's concentrate on getting back over the border. I've brought a passport for you, with a stamp that should work, but I wasn't prepared for him. We'll just have to wrap him in an aluminium blanket and put him in the boot. When we get closer, I'll give him another knock to make sure he's still out. Then all we can do is hope for the best.

'We're not far south of Vyborg,' Bill said. 'What happened to Philby? I assume he was in on the plot from the beginning?'

'I think so,' I said.

Bill gave a short bark of a laugh. 'Never thought any better. Once a traitor, always a traitor – but we had to give it a chance. The reception committee waited for twelve hours and then headed back over the border. I was waiting there. When 859 finally reported in, I realised you'd been taken. Guessed it was Boris. We've got a man in Leningrad – Russian guy, member of the local police. Miraculously, he tracked down your driver and found the house you'd been kept in. He found your signal in the cistern – good thinking, by the way – and

---

* Collateral Fatality Forms.

managed to pick up your scent in Zelenogorsk this morning. When he radioed to us that you appeared to be heading in this direction, I took a chance and came over to wait for you. The others said I was mad. Thank God you showed up.'

'Boris seems to have taken over the operation without permission,' I told him. 'When you were following us earlier, he thought you were his outfit, eager for his blood.'

Bill turned to look at me. 'I wasn't following you earlier,' he said.

It took a minute for that to sink in. We were not out of danger.

'I'm so sorry,' I said. 'I seem to have made a bit of a hash of things.'

Bill reached across for my hand and gave it a squeeze. 'Don't be absurd, Penny. You've done an amazing job. The Old Man's impressed.'

'He is? I didn't get Philby back. Eleanor's still there. I was rumbled by the Russians.'

'Not your fault, old thing. You're here now and that's what's important.' He drove on, his eyes focused on the road ahead. Then something occurred to me.

'Does M know you're here?' As Chief of Staff, Bill was in possession of far too much sensitive information to be allowed far from headquarters.

I could almost feel him grimace. 'Not exactly. Reluctantly gave me permission to go to Finland, with strict instructions not to cross the border under any circumstances. Once I heard you were in trouble, though, I grabbed some equipment, took a car and sped across. Hardly gave it a minute's thought. Knew I had to get you out.'

'My knight in shining armour.'

'Something of the sort. All the same, I'd prefer it if he didn't rumble me. Now, we're approaching Vyborg. Border's just the other side. There are five border gates: three Russian and two Finnish. They won't be any trouble, but at the Russian ones, keep quiet and look relaxed. The story is that we're returning from a day trip to Leningrad. Our papers are in order. As long as they don't look at our man in the boot. Which reminds me . . .'

He stopped the car, got out and went round to the back of the car. I heard a muffled thud and then he was back. 'Shouldn't hear a peep from him for a couple of hours,' he said with a smile. 'Let's go.'

As we were approaching the outskirts of Vyborg, I saw Bill looking in his mirror again. He turned quickly down a side-street and stopped the car.

'Think that might be the KGB,' he said.

I stiffened.

'Don't worry. Chances are they're still looking for Boris's car and heading to the border to warn the guard. We'll stick to our plan. Do your best to appear calm.'

He started the engine again, and within minutes we were approaching a wall of bright lights, haloing a barricade. Knots of uniformed guards stood outside, stamping their feet. I felt the fear flooding back. I willed myself to ignore it. The guards asked for our papers and, as they were studying them, two men in long leather coats came striding towards us. One shone his torch through the window, while his partner slowly circled the car, peering underneath and behind the front grille. I froze a smile on to my face, but, inside, my heart was stuttering. He started asking questions, first in Russian and then in strongly accented English, pointing his torch to my face and then slowly down my body.

Bill kept outwardly calm, but I knew that he, too, must have been horribly aware of the other man, walking slowly towards the back of the car. I felt a lurch as he tried to open the boot, and when he failed, he appeared once more at the window, asking for the keys. Bill looked at me and I could see the suppressed panic in his eyes. There seemed to be no way out. On an impulse, I grabbed the keys and threw them through the window, into the mud-stained slush at their feet. They glared at me, a mixture of fury and pride etched on their faces. I wished I hadn't done it. The taller man leaned towards the window, thrust his face forwards and spat, before turning and marching back into the night. His friend followed.

Bill looked at me in amazement, then quickly recovered. He leapt out of the car, retrieved the keys and we sped away to the next barricade. We were ahead of them now, and with little obstruction, we were through that post and the next and speeding to the Finnish side. In ten minutes we were clear. Bill accelerated away, and when we had rounded the corner, stopped the car, turned and kissed me hard. Then, without a sideways glance, he drove round the corner and pulled into a lay-by, where a car was waiting. As we drew to a stop, all four doors opened and we heard cheers. Four familiar faces emerged in our headlights, walking towards us.

Thursday, 19th March, London

I am nearly up to date* and already it feels as though it happened to someone else. Had I not been forced to dredge up my thoughts, I might have dreamt it into the past. With just over a week of convalescent leave to go, I will have to relive it once more, when I write my report.

I must have slept for several hours after we crossed the border, as when I awoke, we were entering Helsinki. I found myself leaning on Bill's shoulder. He turned his head and smiled when my eyes opened. 'Hello there, Penny. Feeling all right?'

'In another dimension, since you ask,' I replied. 'I prepared myself to die there. I didn't think there was a chance of escape.'

'Disappointed?'

'Deeply,' I replied, before letting my head sink once more on to his shoulder. Then, suddenly, I sat up. 'Where's Boris?'

'In the other car,' Bill replied. 'Didn't want his ugly mug to be the first thing you saw when you woke. He's being taken directly to the Embassy. From there, we'll cable M for instructions, but I imagine it'll take a fair bit of diplomatic unscrambling to work out what to do with him. Apparently, he doesn't care to return to Moscow, but the Finns won't want him and I don't know that we do either.'

---

* Jane Moneypenny does not mention how and when she wrote her account of her time behind the Iron Curtain. However, the diary entries that cover this period were picked out by a document expert as having been written at the same time, which indicates that she filled in the diary from memory after her return.

I shuddered. 'That's what he wanted all along. It's just dawning on me. All the questions about the Office, they were to soften me up for the big one. He needed to get out. I was his passport over the border. That was why . . .'

'Why what?'

For some reason, I didn't feel ready to talk about Pa's grave. I smiled at Bill. 'Nothing, though I wish he'd just asked. It would have saved me a lot of pain.'

'And if he had?'

I suddenly saw Boris, R's killer, begging to be helped across the border. I shuddered.

'I'd sleep better if I never saw him again – but there are some questions I need to ask him.'

Bill looked surprised. 'Not today. You're going straight to bed, as soon as the doc's given you the once-over. You'll be back in London in no time. Then we'll see about your friend Boris.'

I didn't have the energy to argue. For the next few days, Bill cooed and fussed over me like a mother dove. I slept most of the time: I hadn't realised quite how exhausted I was and what luxury it was to be able to close my eyes without fear of someone breaking down my door. I spoke to Helena on the phone, and James and M. Bill had thoughtfully brought a suitcase of my clothes with him from London, and it was wonderful, when I got up, to feel silk and cotton against my skin again. A huge bunch of flowers arrived from the Powder Vine and generally I was treated like a cross between an invalid and a heroine.

I thought about Pa incessantly. Had it really happened? Was it a dream or had I seen his grave and touched the initials he had carved by hand? I needed to know. I needed to talk to Boris.

After a few days of cosseting, I'd had enough and, when Bill once again insisted that there was no way I could see Boris in Helsinki, I asked to be taken home, where I am now, with Rafiki at my feet, looking out at the first buds of spring on the chestnut-trees outside my window. I went into the Office to see M the day I arrived. He was happy enough to see me, I think, though said nothing of the sort, instead ordering me home to rest. Life returns to normal on Monday. I'm off to Cambridge this weekend to help Helena get ready for the wedding next Friday. I thank every deity for giving me the chance to be there.

I am filled with the glorious, tangible feeling of being alive. The last few months have been an extraordinary mixture of horror and exhilaration. I failed to bring Philby home, but I think I found my father, at last.

April

From Moscow, I travelled to St Petersburg by train, as my aunt had done when it was still Leningrad, and from there I hired a driver to take me to the Finnish border. Again, I found the changes to be superficial; the landscape and geography were reassuringly constant. I made the driver stop in Zelenogorsk, where I, too, felt the stares of every pair of eyes. The opening up of Russia, it seems, has not spread far from the major cities. As we wound our way through the pine and silver-birch woods on the road to Finland, following the shore of the frozen sea, I couldn't help but wonder whether, down one of the hundreds of small tracks that branched off to either side, I could have found my grandfather's forgotten grave.

I returned to London excited and invigorated. Russia had worked some magic on me, and I now saw my new home city in a different light: not dull grey, but a subtle shade of dove – like a week-old bruise. I still missed Cambridge, and something bridled inside me whenever I thought of my abrupt dismissal, but I was beginning to feel comfortable in the anonymity of London.

I wrote to Rufina Philby. She had made a real impression on me, with her integrity and quiet dignity. Sitting there, in Burgess's old chair, among Philby's four thousand books, talking to his wife, I'd felt a closer understanding of what my aunt had experienced.

Jane Moneypenny's friend Eleanor Philby left Moscow in 1965, after discovering that her husband was having an affair with Melinda Maclean. By that time, she was desperately unhappy, virtually confined to her flat, prevented from working, and still unable to speak the language. I believe she never recovered from hearing that the party was more important to him than any living person. She went back to northern California and wrote a curiously moving and generous account of that traumatic time: *Kim Philby: The Spy I Loved* (1968). The following year she died of emphysema.

Philby's ménage with Melinda Maclean didn't last long. She returned to her unhappy marriage, while he eventually found lasting happiness with Rufina. He stayed in Moscow, reading *The Times*, following the cricket scores, and spreading Frank Cooper's Oxford Marmalade on his toast. His devotion to the party never publicly wavered, though the KGB remained wary of him until the end, never according him the position or the trust he'd hoped for, and believed he'd earned. Only once, in July 1977, was he invited to the KGB headquarters – now south of the city centre, in Yaseveno – to give a lecture to an audience of more than three hundred officers.

He was trapped in a half-world, between hero and burden. In the 'New Moscow', I visited the KGB Museum on the second floor of the Lubyanka. There I found myself transfixed by a display window devoted to Philby: photographs of him sitting in Burgess's same wing-tipped chair, a medal – the Order of the Friendship of the Peoples – a pipe, and a place mat depicting a scene of Pall Mall. The former KGB colonel who showed me around called him 'the most remarkable counter-espionage agent the KGB had in the West'. But only in death had he finally found full acceptance.

According to his friend Mikhail Lyubimov, when he was alive he was a problem to the KGB, and an expense. He was kept under constant surveillance: his flat and telephones bugged, his correspondence monitored, and a log kept of every contact he made. 'Until the day he died, the KGB lived in terror that Philby would go too far in talking to a British journalist – or, worse, announce that he wanted to return to Britain; what a blow that would have been to Soviet prestige,' Lyubimov wrote in an essay on Philby entitled 'A Martyr to Dogma'.

Philby was careful never to cause trouble – the devoted servant to the day he died, on 11 May 1988. But the KGB's tight rein drove him crazy. 'When he talked about the veil of secrecy in which he had been wrapped in those early Moscow years, his stutter became more noticeable and his eyes burned with rage . . . No normal human being could possibly envy Kim's life,' Lyubimov maintained. 'I am convinced that Kim missed England, even though he was at pains to hide this from even those close to him. He was an Englishman to his fingertips.'

Perhaps, then, his flight north with my aunt was not merely a deception, but a fantasy.

Six weeks after I was unceremoniously dismissed

from the Department of History, I was invited back to the university for a meeting. I was tempted to refuse: my pride had been shattered, and I had no desire to beg the forgiveness of my former boss. But I wanted an opportunity to state my case and to make my peace, if not with the university, then with my home town.

At the end of March, I caught a train bound for Cambridge. Drawing into the station, I found myself smiling at the familiar landscape, the calm immutability of the flat fields and lazy rivers. The department head was waiting for me in his office, flanked by his secretary and the senior professor who, months earlier, had warned me against making 'unsubstantiated allegations concerning matters about which you have no proof'. As I sat in a lone, high-backed wooden chair facing them across the table, I felt as if I was back at school in the headmistress's office.

'Dr Westbrook,' he began. 'There is some feeling in this department that you have been unfairly treated.' I made no response, and he continued. 'While you indisputably contravened a number of university laws, which in anyone else would be an unforgivable offence, in view of your youth, and in memory of your late father's eminence, we would like to offer you the opportunity to regain your junior lectureship.'

'If what?' I asked. It was clearly not a string-free proposition. I had a suspicion what they wanted, and I needed to hear them say it.

He gave a quick glance at the senior professor, who was staring fixedly at me. 'Well . . .' He cleared his throat. 'In view of the not inconsiderable embarrassment that your book is causing the department in certain', he cleared his throat again, 'government circles, we have agreed to reinstate you with immediate effect, on the understanding that you desist from publication of *The Moneypenny Diaries*.'

It was my turn to smile. 'Sir,' I said, in what I hoped was a suitably humble voice. 'I am very grateful to you for your offer. However, I cannot accept, and I wish you had sufficient regard for my integrity as an historian, and', I flashed him a look of contempt, 'my father's daughter, to realise that I would never publish something that I believed to be an untruth. Furthermore, I object vehemently to being blackmailed by an institution that I believe has something to hide, but is unprepared even to answer my phone calls – preferring to threaten me', I turned my gaze to his colleague, 'through so-called back channels.'

At that I stood up and left the room, breaking into a run as I scaled the department steps and emerged into the weak sunshine of a spring day. I ran blindly until I had no breath left, and when I slowed down I found myself on the road to Grantchester, and home. I walked on, and when I reached that dear, familiar cottage I sat on the verge outside and started crying. I cried for my mother and father, for Aunt Jane, for Eleanor and Kim Philby, and finally for me.

Why were they out to get me? I ran my brain back through everything I had learned about the Philbys and my aunt's botched attempt to bring them home. That, surely, was not enough to merit a gagging now, forty-two years later?

Wednesday, 1st April

I knew I couldn't count myself fully back in the Office until I'd run the gauntlet of the Powder Vine. M may be the Chief, but Janet, Pamela and the girls are the inquisitors. They're indefatigable; X Section would be fortunate indeed to have them. I managed to put it off for most of the day.

M arrived at the Office on the dot of nine and walked past my desk with the briefest of greetings and his habitual demand for the signals. When I took them through, he read them and then, without looking up, dictated a slew of replies. 'See that they're sent pronto, Miss Moneypenny,' he said as I walked towards the door. I'm not sure what I was expecting – certainly not roses – but I was so happy to be back that I felt like waltzing straight up and planting a kiss on the polished bald patch on the top of his head. I didn't of course; I just went along with the pretence that I'd never been away. Stupid of me to have thought he might have changed in any way. I've seen a thousand people walk in and out of that door and M has always been just M, captain of this ship and inspiration to us all, but not a man to show outward emotion. I wonder whether he called Joanna 'Miss Moneypenny' in my absence?

Throughout the day, friends from all over the building found excuses to stop by my desk. Bill devoted much of his time to fending them off, hustling up to the door at the hint of a visitor and then glaring at them until they buzzed off. It was a fine role reversal. Over the past few weeks, I've discovered a number of new sides to Bill.

I think he had sensed my reluctance to face the Vine, as at five to one he strode through the door and bore me off to lunch. While I'd been away, spring had sprung. We stopped by Franco's for sandwiches and took them to the park. With our coats on, it was warm enough to sit on the wall at the Palace end of the pond.

'Thank you for inviting me to the wedding,' he said. 'Can't tell you how much I enjoyed it.'

'You already have, dear Bill, about a hundred times. It was both a pleasure and a comfort to have you there.'

'To be welcomed into your family, I can't tell you . . .'

'You have. Instead, please tell me about Boris.'

'No need to worry about him. He's quite safe and he'll never come near you again.'

I felt the relief well up inside me. 'I still dream about him,' I said. 'The greater part of me would be happy if I never saw his face nor heard his voice again. However, there is something I need to ask him. I don't suppose I'll ever have the chance now. Where is he?'

Bill looked over my shoulder as if considering what to tell me. Sometimes, I feel that he treats me like the younger sister he never had.

'Don't mollycoddle me, please. Just tell me.'

'Still in Finland. He's due to be transferred to London next week, where he'll be held in custody.'

'Where?'

'I'm not at liberty to say.'

'Bill, I need to know. It makes it easier, somehow. Otherwise, I'm going to start seeing him round every corner. If you don't tell me, I'm going straight to M to tell him that you disobeyed his strictest orders and drove alone over the border to find me.'

He sighed. 'Nothing's fixed yet, but I assume he'll be taken to X Section for debriefing.'

'Thank you. And Bill . . .'

'Yes?'

'I would never have told M.'

He sighed again. 'I knew that.'

We bumped into James on our way back in. He picked me up in his arms and swung me around like a child on a maypole. Then he gave me a long kiss on the lips and laughed. 'Well, well, well, and so the prodigal has returned.'

'Speak for yourself, 007,' I said, with an attempt at a disapproving frown. Bill was standing behind him with a strange look on his face. I smiled at him and James turned around.

'Bill, old chap. What have you been doing – stealing my favourite girl for an illicit lunch?'

He forced a smile. 'Something of the kind, yes.'

'Well, hands off, she's mine. Aren't you Penny?'

'I don't know about that. I'm not too keen on the harem idea. Judging by the rows upon rows of glamorous women weeping at your memorial service, it's a growing concern. By the way, how's Mary?'

He had the grace to look abashed.

'The picture of domestic contentment in her pretty little villa on the hill. You know, Penny dear, it would be a lucky man indeed who placed a ring on Goodnight's finger.'

I felt an involuntary and surprising stab of jealousy. He must have read it in my face as he laughed. 'Just not me.'

We all joined in, but I could see, behind Bill's eyes, a hint of sadness.

At six, when M had told me to go home twice, I knew further delay was impossible. I could have made a bolt for the front door, but that would have just delayed the inevitable and, if the truth were to be told, I was itching to get back in the thick of the Powder Vine gossip. I just didn't want to be the subject of it.

As I had suspected, no one had gone home. They were all there, lined up by the basins, waiting for me. When I walked in, they broke into applause. 'Hail, the conquering heroine,' said Janet. 'Welcome back, we missed you – but why so thin and wan? Where's that suntan you promised us? Surely, after ten weeks of "leave", at the very least you could have come back with a few freckles? Maybe it wasn't quite so hot where you were?' She gave her best arch smile as the others looked on, like a company of gannets waiting for their feed.

I'd thought about this moment for three weeks, and had prepared any number of careful speeches, but in the end I just laughed, threw up my hands and said, 'The first round's on me at Bully's as long as you don't ask another question.'

Janet pretended to pout. 'Now, Jane, where's the fun in that, for a measly gin and tonic?'

I sighed. 'You win. Champagne all night then.'

She laughed and clapped her hands. 'Jolly good. We've got a pretty clear idea what you've been up to anyway, but still, champagne would be lovely. Come on, girls.'

So it is that I'm writing this at midnight, with an unsteady hand. It is wonderful to be back – I'll never hanker for abroad again. If I could only be sure about Pa. Too many questions. Much as I shrink from the thought, I must find a way to Boris.

Friday, 3rd April

Helena and Lionel's one-week anniversary. What a glorious day it was last week. I couldn't have been happier for Helena as she stood there, beautiful and serene, exchanging vows with the good, kind man she adores and who worships her. I cried, of course, but I always do at weddings. There were moments of reflection too, and when Lionel mentioned Ma and Pa in his speech, saying that he wished they could have been there to share in the happiness, I saw Helena's lip quiver. I wondered again whether I've been right in concealing from her my hunt for Pa. The sad fact is that it's too late now: it's been so long since I started on this quest, I'm not sure I'd know how to begin to explain it all.

Focused as I was on Helena and Lionel, the image of R still managed to flit across my mind. Even that was a strange kind of comfort: he came not as a ghost, but as a welcome guest at the festivities. Better in person, of course, but also better than nothing. Then there was Bill – dear Bill.

I can hardly bring myself to contemplate the idea that his feelings for me are anything other than brotherly. Day after day, we sit twenty feet apart, separated only by a door, which is as often open as shut. He's wonderful, my dearest friend, and I trust him more than any man, but, after everything, he's still Bill. I'm trying to push the thought from my mind, but the more it refuses to budge, the more the signs seem to add up. Last year, he put himself in considerable professional jeopardy to cover for me when he needn't have. He's always shown what I sometimes regard as excessive concern for my welfare – he almost begged me not to go to Berlin. And that strange look when I was flirting with James . . . Surely it couldn't have been jealousy? But am I being straight with myself? Deep down, haven't I always known?

Saturday, 11th April

Boris has arrived in London. I learnt quite by chance. I asked for his file from Records, to check on the spelling of his full name for my final report, only to be told that it had been signed out. It took me a good ten minutes of gossip with Harry to learn that it was with X Section. Another fifteen – and a promise to fix up a drink with Jo Comely – before he grudgingly admitted that he'd overheard them saying that 'Moneypenny's Russian colonel' was 'due a good grilling by X next week'. *My* Russian colonel? So much for office security. No wonder news of my mission reached Moscow. I'm surprised it didn't make the front page of the *Express*.

I must find some way of talking to him – but how? I have no clearance for Kensington Cloisters.

Thursday, 16th April

The last few days have been like a Russian cultural exchange. First, M accompanied the Minister to a meeting with the Russian Ambassador at Kensington Gardens. Then he went to the Ministry for another, this time with their 'Cultural Attaché', who everyone knows is their KGB supremo over here, and today he lunched at Blades with yet another Russian, who apparently flew in from Moscow for the pleasure. You would never have known we were deadly enemies.

The more I think about Boris, the more I need to know. Pa's last days are haunting me. I've come so far and searched so long, I cannot stop here. Even Bill won't tell me what's happening.

Friday, 17th April

Bill has just left after a most enjoyable evening. I roasted a chicken and we had green beans and roast potatoes, with oranges in sugar syrup for pudding. He was charming and attentive, but it still wasn't easy to persuade him to unburden himself of the latest news on Boris. It took three schooners of brandy and two fierce games of Scrabble (I let him win the second) before I got anywhere.

'Seems that, as he fears, the Russians want him back,' said Bill, with the merest hint of a slur to his normally clipped voice. 'Probably Mater Boris putting pressure on her current husband. M said no at first, but now that they've offered us Greville Wynne in exchange, he's considering it.'

'Will he go for it?' I asked. I felt suddenly sick at the idea of Boris disappearing back to Moscow – or, more probably, to a labour camp in Siberia – without having had the chance to ask him about Pa.

'Honestly don't know. It's a strong possibility. Frankly, after what he did to you – and let's not forget that he taunted you with R's murder – I think we should wash our hands of him.'

'He delivered me to you,' I said.

'To suit his own ends. From what we've heard from our sources over here, he'd got himself into deep you-know-what in Moscow. It wasn't just the failed missions: there was talk of uncontrollable drinking, marital indiscretions – the sort of things that the Centre can't abide. He wanted to get out, Penny. He needed you to show him the way.'

'He took me to my father's grave.'

Bill gave a short laugh that was far from mirthful. 'So he said.'

'He did,' I insisted. 'Our initials were carved on the wall behind the bed.'

'You don't think the Centre could have organised that? You were the object of an attempted entrapment two years ago, using your father as bait. You don't think they would have put all the pieces in place before that began?'

'It was his grave. I felt it. I knew that Pa had been there.'

'Why? How?'

'I don't know. That's what I need to talk to Boris about. Please, Bill, I've thought about it long and hard. It's my chance to find out once and for all. If I ask you one thing, please arrange for me to see him.'

He harrumphed and said he'd think about it. Then, after a habitual peck on the cheek, he left. I must have been wrong. He's back to acting like a brother. It's a relief, I think. Hopefully, brotherly love will persuade him to help me.

Tuesday, 21st April

I received a postcard at home this morning. It was post-marked Copenhagen, and contained just three words, in tiny, neat script: 'Sorry old girl.' It can only have been from Philby, smuggled out by someone he trusts. Eleanor must have given him my address. It means that my return home is generally known. Also, that he didn't want the Centre to know he was writing to me; he must have entered into the operation under some pressure. Every day since I've been back, I've wondered about Eleanor: how she's doing, whether she suffered any consequences from our escapade, whether she's learnt the Cyrillic alphabet yet.

I want to write to her. I have their address engraved on my brain – Box 509, CPO, Moscow – but I don't think I dare. Their mail, more now than ever, will be systemati-cally read and censored by the KGB. I've got her in enough trouble already; I cannot risk making it worse.

Thursday, 23rd April

This morning, M called me into his office. Bill was already there, sitting in front of the desk, looking, I thought, a little sheepish.

'Miss Moneypenny, it is Chief of Staff's opinion that you deserve some sort of update on the situation regarding the man who, for the sake of simplicity, we shall continue to call Colonel Boris.' I saw Bill frown.

'I would be very grateful, sir.'

'That's all very well, but this concerns matters of great delicacy and national importance.'

'Sir, you can trust me, I assure you.'

'I hope I can, but I'm still not convinced that you need to know.'

'Whatever you think is best, sir. I would not want to jeopardise any operation. It's just that, after all I went through in Russia, I would very much like to learn the outcome.'

M slowly got out his pipe, tapped it on the desk, filled it with a pinch of tobacco from the jar at the base of the fourteen-pounder shell he'd brought back from his successful Baltic campaign, tamped it down and then lit it. It was his favourite delaying tactic, a sure sign that he was turning something over in that extraordinary mind of his. I sat quietly, mentally rehearsing the drubbing Bill would get when we were out. Why had he gone to the Old Man? He could have just told me himself.

'Very well, then,' he said, finally, 'but this is to be the last of it. You are not to ask again or to indicate to anyone what you have learnt. Is this clear?'

'Yes, sir.'

'Your Boris has made a formal request to defect.' I stifled a gasp and M glared at me. 'I don't need to assure you that we have no intention of complying, even though he could be a valuable asset. After his actions last year and then again in Moscow, the only place he'd end up here would be in a maximum-security prison. Moscow, meanwhile, is keen to have him back and, as I know Chief of Staff has informed you, has offered Wynne in exchange. I suppose we are going to have to deal with them, though I'd rather hoped we'd got rid of that arrogant amateur, for the next few years, at least.'

He leant back in his chair, appearing to contemplate the painting over the fireplace. Then he looked up.

'We're not showing our hand to Boris at this point. There's just a chance that he might have something to offer us that we would be most interested in. X has been working on him for the last few days, but he's getting nowhere. He's baited the hook, but Boris isn't biting – just keeps spouting some nonsense about how Penkovsky was a double all along, being run by the Centre, and, far from being executed last year, is living out honourable retirement under an assumed name in a villa on the Black Sea. Can't give much credence to that – certainly it won't buy him a ticket to freedom. We told him as much. He says that if we want more – and he assures us he has some bombshells to impart – we will first have to release him, give him a new identity, new nose, all that sort of thing. We've told him in the strongest terms that it doesn't work that way round, but all he says is that we would be more than happy with what he's got to tell.

'We had reached a stand-off and were on the point of booking his ticket home, when', M looked into my eyes and paused, 'he said he wanted to talk to you.'

My head snapped up in surprise. Twice now, I've been the agent of his destruction. He must hate me every bit as much as I loathe and despise him. Yet he showed me my father's grave. I was in his debt. I gave an involuntary shiver. Bill must have noticed.

'Sir, I honestly can't recommend it,' he said. 'Let's just send him back.'

M regarded him with half-cocked eyebrows.

'I know your feelings, Chief of Staff. Now I want to hear Miss Moneypenny's.'

Every nerve in my body recoiled from the idea of seeing that face again. It was enough that he trespassed on my sleep. But the little cross by the stream also haunted me. Talking to Boris was my one chance to lay Pa's ghost to rest.

'I'll do it, sir. I'll talk to him and tell him whatever you say. However, I have one condition.' M looked up, frowning. 'I want to see him alone. I'll take a panic button and will report in full. You can wire me up and play the tape later, but I don't want anyone watching or listening at the time.'

'I don't think that's a good idea,' Bill interjected.

M shook his head and drew on his pipe, while apparently contemplating my request. 'Very well, then. We've got nothing to lose. Open up the jibs and turn to the wind. The Russians are breathing down my neck. Get X over here this afternoon for a briefing and you can go early tomorrow morning, before the body of staff has arrived. Should be nice and quiet. Chief of Staff and X and I will be in the building, but out of earshot. Does that suit you?'

I nodded and got to my feet. 'I'd better fetch the morning signals, sir.'

'Yes, very good. Go ahead, Miss Moneypenny.'

It's now past midnight and my alarm is set for five. I've tried to sleep, but given up. Different scenarios for the morning keep intruding into my thoughts – conversations, outcomes, fears. X described the meeting-room for me, a small cell in the basement of Kensington Cloisters, with a bare table and chair and no external light. It's next to the cell in which Boris has been kept, deprived of a watch or any way of telling day from night. 'Keeps them off balance,' X explained. 'Once they lose track of time, they begin to doubt what is real and will often start talking just for the glimpse of a watch or a calendar. Nothing to prevent it in the Geneva Convention, I assure you,' he added, when I looked a bit dubious.

He advised me to wear red lipstick and my brightest, most confident clothes. 'Whatever you do, show no sign of fear. That's of utmost importance, especially for a woman interrogator. You want to portray yourself as a sympathetic ear. I know you've got some history with this chap, but put that out of your head as far as possible. The tables have been turned; you're on home ground now and you're in charge. He's the one in jeopardy. Remember that.'

It won't be easy. My first encounter with Boris involved a shoot-out in my bedroom; in the second, I was bound to a bed in Leningrad and driven across the frozen wastelands to my father's grave, after which the driver was shot and killed. Those are hard images to banish, but I will have to try. This is my opportunity to make amends for the Philby débâcle and to lay Pa to rest – not to mention R. I need to be strong.

Saturday, 25th April

I was too shattered yesterday to write anything. I went back to the Office after the session with Boris, but I couldn't think straight. Fortunately, M and Bill spent the rest of the morning at X Section, presumably listening to the recording, and went straight from there to the Ministry and goodness knows where. I took advantage of their absence and left early. All I wanted was a long soak in the bath. I felt like Lady Macbeth, scrubbing my evils away. I am not proud of what I did.

Bill had arranged for a car to collect me at six. London was waking up with the sun as we drove the short distance west along the park to Kensington Cloisters. As the car pulled to a stop in the quiet mews behind a dull-red Victorian mansion-block, I wondered whether Boris and his Soviet compatriots at the Embassy were aware of their propinquity. The door was opened before I rang the bell, by a large, muscled doorman, who took my coat and said that M was waiting in the basement. He led me along a thickly carpeted corridor into the cage lift and, after pushing the button labelled 'B', clanged the door shut behind me. As the machinery moaned into action, I couldn't escape the feeling that I was descending into the fires of hell.

Bill was waiting when I got out, with a hearty smile on his face which failed to reach his eyes. 'Morning, Penny. Ready for the ordeal?'

'Put like that, how can a lady resist?' I retorted, feeling far from confident.

'M's in the waiting-room, drinking tea. I've got you warm milk. Is that right?' he asked anxiously.

'Perfect. I'm ready to go whenever you are. The sooner the better, to tell the truth.'

'Look, old girl,' he took my arm, 'there's really no need to push him. He's probably just stringing us along, playing silly buggers to get a reaction out of you. Be careful, please. It doesn't matter a hoot if you don't get anything, as long as he doesn't hurt you. Do you understand?'

I nodded. He assured me that I could start just as soon as the boffins had wired me up to the panic button.

The interrogation room wasn't as bad as I'd expected. There was green lino on the floor and a 1962 calendar displaying a picture of JFK and Jackie, smiling at his inauguration. I walked in and sat down on one of the chairs. Bill said that Boris would be there in a few minutes, and showed me, once again, how to activate the alarm. I told him to stop fussing, that no harm could possibly come to me here, but he didn't look convinced and his palpable tension did nothing to ease mine. I sat down and took some deep breaths, trying to compose my face into a mask of serenity.

I heard the keys jangling in the lock next door and then a crescendo of footsteps approaching the room. Finally, the door was opened and he walked in, his shoulders thrown back and chest puffed out. He was wearing the same suit as when I had last seen him, at the Finnish border a month before, but the look in his pale eyes was anything but crumpled. 'Jane Moneypenny, how good of you to come,' he said, as if I had accepted an invitation to his house. I was immediately on the back foot. I took a deep breath and reminded myself of X's advice.

'Colonel Boris,' I replied. 'It is good to see you in my country. I trust you have been well looked after?'

'Adequately, although I would be happier with my freedom. I like your country, you see, and would very much like to stay here.'

'Perhaps,' I said, sticking close to the script I'd been given, 'perhaps we could find a way to make that possible?'

He gave his chilly imitation of a smile. 'I think you can help me. You owe it to me to do so. I took you to your father.'

'You took me to a wooden cross in the middle of the countryside. Do you expect me to believe that it was my father's grave, with no explanation? To take your word for it – the word of a man who has systematically lied and deceived me, and who killed a dear friend?' As soon as I'd said it, I knew it was a mistake. X had warned me against stoking his antagonism. I took a deep breath and smiled. 'However, if you were to tell me what happened to my father, I might be able to use my influence to ask for your asylum case to be reconsidered.'

That was a clear deviation from the script: M had no interest in the fate of my father.

I think I caught a glimmer of relief beneath the hauteur. He sat down opposite me and started to talk. 'When I graduated from KGB college, I was assigned to Section N, the department devoted to running the illegals . . .' Hundreds of officers were employed in 'N', creating *ligenta biografica* – invented biographies – for each agent, who would then be sent abroad, in his new guise, to wait for World War Three to break out. In Britain, Boris told me, these agents were known as 'sleepers'.

His first job was to sort through biographies which for some reason or another had not been used. It was during this time that he came across a file named 'Hugh Moneypenny (aka Hugh Sterling)'. It had caught his eye because he had always been an Anglophile and had ambitions to go to England as an illegal himself. 'I started researching Hugh Moneypenny's file and became fascinated by him. For a time, I believed I would be able to adopt his name. As you have discovered, he survived the British operation against the Germans. From there, he was taken as a prisoner of war, some years later ending up in Oflag 4C.'

'Colditz,' I said. He looked a little surprised that I knew.

'There he systematically maintained that his name was Hugh Sterling – in line with his instructions as an intelligence officer. In January 1945, just three months before the Americans liberated the camp, he escaped from Colditz. His absence was concealed by his fellow officers. From the radio reports they listened to illicitly, they must have known the end was near. It was a strange thing to do. He would have been home and happy with his family by summer had he not made that foolish bid for freedom. It would appear that he was trying to head north out of Germany. He spoke the language fluently and was making good progress. In April 1945, however, he had the misfortune to run into an advance troop of the Russian army. They detained him. They refused to believe he was a British officer – he was dressed in German clothes and, when they picked him up, he was speaking German. They thought he was one of Hitler's spies. They took him first to Berlin and from there to Moscow for further interrogation.' He paused. 'Do I have your interest now?'

He did and he knew it. I took a deep breath and tried to quell my mounting excitement. Boris looked at me.

'My dear Jane, I think you would like me to continue. Am I right?' I repressed a shudder at his use of my first name and nodded.

'I think you have heard of SMERSH?' I nodded again. 'As a suspected spy, your father was under their authority. He was being held at their Moscow headquarters. It was a busy time for SMERSH, however, and their forces were spread thin. On May 20th, 1945, he managed to escape from custody. To this day, no one knows how he did so. It had never happened before and, to the best of my knowledge, never happened again. You can imagine the uproar it caused.'

I could. In my mind, I had ciné film playing of my father running along those grey Moscow streets, trying to hide from the myriad eyes and ears of Stalin's secret forces. Although, since discovering that he had been in Colditz, I had tried to numb myself to imaginings of what he must have suffered, my memories of Moscow were too fresh and too chilling to suppress. Boris was watching me closely; I forced myself to appear calm.

'A general alert was sent out from SMERSH to the army and NKVD,* with your father's description and instructions to capture him, dead or alive. You understand, they still believed he was a German spy. They were unsuccessful.' I looked up with surprise and a dawning sense of pride.

He continued: 'This is all detailed in his *zapiska*. From Moscow, he managed to find his way to Leningrad – I have no idea how, since I do not believe he spoke much Russian. He did not stay long, but headed north out of the city towards the Finnish border, along the same route that we took. He might have made it, but for his failing health. He had contracted pneumonia in the prison camp, and had never fully recovered. He found refuge with a family of peasant farmers, who had once worked on the Tsar's estates. This family looked after him, at considerable risk

---

* The Soviet security directorate and secret police, forerunner of the KGB. The NKVD's major responsibility was to deal with 'enemies of the people'. In the two decades before its name change in 1946, millions were rounded up and sent to the Gulag and hundreds of thousands were executed by the NKVD.

to themselves. When they were visited by the search parties, they hid him in a well by the pig shed. Unfortunately his health deteriorated and they were too afraid to send for medical assistance. On August 16th, 1945, he died of his illness.'

I gave a start. He had died a week after my fourteenth birthday. I remember it particularly well. We were still in Kenya and, to celebrate the end of the war, Ma had given me a pony, Tsarvo. I would go for long rides on her into the Maguga forest and on the surrounding farms, in search of giraffes and zebras and impala, which I would race across the plains. Those rides were some of my happiest times, when I felt most free and when Pa felt closest to me. He had taught me how to ride and, before he left, we would go for long rides together, sometimes camping overnight; while Helena stayed at home with Ma. I had kept Tsarvo long after I grew too tall for her, and when we eventually left Kenya, I entrusted her to Moses, the chief syce on our farm, and he, in turn, had taken her with him to Daisy's. Tsarvo and Pa will be joined for ever in my thoughts at my fourteenth birthday.

I pulled myself out of that land of childhood dreams when I felt Boris's eyes on me. 'It was only after his death that SMERSH discovered your father's true identity,' he said. 'But by then it was too late, and we could not inform the British. Some neighbour of the family he was living with had informed the local NKVD that there was a for-eigner on the farm. By the time they got there, your father had been buried. The family was punished – ordered east to the oilfields. Ten years later, they returned to their farm, but they had not forgotten him. They erected the small cross I showed you. It was the father of the peasant you met. I discovered this when I was researching the file, to see if I could use it as my legend. I was desperate then to come to this country. I feared the family might have lied about his death, so I forced them to reveal the grave site. They thought I would punish them for putting up the memorial. I decided to spare them,' he said, with a return of his customary arrogance.

'Thank you.' I realised that tears were falling unbidden from my face. After all my hopes and fears, Pa's last days and weeks had been, if not happy, then at least free. He had not died in custody, nor had he been shot – both possibilities that had been circling my thoughts. He had been trying to get back to us.

'He was known to SMERSH as "The Great Escaper",' Boris said. I realised, as I looked up at him through a wall of tears, that he had admired Pa, and that perhaps it was because I was his daughter that Boris had pursued me with such determination. I knew he had told me the truth. For a fleeting moment, I allowed myself to feel sympathy for him. He had indeed fulfilled his side of the bargain.

I made myself think of R. I tapped my fingers on the desk and, when I spoke again, my voice was steady. 'Colonel,' I said, 'you realise that it is not in my power to authorise your release, whatever you tell me about my father? I can make a recommendation, but the final decision rests with my superiors and they aren't interested in how my father died. They need something more than that – something that will benefit our intelligence activities.'

He raised one eyebrow and gave me the dubious benefit of one of his attempts at a smile. 'What might that be, my dear Jane?'

I swallowed back the revulsion. 'You tell me and then perhaps we can start to negotiate an extension to your stay here.'

He shook his head. 'I cannot,' he replied – 'not until I have an assurance from you that I will be protected in this country. Do you not see what a position I am in? My people want me back because they are scared I know something that would be of inestimable value to you. Something, for instance, like the identity of an agent working for your organisation.'

I drew in breath: this must have been what M was looking for. I couldn't afford to let Boris know that we suspected an internal mole. I attempted to look sceptical. 'Do you have information about such a person?' I asked.

'I do.'

'Would you tell me the identity of this person?'

'Possibly – but then again, possibly not. It would be foolish of me to give away my best bargaining chip. You would need to assure me first that I could stay here and that I would be protected from my people.'

I shook my head. 'That is not within my power to do. If you tell me, however, I promise to do my best.'

It was his turn to shake his head. 'Please do not let them send me back there. I will be executed.'

For the first time, stripped of his veneer of confidence, Boris seemed almost vulnerable.

'I will do what I can,' I said.

'You promise?'

'I promise,' I replied, though I knew I had no right to do so, nor any real desire to succeed. I got up to knock on the door, to inform the guard that we were finished.

As the door began to open, he spoke again: 'If you do not help me, I will hunt you down wherever you are, for as long as it takes. Then I will take great pleasure in killing you, as I did your "dear friend".' He spat out the last words. Without turning around, I walked through the door and down the corridor, where I saw Bill waiting. He looked anxious. 'Did he tell you?' he asked. I shook my head and, for the second time in as many months, fell into his arms, sobbing.

He held me and stroked my hair. 'Hush,' he said. 'Don't worry. We will not give in to his blackmail. There is no way that we will give him asylum. I promise you that. Don't worry.'

'What if he knows, though? We need to find the mole.'

'It's a bluff,' Bill said quickly. 'He wouldn't have been privy to that sort of sensitive information. Bookie says it's impossible. We all agree. Don't worry – he is going back to face the music.'

Now I am home, out of that terrible place, I feel both brimful of emotion and strangely empty. Not for the first time, I wish I had someone to confide in. Bill is the only one, but for some reason I don't want to, as if it would plunge us further into a complex intimacy. Discovering the truth about Pa has been the most extraordinary relief – it is a chapter that I can now close, with some satisfaction. I can think of him at peace by that pretty stream, rather than incarcerated in a prison or in the torture chamber of some rotten organisation. He is dead, and long since mourned. I can now treasure my memories of him, with enjoyment and without anguish.

That is what I will concentrate on now. I cannot let myself dwell on that last, threatening glimpse of Boris. I will not.

Monday, 27th April

Greville Wynne is back. His plane arrived at Brize Norton early on Sunday morning. It should have been a secret, but someone had tipped off the press, who were waiting at the gates to photograph him. Of course, he couldn't help but talk to them.

Boris is in Moscow. I suppose I shouldn't have been surprised. Bill admitted this morning that his flight had been long since organised. M, he said, had made the decision to send him back even before I talked to him. Nothing he could have said to me would have made any difference. He would face certain punishment on his return, Bill assured me.

It was not fear that I was feeling, though – more relief, mixed with a shiver of shame. I didn't doubt that he had gone to the right place and, for what he did to R, he deserved the worst the KGB had to offer. I just wish I hadn't given my promise.

Wednesday, 29th April

M received a top-secret cable from Dikko Henderson in Tokyo, which I decrypted this morning. He had been sent to South Korea on a mission and returned by boat to Kyushu, Japan's south island. While there, he thought he might as well pay a visit to Kissy Suzuki on Kuro island. It took him some time to find her. The villagers appeared determined to hide her whereabouts, but he eventually tracked her down to a small house on a hill in the island's interior. She appeared shocked to see him, but not as surprised as he was when he saw, in her arms, a five-month-old baby boy: 'WOULD WAGER MY LAST SHIRT WAS BONDSAN NIPPER STOP WHAT ACTION REQUIRED QUERY HENDERSON'.

I showed it first to Bill, who burst out laughing. 'Pretty pickle he's got himself in now,' he said. 'Mind you, I'd be surprised if it was his first. Now we can solve the mystery of the memory-inhibiting drugs: they weren't part of some international plot, just a woman desperate to hold on to her man.' He laughed. 'James: how does he do it?'

'What do you think M will do?' I asked, though I knew what the answer would be.

'Tell Henderson to ignore it. She's obviously happy enough and James isn't exactly going to drop his oo, don a dress and return to the pearl-hunters, is he?'

The image made me smile. I'm sure Bill was right, but still, surely James had the right to know?

'Wouldn't you want to?' I asked.

'Yes, but I'm not James, however much I might want to be.'

'Don't,' I found myself saying. 'Don't ever change. You're just right the way you are.'

His eyes lit up for a moment, before he shook his head a little sadly. 'Oh, Penny, I wish I was. I wish I was.' Then he smiled again. 'Tell you what. Seems to me this young Bond-san needs to be celebrated. James is off to Casablanca tomorrow, but why don't we dress up and go somewhere swell on Saturday night to toast him with fine champagne and good music?'

'An excellent idea,' I said. 'I could do with a bit of fun. I'll buy a new frock for the occasion.'

As I went back to my desk, I couldn't help but feel a buzz of excitement at the thought, but whether it was the prospect of a new dress, or a night out with Bill, I couldn't say.

Thursday, 30th April

James was on fine form as he swept past my desk on his way to collect his final orders from M. He perched on my chair and gave my bottom a friendly tweak as M opened the door to call him in.

As he came out, the light was back in his eyes. 'Come with me, Penny, please. We could make whoopee in the sand dunes.'

'I think you've done quite enough of that already,' I couldn't resist saying. 'Isn't it time you settled down with a nice girl and made lovely little James babies?'

He pretended to frown. 'Only if you're sure you're ready. I wouldn't want to force you to give up all this. What would the Old Man do without his Moneypenny?'

With a final smile, he was out of the door. Dear James, he needs a mother more than a wife, but that's exactly what he doesn't want. I fear he's destined to remain one of life's bachelors – desired but never contained.

I found a puzzling document today. It was the minutes of a top-secret meeting held a week ago, in which Boris's future was debated and decided. There had been a vote at the end. Bookie, Dorothy and Bill had been in favour of sending him directly back to Moscow; X and M had wanted to detain him for further interrogation. Why had Bill lied to me?

The last page in this diary. I will have to go to Smythson's tomorrow to buy the next, fresh with the promise of new episodes in a life that could never be called dull. In the last year, I have lost a lover, but gained a brother-in-law and, in Eleanor, a friend. I have also laid my father to rest. Boris, I hope, is out of my life, but Bill seems set on working his way further in. Dinner on Saturday night. We shall have to wait and see.

Afterword

I am in Kenya now, staying with my mother's old school-friend on her beautiful game ranch in the lee of Mount Kenya, only an hour's drive from where Miles Pitman used to live.

A week after I had walked out of that meeting with the university Department of History – effectively burning my academic boats, perhaps for ever – I received a phone call from Ferdy Macintyre's secretary at MI6. 'He wants to see you,' she told me. 'Four o'clock today at the Oxford and Cambridge Club.'

Macintyre was younger than I had expected – perhaps in his late thirties – with floppy blond hair and cutting-edge glasses. He smiled as he stood to shake my hand. 'Good to meet you, Dr Westbrook. Tea? Coffee? Something stronger?'

I opted for mint tea and settled into an armchair opposite him. There was silence for a minute: I was determined to ensure he made the running. He sat there, looking at me, with a half-smile on his face. Finally he raised his eyebrows a few millimetres and said, 'You wanted to talk to me.'

'That was some months ago,' I replied. 'It was you who ordered this meeting, I believe.'

'Requested, not ordered. That's by the by. I understand that you are editing Jane Moneypenny's diaries,' he said.

'Yes.'

'May I ask what period they tackle?'

I smiled. 'You may ask, but I don't feel inclined to tell you.'

He cleared his throat. 'Fair enough. In view of our email correspondence, however, might I be correct in surmising that you will be covering the issue of Prenderghast – his trial and so on?'

I inclined my head.

'You made a request for information about a colleague he may have had within the Office at that period.'

'Yes, I did. You didn't respond.'

'I apologise. I know you're keen for your book to be as accurate as possible, but, as you undoubtedly know, its publication is in contravention of the Official Secrets Act. Nevertheless, I thought it would be best to meet and clear up a few things. There was no further penetration of SIS at that time, and I would hate you to waste more of your valuable time searching for it.'

'My time, Mr Macintyre, as you undoubtedly know and probably thanks to you, is not as valuable as it once was. Since I was dismissed from my job, I have been able to devote all my energies to my aunt's diaries.'

'But you have found no proof of this mythical mole?'

'If, as you claim, it did not exist, how could I have found proof?'

Macintyre smiled, with what looked like genuine amusement. 'As you say. I just wanted to ensure that you wouldn't cause any trouble for yourself by making unwarranted guesses. If you did – and particularly if you were to mention any names – I am bound to inform you that we would have no hesitation in invoking the full powers of the law. The penalties for what would qualify as a Section 5 offence would be six months' imprisonment and a fine.'

'Are you threatening me, Mr Macintyre?'

The smile didn't leave his face. 'Of course not, Dr Westbrook. My aim is merely to help you.'

'Then I can assure you that I will not publish any unsubstantiated allegations.'

'Thank you. Perhaps it would be of some assistance if we were to read your manuscript before publication?'

I shook my head and laughed.

'Well, perhaps I could invite you to meet me for lunch one day?'

I was momentarily wrong-footed. 'Perhaps you could. Until then, thank you for the, er, help.' I stood up, turned, and left without shaking his hand.

That weekend I drove down to Wiltshire to see Bill Tanner. I told him what had happened. I told him that I had been warned, that his old firm appeared keen to block publication of the book. He sat quietly throughout, occasionally nodding. He exhibited no surprise.

'You knew this was happening,' I said finally.

He nodded. 'I had heard.'

'The "sieve", as you named it, did exist?'

'I wouldn't go that far. Perhaps even just the possibility is enough to frighten the Office.'

I shook my head. 'I don't think so. I think he – or she – was a reality. And that the revelation of their existence would provoke more embarrassment to your outfit than they are prepared to endure.'

He got up and walked over to the drinks tray, where he poured himself a tumbler of whisky out of a cut-glass decanter, before walking back to the fireplace. 'You remind me in so many ways of your aunt,' he said. 'She was convinced there was a mole too. I implore you to be careful. The consequences of arousing the ire of some of these people could be fatal.'

I sat down as the implications of his carefully chosen words sunk in. I shook my head in disbelief, the words coming out slowly: 'She died when her boat upended in a storm. There was an inquest. The coroner returned a verdict of accidental death.'

'On what date did she lodge her papers and diary with the lawyers?' he asked.

'The letter she wrote to me was dated September 15th, 1990,' I said, shaking my head again – 'three and a half weeks before she died. No. It can't be true.'

He just looked at me. 'Why don't you go away somewhere and think it all through,' he said gently. 'You don't know for sure that she wrote them at the time. You don't know she didn't add things to further her case. Think about what happened and whether you think your aunt's version of history is worth fighting for.'

Sitting here in Kenya, I cannot pretend that the option of burning this manuscript and going back to Cambridge to beg for my old job has not been playing at the front of my mind. But it is not an easy decision. I believe that these diaries may provide the only contemporary, unedited account of the day-to-day dramas in the Secret Intelligence Service. I believe they contain the clues that will lead me to a mole. The idea that my aunt may have been killed – perhaps for her conviction that this mole did exist; perhaps by Boris, in retribution for betraying him; perhaps by someone completely different – haunts me. I do not want to believe that, but I cannot ignore its possibility.

In a way, however, it has made the decision for me. If she died because she knew who this mole was, I cannot let her death be for nothing; if she did not, then I have nothing to fear. I am almost certain that the mole existed, that Prenderghast had an ally within the Secret Intelligence Service, and I have a hunch that my aunt had worked out who it was. I have drawn up a short list of suspects, colleagues of hers close to the hub of power with access to highly classified information, and have resolved to devote the next year to following the clues left in the diaries. Many are unwitting, of use only with the benefit of hindsight; others, I believe, she deliberately hid within her words, wary as always of the possibility that her secret diaries might someday be read, perhaps against her wishes. By the end of one year, if I am no closer to the truth, then I will cease the chase.

But a lot can happen in a year.